Sinning with Los Santos
By Marina Black

Dedicated to my tireless editor, to whom I owe everything! And to my PK girls who are always there when I need them. This one's for you!

Chapter One

"*Oye*, Rogelio!" Cecelia Santos's voice carried as she barreled through the front door of Black Ink. Her vibrant pink hair had been braided and pinned to her head so it wouldn't get in the way while she was riding. Hazel eyes flicked around the interior of the tattoo parlor; the walls were painted black and each artist's station decorated with samples of their designs. Posters for concerts, local sales, and lost cats hung on an ancient bulletin board, covering older flyers and announcements. Usually every station was full and a line of customers waited their turn. Cece was surprised to find the place deserted. She took it upon herself to snoop around for any clue as to why her brother had called her cell phone ten times but hadn't left a message. Rogelio almost never called her...and that's what concerned Cece the most.

Absently running her fingers over the crescent shaped scar on her cheek, Cecelia let out a shaky breath. Her posture tensed when her brother's on-again-off-again ex-girlfriend nonchalantly pushed open the door to the break room. As usual, Gina was loudly smacking her bubblegum and trying to suck the last few sips out of a soda she'd purchased from the Taco Loco across the street. "Hey, have you seen Rogelio?" Cece called.

"Not since this morning," Gina replied with a shrug. "He missed two appointments. I tried to call Luis to cover for him but he's in Chino with the flavor of the month. I had to call and cancel everybody today."

Rogelio wasn't the most reliable boyfriend—or brother—but he took his business very seriously. Cecelia had never heard of him missing appointments like that. Her frustration was palpable as she paced the length of the store. "First this damn motorcycle accident and now a disappearing act?" Cecelia huffed. "Something is not right here."

Gina turned suddenly, her thin brows knitted. "Motorcycle accident? What are you talking about?"

Cecelia scoffed, "Don't tell me you didn't notice my brother's face all bashed in, his arm in a cast? *Madre de Dios*! You need to cut back on the weed, *chica*!" She scolded, the annoyance giving way to a throbbing headache right between the eyes.

A scowl crossed Gina's features. "Hey, I ain't smoked since before Raphael was born!" She countered, resting on her hands on rounded hips. "I don't know what Rogelio told you but he wasn't in no damn motorcycle accident. His face got all busted up when some guys came barging in here and took him out back."

Cecelia's expression turned murderous. The unbridled anger that swirled in her gut was making her vision start to blur. Things started making sense...after the so-called '*accident*' Rogelio waited until he was discharged from the hospital to call, claiming he didn't want to bother her. What *really* bothered her was her brother hadn't thought her strong enough to be there for him in his hour of need. It had taken Cece a long time to come to terms with what

Sofía Salma and the Black Jacks had done to her in Reno but she was getting better every day.

When she first returned to La Verdad—after being released from the Black Jack compound—Cecelia allowed herself a few months to heal. It wasn't just the fact that her freedom had been stripped away; her attempt at escape nearly got the left side of her face ripped off, leaving her with a lasting physical reminder of her torture. Over time, Cece learned to embrace the scar as part of who she was but it didn't make life any easier. She worked part time at Black Ink, dusted off her résumé, and threw herself back into the wonderful world of engineering. It wasn't long before a great job in Atlanta popped up and Cecelia was their first choice. Although Los Santos didn't have any contacts in the Georgia area, Archie and the Devil's Own had sister charters in Jackson, Shreveport, and Dallas. If she had mentioned the job to Daniel Harding, Vice President of the Devil's Own—and the man who was in love with her—she could've had all the protection she wanted. But Cecelia didn't want to be coddled. As always, she wanted to do everything on her own.

It had been difficult obtaining the security clearances she needed to go accept the job in Georgia. Rogelio had never been the type to walk the straight and narrow; he'd spent most of his teen years in and out of juvie. It wasn't until his son was born that Rog seemed to understand he needed to be better. Despite being a blood-sworn member of Los Santos—or maybe because of it—Cecelia managed to get certified and shipped out shortly thereafter. With a single suitcase strapped to the back of her bike and her concealed weapons permit holstered with her gun, she rode off into the sunset.

Atlanta in August was the stuff of nightmares. Cece was used to heat, but had no idea what to do with the humidity the deep south was bathed in. Given she was under contract with the government, she was forced to wash her signature blue hair dye out. She kept her hair in a tight bun, with several strands kept loose to cover the part of her face that would never really heal. Right after she returned to California, she'd seen a plastic surgeon at her brother's behest. Cece balked at the mere thought of it...there was *no* way she was going to let a doctor cut off a piece of her ass and put it on her face. No fucking thank you. Cecelia Santos as no butt-face. She preferred the scar.

When push came to shove, Cece wasn't losing any friends over it anyway. She was, however, not an office favorite due to her gruff attitude and brutal perfectionism. Even dressed up in a pencil skirt and crisp black button-down, she didn't quite pass. They could take the girl away from her MC but they couldn't take the MC out of the girl. It didn't help she hated the work she was doing. Cece was an electrical engineer, yet the team she was working with seemed to be focused on nuclear fission and making missiles and bombs that would explode faster and decimate more ground than regular artillery. It made her remember the chaos Sofía wanted to inflict on the world and left a bad taste in Cece's mouth.

It was a relief when she got the call from Rogelio that he needed her at home. He hadn't said it in so many words but she could hear the fear in his voice when he told her about his accident. Cece gave her resignation the very next day, signed all the confidentiality waivers the US government could throw at her, and headed back to La Verdad.

The first thing Cecelia did was to hit the hairdresser to get her hair back to normal. Her signature color was blue but she decided to go with a sassy, vibrant pink for a change of pace. Now she wished she'd gone with red or left it black to match her dark mood.

"Gina, I ain't going to ask you again: what the fuck are you talking about?" Cece's hazel eyes flashed with danger. The little slut had the good sense to cower, skittering away when Cece advanced. She reached out, poised to throttle Gina when the bell above the door chimed and shuffling footsteps entered the shop. Time seemed to slow to a screeching halt when Cecelia turned, her entire body tensing as she drank in the sight of a man she'd been trying to forget since she'd left him in Errol.

Daniel Harding seemed to fill the entire tattoo shop with his presence. His jaw was set and his warm blue eyes hardened as he stared her down. "I think I have something that belongs to you," he coughed, letting Rogelio's limp body fall onto the ground in front of them. "We need to talk."

Gina gasped and rushed to tend to Rogelio's invisible wounds. Cecelia, on the other hand, stood frozen, her fists clenched and her spine taut with anger. "I've said everything—"

9

"Not about you and me," Danny cut her off brutally. He stepped over Rogelio's body and closed the distance between them. "This is bigger than us. I just talked to Marco Caraway and he told me your brother's been borrowing money from Los Lobos."

Panic speared through Cece and spread like wildfire. She descended into a violent string of curses that would've made the devil himself blush...but the Devil in front of her understood immediately. Danny reached out as a gesture of comfort, but seemed to think better of it and dropped his hand. Cece swallowed back the emotion in her throat and composed herself again. "Thank you for bringing my idiot brother back. I'll make sure Ramón reimburses you for gas and food."

Danny scoffed. "I don't want your fucking gas money, Cece. I want to help you. You can't take on Los Lobos alone!"

Cecelia waved him off. "Sofía Salma didn't scare me and neither do these clowns." She frowned deeper. "I'm not looking for another showdown, *vaquero*. Los Santos can handle their own problems. I don't need the Devil's Own and I sure as shit don't need you."

Oh, Danny was well aware of that. After he and Cece got back from Reno, he foolishly thought he meant something to her. While he was busy falling in love, she was planning the fastest way to rip out his heart and stomp it to pieces. For the first time ever, Daniel actually wanted to take his mother's engagement ring out of his sock drawer and pledge himself to another person for the rest of his life. Cecelia scared him in ways he couldn't even begin to quantify but living without her was a terror even worse. When she told him—in no uncertain times—they had no future and rode off into the sunset, he was heartbroken.

Daniel realized standing in this shop, arguing with her was the first time he'd felt anything in a *year*. He'd buried himself in his mechanic work, booze, and in Devil Eaters. He hadn't taken the same woman in bed in just as much time. Now that he was standing in front of her again, his heart ached. "I don't really give a fuck what you need, Cecelia. I'm going to be staying in La Verdad whether you like it or not..."

"You can't stay in Los Santos territory without my permission!" Cecelia took a menacing step forward. "You wanna start a war, *asquero*?"

Danny refused to be intimidated. She was millimeters from him and he could smell the sweetness of her breath. Every cell in his body yearned to bend down and taste her, but he dug his short nails deeper into his palms. "You think you can protect yourself from Los Lobos *and* the Devils?" He laughed derisively. "Not a fucking chance, sweetheart. You need me whether you want to believe it or not."

Damn it if he wasn't right...but she still refused to yield. Instead, in true Cecelia fashion, she turned and stomped out of the room.

Daniel folded his arms across his broad chest and sighed heavily. A low whistle dragged his attention away from the empty doorway she left behind. "You're much braver than I am..." Gina made the sign of the cross. "I pray for your soul. She may come in the night and kill you in your sleep."

"Let her try," Danny replied coolly. Sighing, he moved over to where Rogelio was still passed out. He crouched beside him, frowning. "You think he needs to go to the hospital?" The man on the ground was probably handsome in his youth, with black hair slicked back and a toothy smile. Now he was at least forty pounds overweight, balding, and reeked of body odor, marijuana, and tequila.

Gina shook her head fiercely. "No, he just needs to sleep it off." She looked down at her feet in shame. "I don't want Raphael to see him this way. Can you help me get him to the back room?"

He nodded, hefting Rogelio over his shoulder like a giant sack of potatoes. With a slight grunt, Danny managed to get the disgraced Presidente onto the bed before he rolled onto his side and retched. Danny darted out of the way but barely missed getting splattered. "Best of luck with that." He left the room with alarming celerity, wincing as Gina threw herself into the line of fire to minister to a man she clearly loved more than he deserved.

By the time he got outside Cecelia was nowhere to be found and Danny wasn't going to waste his time chasing after her again. Striding into the fading daylight, he threw his leg over his Harley and fumbled with his cellphone. A friendly voice picked up after just one ring and he grinned to himself. At least he hadn't lost his touch with the rest of the female population. "Hey, I'm in La Verdad. You mind if I crash tonight?"

"Come on over," the feminine voice answered warmly.

Danny didn't bother thanking her. He cut off the call and kicked his bike into gear. Glancing back one more time at the Black Ink, he sighed and eased his way into the worst traffic he'd ever seen. Suddenly he missed Errol and its small town way of life. He missed knowing everyone and waving to his neighbors. He missed Marge's famous burgers and milkshakes. But mostly he missed being able to go more than two miles an hour on his bike. The 405 was a fucking disaster...

Eventually, he managed to get off the freeway and meandered along a two-lane highway that led him past the beach and the pueblos by the sea. It was pitch black out by the time he reached his destination. Danny parked haphazardly in front of the house. He barely had his leg over before the front door whipped open and the occupant rushed outside, throwing her arms and legs around him.

"It's been a long time," the blonde whispered, her blue eyes slightly glazed. Sliding her fingers down the chiseled expanse of his body, she grabbed him by the lapels of his cut and pulled him toward the door.

Danny was lost. Her blonde locks were perfectly coiffed, not a hair out of place. She was wearing a pink silk robe that gapped open to reveal the purple lacy bra beneath cupped silicone breasts. He couldn't remember if she was a yoga instructor...or maybe a paralegal? Danny couldn't remember. He didn't really care. The only part of him paying any attention to her at all was '*Lil' Danny*' and he was definitely interested.

Stumbling up the front steps, Danny closed the door behind them and nailed her to it. As the woman sobbed her orgasms into his ear, he pictured the one who he loved more than life itself. He ached for fulfillment, for emotion, for connection. None of that was available to him now, though, so he settled for meaningless sex with another meaningless chick. Danny held out hope she be the one to finally fill up the Cecelia sized hole in his chest...

It was never going to happen.

Chapter Two

Cecelia fumed all the way back to the two bedroom apartment on the waterfront she had called home for the last few years. On several occasions she'd been told it didn't suit her personality...Cece didn't know what that meant. Was she expected to live in some kind of hovel with a wooden door like the one her *abuelos* had grown up in? She was forced to remind friends and family she was a *bitch*, not a *witch*. She didn't need any goats in the yard, or shrunken heads on the wall to augment her strength; she had all the power she needed from being part of Los Santos.

Pulling her bike into the sheltered parking garage, Cece eased into her assigned space. With her helmet tucked under her arm, she nodded hello to an elderly neighbor and stabbed at the elevator button to take her to the twelfth floor. A golden glow wrapped around her as she started her ascent and she found herself staring at her reflection. Cecelia's hazel eyes were flecked with amber, her pink hair drew attention to her olive skin, and her scar seemed more prominent in fluorescent lighting. Once upon a time she might've been beautiful but it was clear by the warped visage staring back at her those days had long passed...

When the doors opened, Cece dug into her pocket for the keys. A bead of apprehension curled in her chest when she approached the home she'd been away from for so long. Who knew what was lurking behind the doors? With one hand she slid the key into the lock, her other instinctively came resting on her firearm. She inched the door open and her heart slammed into her chest when a collection of men came into view. Whipping her pistol out, she aimed and very nearly fired.

"SURPRISE!" Luis Delgado grinned boyishly, blowing into a noisemaker as she walked in the door with her weapon drawn. Quickly that enthusiasm turned to fear. "Cece! It's just us!"

Heart pounding in her chest, Cecelia stormed over and smacked Luis, Diego, and Martín in the back of the head. "Do I look like the kinda bitch who loves surprises? *Hijos de puta!*" She holstered her weapon again, against her better judgment. To their credit, the boys had cleaned because there wasn't a speck of dust on any surface— Cece was sure she had Luis to thank for that. At least the three stooges knew better than to track dirt onto her pristine white carpet. Sighing, she reached out and embraced the three of them tightly. "I missed you, *cojones.*"

Diego beamed but there was something in his smile that made Cece feel uneasy. He shuffled mismatched socks around the carpet, herding the boys over to the plush leather furniture in the living room. "We missed you too, Cecelia."

"I wish I could offer you something but anything left in the fridge has gotta be expired by now." She slipped into the galley kitchen that overlooked the living room. Stainless steel appliances gleamed, accentuating the gorgeous azul marble of her countertops. Cece didn't do much cooking but she liked having a pretty space to work in.

"We got some stuff," Martín offered. "I'm not sure it's what you woulda picked out for yourself, but we didn't want you to starve."

Raising a perfectly sculpted eyebrow at him, Cece explored the contents of her fridge. There was a ton of booze, cold cuts, rolls for sandwiches, the Dijon mustard she loved, lettuce, tomato, onion, tortillas, cheese, salsa, and just about every junk food imaginable. She grabbed several beers and handed them out before flopping next to Diego. He immediately wrapped his arm around her, pressing a tender kiss to the top of her head.

Cecelia clinked her bottle against his before taking a long pull from the neck. She could tell this wasn't purely a welcome home party from the way Martín kept wiggling in his seat. Although they were technically her cousins, these three men were much more like brothers; she'd grown up by their side and knew their tells better than anyone. "I saw Rogelio tonight. He was wrecked. I don't know if he's on the rock or the bottle or if he's just a fuckin' tool, but I'm worried." When she frowned, her scar seemed more pronounced. "I'm thinking this ain't a social call. You got something to tell me and I need to hear it."

The three men shared a look, as if silently deciding who would be the one to break the news. It was Diego who finally spoke up. "It started a while ago, after you went to Reno. The business wasn't doing well and Rog was

17

looking for a quick infusion of cash. Los Lobos offered him an easy gig...but it was bait, leverage to hold over his head to keep us doing their bidding." He examined his hands in great detail. "It's getting worse. Rog ain't no gangster. He wasn't interested in drugs and guns being sold on the street where Raphaelito goes to school...but when he told them he wanted out, they put him in the hospital. They ain't playin', Cecelia."

Dragging a hand over her face, Cece gulped down the rest of her beer. "Where was Ramón in all this? Rogelio can't go around makin' unilateral decisions." She gritted her teeth, watching as her cousins seemed to shrink. "You were all lookin' for a quick buck, eh? Signed on without thinkin'?"

Silence descended on the room again. It terrified the three men who sat around her. They expected rage and violence and cursing...a quiet Cecelia was a deadly Cecelia.

Diego inched away from her, as if expecting to get shanked and Martín nearly knocked his beer over with his jerky movements. Only Luis seemed brave enough to weather the storm that was brewing. He inclined his head, sending the other guys out of the line of fire. They didn't need to be told twice. While his cousins ran for their lives, Luis picked up the empty bottles and settled them on the counter. He didn't want there to be anything to throw if Cece should suddenly fly off the handle. She was passionate and often acted before thinking, then deeply regretted it later; but this didn't seem to be one of those occasions. She seemed suspended in time, mesmerized by the bay window overlooking the ocean. "You want to take a walk?" He offered.

"Yeah," Cecelia replied coolly. Instead of her leather riding boots, she opted for a pair of black flip-flops. They headed along the hall to a private exit that led to the beach. When she reached the water's edge, she kicked off her shoes and dug her toes into the sand. Cecelia closed her eyes tightly and inhaled the salty scent of sea air. This was her happy place. She rolled up the legs of her dark jeans and let the waves lap at her ankles as they strolled down the beach. "I've always trusted you, Luis. You've got a good head on your shoulders," she paused, "that's why I'm even more pissed off at you than the rest of them."

A heavy sigh rumbled from deep in Luis's chest. "Cece—"

"*Don't* interrupt me, Luis," she snarled at him. "At any time you could've called or texted or e-mailed or sent up a fuckin' smoke signal and I'd have come running. Rogelio may wear the Presidente badge on his cut but we both know who runs Los Santos." Cece gazed at the sun as it hovered above the cerulean water. Darkness was descending quickly around them and the dusk cast an eerie glow over her face.

Luis shifted uncomfortably. "I was under strict orders—"

Cecelia wouldn't let him get a word in edgewise. "*Fuck* your orders!" she exploded. "You think I don't see how things are going around here?" Cece jabbed a finger into his chest. "Los Santos own this town because we keep the peace, keep smack off the streets, and our borders secure. Now we're going to be lumped in with dogs killing and raping the carcasses they leave behind? *No,*" she shook her head violently, "It ends now. It ain't gonna be a puppet show anymore. This is a hostile takeover and you're either with me or you're against me." Cecelia returned her hands to her pockets. "What's it going to be?"

This time, there was no hesitation at all. Luis's chocolate brown eyes caught and held hers, nodding his head. It was a sacred contract. "We're with you. You know we've got your back and I'll convince Horatio...the rest is up to you." The unspoken understanding was Luis was not going anywhere near the V.P. of Los Santos; Cecelia may have been terrifying but Ramón Diaz was so much worse.

Cecelia squared her shoulders. "I'll take care of it tomorrow." Right now, she was far too tired to deal with anything else.

Cece and Luis walked along the beach in silence, turning back toward her condo complex. She remained barefoot with her shoes still dangling from her fingertips as they wound their way back up. Wiping her feet on the mat outside, Cece paused to brush away any visible sand that remained. Reaching out, Luis wrapped his arms around Cecelia, resting his head against her shoulder for a long moment. "*Te amo, prima.*"

Snorting softly, Cece slid her fingers over Luis's dark hair. "This ain't goodbye, *cabrón.* Everything is gonna be fine...but I love you too." She pecked him on the cheek before disengaging from the hug. "*Hasta mañana.*"

Cecelia waited until Luis was out of sight before she went back inside. She was finally alone and it was bliss. Inhaling deeply, she leaned against the door and closed her eyes tightly. The events of the day began to crash over her like the ocean waves whooshing outside. Cece's thoughts drifted away from Los Santos drama to the man who walked back into her life today and ripped open the wounds she thought she'd healed.

She was only lying to herself.

Cecelia wasn't healed. Her wounds festered beneath their rough stitching, the infection raging in her blood and poisoning her mind. Things hadn't ended well between her and Danny and it was *completely* her fault. Danny had grown up with a mother and father who loved him and told him he could be anything he wanted. He distracted himself with pussy and flirting but deep down, he wanted the marriage, the kids, and the fucking white picket fence. He deserved it. It was too bad Cecelia couldn't give it to him.

Making the best attempt she could to shake off the pain, Cecelia headed for the bedroom. The soft blue walls calmed the fire that raged inside of her, for a moment at least. She dug in a chest of drawers to find a familiar pair of red flannel pajamas. Turning on the shower full blast, she dragged her clothes off and deposited them into the empty hamper. Steam began to cloud the room but not before she caught a glimpse of herself in the mirror...

The scar on Cece's cheek wasn't the only mark on her body. Sofía had inflicted some of the damage, and those blemishes were still lividly pink. Yet there were older scars, ones so faded it wasn't obvious that they were even wounds anymore. Long ago, Cece had learned that the world was a cruel place. She grew up, got tough, and learned to protect herself; she learned to put on her armor before anyone could get to the tender flesh beneath the surface. A year held hostage by the Black Jacks only made her harder and more inflexible. Any sweetness or kindness or humanity she kept locked behind those hazel eyes had been burned away for good.

Fog covered the mirror, obscuring her visage as she slid beneath the brutally hot spray. Cecelia inhaled sharply, her lips parting just slightly. She reveled in the water beating against her body and washing away sand and dirt and several layers of her skin. Cece stared down, watching some of the pink dye washing out of her hair and tinting the water as it flowed down the drain. Part of her wished she could disappear down the cracks and rest there, hidden from the world.

It was a long time before Cecelia finally gathered her courage and stepped out of the shower. She ran a comb through her hair before throwing it up in a bun and aggressively brushing her teeth. The hour was still early but Cece didn't care. She pulled a clean set of sheets out of the closet and made up the bed, throwing the fluffy white down comforter over the top before she flopped down on it. The sound of waves outside and the song of seagulls enveloped her. Cecelia switched out the light and was asleep moments later. That night, she was plagued by dreams of Danny and how happy she was in his arms; those dreams descended into nightmares as she relived their last night together. If she'd known that was the end, she'd have loved him harder, kissed him sweeter, and held him tighter.

Cecelia awoke the next morning with wet cheeks and a knot in her stomach. Sliding her legs over the edge of the bed, she leaned over and buried her head in her hands. Right now she had much bigger problems than Daniel Harding and his power over her. She had to deal with Ramón first and that required at least one pot of coffee. Padding into the kitchen, she pulled grounds out of the freezer and sniffed at them before deeming them acceptable. Hopefully they'd give her the courage she needed today. As the coffee percolated, Cece moved to the bay window and watched the vibrant orange sun peek over the horizon.

She made the sign of the cross and then folded her hands in her lap. Cecelia wasn't exactly sure what she was praying for or if God was evening listening. The only thing she knew for certain was that she was going to need all the help she could get.

Chapter Three

Black Ink's parking lot stood empty and silent except for a pristinely kept BMW tucked around the corner. Ramón Diaz had been forced to give up riding a motorcycle after a severe accident in his twenties that left him permanently damaged. He'd been in a coma for a month, circled the drain too many times to count, and required nearly a hundred days in a hospital, plus six months in a rehabilitation facility to get some semblance of function back. He'd had to use a walker for eight months after returning home and two years of cognitive-behavioral therapy for him to be able to eat, drink, speak, and take a shit without assistance. Ramón would never be truly normal again, but over the last ten years he'd learned how to subsist.

The low hum of an engine drew Ramón's attention. He pulled his glasses away from his face and set them on the table. He stood up, pausing to let his equilibrium balance before he went to investigate who was coming by so early. A smile cracked his face as Cecelia sauntered to the door. He met her eagerly, opening his arms and enveloping her in a tight hug. He inhaled the scent of her shampoo and the warm leather of her cut, Ramón melted against her. "Hola, *mujer*," he murmured into her shoulder. "It's so good to see you."

Cecelia tensed only slightly, allowing him to embrace her a moment longer before she wiggled out of his grasp. "Good to see you too, Ramón." She locked the door behind them before moving out of his reach. "You talk to Rogelio yet this morning?"

"No, *por qué?*" Ramón pressed, settling back into the office chair. Cecelia didn't immediately answer him and his smile began to fade, his dark eyes glinting coldly. "What happened?"

"Why don't you tell me?" Cecelia countered. "I heard a rumor this club's been in bed with Los Lobos. You wanna explain that to me?"

The muscle in Ramón's jaw began to jump menacingly. "Who told you that? Diego?" he growled low in his throat. "*Hijo de puta!*" Without warning, he ripped the keyboard away from the desk and hurled it across the room. Ever since the traumatic brain injury, Ramón had no impulse control and his temper raged hot and violent. The lability of his moods and instability of his personality were a truly terrifying sight to behold.

As hard as she tried not to, Cecelia flinched and he noticed. Her entire body was tensed and ready for his violence to turn on her but Ramón remained firmly planted in his chair. Suddenly his rage was replaced with a deluge of tears. "I would *never* hurt you, Cecelia." He reached for her, his hands sliding over her hips as he dropped to his knees in front of her. "I've been waiting for you to come back for so long, to show you I've changed. I'm a different man. I got help...I'm *better* now." He sobbed.

Cecelia's spine was so tense she was afraid her whole body would crack. "It was a long time ago, Ramón. I'm worried about the club—"

"It wasn't that long ago!" Ramón whimpered. "I was happy. *We* were happy." Gazing up at her, he slid his palms up and down her thighs to comfort and entice. "It can be like that again, Cece. We can start over and you can come home...we can *try* again."

"I don't want to try again, Ramón!" Cecelia thundered. She moved away but Ramón refused to move. He kept his arms wrapped around her waist, his head resting against her barren womb. Salty tears soaked through her t-shirt, moistening the skin beneath. Cece squeezed her eyes shut and pretended she was anywhere but here. This was not the first time Ramón fell at her feet and begged her to start over. Each and every time, he promised her the world; she had given him so many chances, honoring the vows they made. She couldn't do it again...but she also couldn't deny she desperately needed him to support her in this vote. Cecelia's hazel eyes narrowed, "I need something."

Ramón's words came out in a garbled slur of tears and snot. "*Anything*," he promised.

Cecelia licked her lips. "I want to be la Presidente de Los Santos..." Staring down at him, she watched the wheels in Ramón's head begin to turn. Rogelio wasn't an effective leader, so Ramón got to do whatever he wanted. Cecelia taking over would be a very different power dynamic, since she wouldn't put up with any of his extra curricular

26

activities and she could tell he was wary...but he hadn't said no yet. She still had a shot.

Ramón pulled himself to standing. He was an inch taller than Cecelia and built like a tank. Unlike Rogelio—who had allowed himself get soft—Ramón went to the gym every day to keep his strength up. He was handsome in a brutal sort of way with thick, wavy black hair hanging just above his shoulders. He wore a black t-shirt that hugged his biceps tightly and accentuated his perfect pecs just peeking from beneath his cut. A pair of black jeans and a thick belt with a silver buckle completed his signature look. If not for the deadness behind those chocolate brown eyes, he might've been handsome.

"You're not wearing your rings." He licked his lips menacingly.

"We ain't been married in a long time, Ramón..."

"I told you before, I ain't signing those divorce papers, Cecelia. You're still my wife in God's eyes...and in the eyes of the law." He glowered. "I'm going to make this right between us. I'm just asking for one more chance." Ramón reached for her and gripped her hand tightly. "I'll vote for you if you move back home. And if I screw it up again, I give you permission to walk out and never come back. *Mi corazón, mi amor, mi esposa*...please." His eyes were shimmering with emotion again.

Unsheathing the double-edged sword from its hilt, Cecelia stood on the precipice of her own personal cliff. She promised never to go back here but if she didn't do something, her life would be forfeit anyway. The devil she knew was better than the devil she didn't...

Cece's mind wandered to Danny again; his sweet touch, his hot kisses and even hotter temper haunted her dreams. She'd already ended their relationship and stomped on his heart. Holding out on the hope he might see past the walls she'd erected to protect herself was a fallacy. She was better off doing what was right for her club...they were her family, and the ones who needed her the most. Exhaling sharply, Cece dug her nails into her palms until they left livid crescent shaped marks and droplets of blood welled to the surface. The physical pain was a welcome relief from the onslaught of emotion that raged inside her.

Ramón was staring her down, looking so broken yet so hopeful. A whisper of footsteps dragged Cecelia's attention away. Gina slipped out of the back room, exhausted from a night of caring for Rogelio. She reeked of vomit and her eyes were red and puffy from crying. The door gapped open, giving Cece a clear view of her brother, laying on his side and shivering beneath a blanket. It made her decision easier somehow.

"You've got a deal."

And just like that, the life she'd worked so hard to make for herself disappeared into Ramón's crushing hug. She closed her eyes and hoped her soul would not so easily follow suit...

* * *

It was well after noon before Daniel Harding stirred. He probably wouldn't have moved but the bed dipped and…Sherrie?…Sheila?…Denise?…the *woman* curled up at his side. She was too warm and had clearly just bathed in perfume and hairspray. He rolled to the side, coughing and sputtering.

"Morning, honey," she purred.

For the first time, Danny really *looked* at her. The girl was pretty but she was all silicone and plastic, perfectly proportioned and blonde. She was exactly the opposite of Cecelia who was dark haired with soft curves that melted against him. Of course the girl resting next to him was pretty but she couldn't outshine the love of his life. "Hey," he grunted at her. "I need a shower."

"Oh." The disappointment in her voice was palpable, but she didn't complain. "Sure, there's an extra towel in the closet and a few toiletries. It's mostly stuff I picked up in hotels."

Danny didn't thank her. He scratched his balls and lumbered into the bathroom, slamming the door behind him and locking it in case she got any ideas about joining him. Cranking the shower on, he stepped beneath the icy spray. He didn't deserve a hot shower; he deserved to suffer for the mistakes he kept making. Grabbing the bar of soap, he dragged it over his skin until he couldn't smell the woman on his body anymore. Once he was finished washing his shame away, he settled a towel loosely

29

around his hips. Digging through the medicine cabinet he pulled out a plastic disk and glanced at the name. "*Jenna.*" Whoa, he'd been *way* off base with her name…

A knock on the door startled him and he dropped the pack into a small puddle in the sink. "Shit!"

"Danny? Are you okay?"

He fumbled for the birth control pills, wiped the container off, and stuffed it back in its place. "Yeah!" he called back. His heart was thundering in chest and he shook his head. "She has ears like a damn bat," he muttered under his breath.

Jenna pressed tighter against the door. "Did you say something?"

"NO!"

"Oh…okay, well, I made brunch. When you're done, come down and get something to eat," she urged. "I didn't know what you wanted so, I just threw a couple things together."

Danny ran a comb through his shaggy reddish-blonde hair and scratched the stubble on his jaw. He was starting to look like a Leprechaun, as Archie would've said. He needed a shave and a haircut but that was for another day. Laziness won out and he shuffled into the bedroom to find a spare pair of boxer shorts and t-shirt waiting for him. The smell of breakfast wafted through the house and his stomach growled. Jogging down the stairs, he let his nose lead him to the kitchen and his eyes widened in shock.

Jenna's version of 'throwing things together' happened to be whipping up enough eggs, pancakes, bacon and fruit salad to feed a small army. "I hope you're hungry," she beamed. Sidling over to him, she pressed a lingering kiss to his lips. "There's coffee on the table."

"Uh, yeah..." Danny plopped down at the table. Eight sugar packets were lined up, waiting for him. How the hell had she known he liked his coffee so sweet? He watched her bustle around. "Are you expecting guests or something?"

Jenna glanced over her shoulder at him. "Nope, just you." She turned back to the stove. "How is everything?"

"Great," he said through a mouthful of pancakes and bacon. "I didn't know you cooked."

Jenna cocked her head at him. "I'm a chef, Danny. I own La Trattoria. That's where we met."

The fork in Danny's hand dangled and then fell. "Wait, Jenna *Dayton*?"

Pretense gone, she turned the burner off and took a shaky breath. "Yes?" Crossing her arms over her chest, she squeezed herself tightly as if trying to keep herself from tearing apart. He sat there, gaping at her and it only made her angrier. "Who did you think I was, Daniel? I want an answer!"

Daniel shifted uncomfortably under her hot gaze. "I had you filed under *'Girl in La Verdad'*...and I was in La Verdad so I called you, okay?"

The vein in Jenna's head was throbbing so badly Danny was afraid it was going to rupture. He seemed to shrink back from her as she reached across the table. Instead of inflicting unspeakable violence, she grabbed the plate of pancakes away from him and turned to the sink.

"I think you better go."

Danny didn't need an engraved invitation. He jogged upstairs. He found his pants and both his socks, but no matter how hard he looked, he couldn't find his cut. His head was three quarters of the way under the bed when he caught sight of bubblegum pink toenails in the doorway. He poked his head out, finding Jenna holding the garment in her hand. "Thanks."

"Don't mention it," Jenna replied coldly and tossed it at him. She had changed out of her robe and lingerie and threw on a pair of baggy jeans and a t-shirt. Tucking a lock of hair behind her ear, she chewed her bottom lip. Danny moved to brush past her and she stepped into his path. "Before you go, there's something I want to know—"

"It didn't mean anything to me and I'm not going to call you tomorrow."

Jenna laughed bitterly. "I'm blonde, not *stupid*." Resisting the urge to strangle him was getting harder with each passing moment. "The first time? You weren't wearing a condom...do I have anything to be worried about?"

Danny broke into a cold sweat. He'd been so eager to bury his pain inside of her he'd gone bareback when he took her against the front door. "I don't have anything, if that's what you're worried about." He dragged a hand over his face. "Do I have anything to be worried about? Not like...*diseases*. I know you're clean, but..." He couldn't bring himself to say it.

"I'm on the pill," Jenna offered. "It was just that once without a condom. The other two times we did." She chewed her bottom lip. "Even if there was some kind of freak accident, you don't have to worry. I, um, I *can't*...not for another two years, at least."

"Two years?" Danny arched an eyebrow at her. "You got some kind of rigid life plan or something?"

Jenna stared down at her feet. "No, but my oncologist was very clear I shouldn't get pregnant while on Tamoxifen."

"Oncology is like *cancer*, right?" Danny couldn't breathe. "Shit, are you dying?"

A bubble of laughter lodged itself in her chest. "Not today," Jenna smirked. "After my mother got diagnosed with breast cancer, I got tested as a precaution. It was supposed to be a routine exam but they found stage two cancer in my left breast and in situ markers in my right. I underwent a radical mastectomy. Thankfully I didn't have to do any heavy duty radiation, but because my mother, my paternal aunt, and great grandmother died of cancer, we decided to do a course of Tamoxifen and I...don't know why I'm telling you all this."

Danny stood there, thunderstruck. "So that's why you have fake tits then?"

"In short, yes...though I have to say, these are a big improvement over the old ones." A smile crinkled the corners of Jenna's warm eyes.

"You can say that again," Danny muttered. He scratched his jaw. "Look, I'm a fucking dick. I think I remember your restaurant and the party after. You were nice to me and I didn't want to break your heart, so I went home with your sister."

"I don't have a sister, Danny..." Side-stepping to let him pass, she patted him on the back a bit more forcefully than necessary. "Get out of my house."

"I think that'd be for the best," Danny coughed.

He took the stairs two at a time and was out the door before she even left the room. God, he was the lowest scum on the face of the earth. Digging his keys out of his pocket, his bike roared to life and sped off into the hazy afternoon sunshine. Even zipping around cars on the freeway didn't unburden him of his guilt. He kept thinking about Jenna and Cece and what Lucy would say if she could see him right now. His sister had been on his case for a long time to change his rakish ways. She didn't care if he settled down, but she was sick of the endless parade of women coming in and out of the house they'd grown up in. Honestly, Danny was sick of it too. Unfortunately, the only woman he wanted to settle down with wanted nothing to do with him.

Pulling off the highway, he found a coffee shop and stopped for a cup before heading to Black Ink. Even if Cecelia didn't want to be with him, he wasn't going to let her get killed by Los Lobos either. There was a menagerie of cars and bikes parked in the store's lot but Danny managed to find a space. He headed into the shop, eight sets of eyes swiveled to meet his. It seemed Los Santos were having a powwow.

"Danielito!" Ramón called, closing the distance between them and shaking his hand tightly. "*Qué pasa, hermano*?" Pulling Danny into a tight hug, he beamed. "We're just celebrating a new era. Come on! Have a drink!" He dragged Danny along, pulling him directly in front of Cecelia.

Rogelio was curled in a chair, Gina gingerly soothing his dark hair. Luis, Horatio, Martín, and Diego looked grim and uneasy. Daniel could tell he'd walked in on something. On his way by, he glanced at Cece and his eyes widened at the new Presidente patch that was emblazoned over her breast pocket. "You—"

"Got it under control," Cecelia finished for him. "I told you there was nothing to worry about, *vaquero*." She set her

35

jaw. "Seems you caught us in a celebratin' mood. Have a drink, enjoy La Verdad, but tomorrow you go home. *Entiendes?*"

"Coming in loud and clear, sweetheart." Danny replied coolly.

Ramón stopped to watch the exchange, but his expression betrayed nothing. His eyes kept flicking between Cecelia and Danny as they engaged in a staring contest. After almost a minute, he laughed a little too loud. "Come on, that tequila ain't gonna drink itself!"

Danny cast one last glance back before following the boys to a bar across the alley from the tattoo parlor. Cece's back was turned and her fists clenched. In the waning sunshine he could see the shadow of the scar on her cheek and the sweetness of her lips. Drowning himself in pussy hadn't worked last night, so booze would have to suffice. In the morning he'd return to Errol and the emptiness that threatened to devour him, to the house his parents once lived in, to his sister, niece, and the club he used to love. Damn, the tequila couldn't get to the table fast enough. Tonight, he just wanted to forget.

Chapter Four

It was a nine hour ride from La Verdad, California to Errol, Nevada and Danny could've ridden through without stopping but his annoying sister insisted he rest and refuel. It just so happened Marco Caraway, Lucy's godfather and the closest thing they had to an uncle, lived just outside of Fresno—almost exactly four and a half hours between Point A and Point B. Argument was futile. Danny would just have to suck it up.

Marco greeted Danny with a bear hug when he arrived. As President of the Devils of California, he had a pretty sweet setup. The contemporary home was a fashioned from glass, wood, brick, and stately Doric columns, but each medium came together perfectly to create a warm, inviting façade. Jogging up the three steps into the house, Danny smiled as the dogs came running from every end of the house, yapping and dancing around him. Nobody would believe big, bad Marco Caraway had such a soft spot for stubby, squishy-faced pups but Danny knew the truth.

"Hey guys." Danny crouched, scratching behind Regina's floppy brown and white ears; she was aptly named, since it was clear she ruled this roost. Marco rescued the bulldog when she was only three months old. She'd been horribly abused and lost an eye to infection. The vet told him she probably wouldn't last the night but Marco had gotten up every hour on the hour to feed her from a tiny dropper and continued to do so until she was a chubby, wriggling puppy who followed him everywhere he went. Regina was almost seven now and Marco was still her best friend. Two cream-colored Chihuahuas called Chip and Dale pawed at Danny's legs, and when he bent to greet them, Rufus—an eleven-year-old Boxer—pressed his nose right into his crotch. "Yow!" Danny swatted at him, covering his junk for propriety's sake. "Shit, man, how many dogs do you have now?"

"Can't you count?" Marco called from the other room. "You want something to drink? Water? Lemonade?"

"You got anything stronger?" Danny followed Marco's voice into the kitchen, narrowly avoiding stepping on Chip...or was that one Dale?

Marco disappeared and then returned with an expensive looking bottle. "I'll have a room made up." He patted Danny on the shoulder before yelling for the maid. Thankfully his regular girl was on vacation. Marco didn't trust Danny not to try and nail the younger one, but Señora Vasquez was a happily married woman and pushing seventy; it was one less thing to worry about. He poured two snifters of whiskey, handing Danny one before taking a sip of his own. "You want to tell me what you were doing in La Verdad?"

"Field trip?" He took a sloppy sip of whiskey and wiped the remnants on the back of his arm.

Marco's expression hardened. "Nice try, Daniel, but that's Los Santos territory."

Sauntering over to the breakfast nook, Danny flopped onto the plush wraparound booth. "I wasn't breaking any rules. We've had a truce with them for a while now." It was a technicality and they both knew it. Ever since Los Santos, the Devils, the Redhawks, and the Nightriders joined forces to take down the Black Jacks, MC relations were at an all-time high; but decades of bad blood weren't so easily forgotten.

The Devil's Own, which operated out of Nevada, didn't have any particular history with Los Santos...but the Devils of California most certainly did. There had been scuffles in the not-so-distant past and some nasty words exchanged. If not for a greater threat looming on the horizon, Marco would've told Danny to drop it and leave town but there were rumors that Los Santos had been in bed with Los Lobos for a while now. The drug cartel had infiltrated the border several years ago and made a play for Devil territory. Marco shut them down several times and they eventually retreated but not before shedding innocent blood. When he heard their name whispered in conjunction with Los Santos, Marco began to worry. Then when a reliable source told him they'd gotten to Rogelio Santos, he couldn't ignore the signs anymore. This visit was as much a chance to catch up as it was to get more information.

Marco settled down across the table from Danny. "So, how's Rogelio?"

"Probably not too great considering he was just voted out of the President spot." Danny chuckled into his glass of whiskey. He watched the concern cross Marco's features and he furrowed his eyebrows. "Come on, man, we all know Cece was holding that club together. Now it's just official."

"And Ramón allowed that to pass? That spot was rightfully his."

"Cecelia *is* a Santos." Danny frowned. "Look, I walked in on the tail end of the vote. Rogelio looked rough, Ramón wanted to celebrate, and Cece…well, you know Cece."

Marco did know; he also knew how Danny felt about the girl. "Did you two get a chance to talk?"

Danny's posture tightened. "There's nothing to talk about." Downing the rest of his whiskey, he avoided eye contact, as if that would make the lies easier to swallow. "I'm better off anyway. There are lots of women in the world and I don't want to be tied down. It ain't like she's got a magic pussy or something."

"The way Lucy tells it, you're in love with Cecelia." Marco was not going to sugarcoat the truth; it didn't benefit either of them. Years ago, he'd made the mistake of not fighting for the woman he loved and he lost her. Candy still haunted his dreams after all these years. Marco would be damned if he condemn another to the longing and regret he had to live with day in and day out. "What? Not going to argue?"

Tightening his hand around the empty glass, Danny cursed. "Lucy's got a big fucking mouth." He leaned back, his head smacking against the back of the booth. "I don't get it, Marco. Cece is brutal and brash and mean, most of the time but when she lets down her guard, the woman underneath is so beautiful I want to fucking *cry*." Danny buried his face in his hands. "When I'm with her, I actually want to be better."

Pain was etched into the lines on Marco's face. He reached over, resting a hand on Danny's shoulder. "So you went down there to make amends?"

"No, I went because Rogelio called me," Danny confessed. "He left me a voicemail that made no damn sense. He was slurring his words and all I got out of it was an address so I decided to head down and check it out. When I got into La Verdad, I found Rogelio crumpled in a heap in the middle of an abandoned warehouse." He paused. "I didn't know Rogelio had been recently released from the hospital. I also had no idea Cece was back from Atlanta...but she is and she's the President and, honestly, I think everyone's better off without me around."

Marco refilled both their glasses to the very top and took a long swallow of whiskey. "You remember I warned you about Los Lobos?"

Danny shifted uncomfortably. "Yeah..." When Marco didn't immediately respond, he let out a puff of air from his lungs. "Gina told me you talked to her. Believe me, I get it. Nobody wants those gangsters around. Lucky for you, Cece's taking over now and she'll put a stop to it."

"What makes you think she's going to be successful?" Marco narrowed his eyes. "There are seven members of Los Santos, maybe less now that Rogelio is out of commission. They don't have the network the Devils have. They're a small, family-run operation. They can't fend off Los Lobos."

"Yeah well, Cece made it clear I'm not welcome." Danny didn't want to piss her off any more than he already had. Besides, being in the same zip code and unable to touch her was more painful than he'd anticipated. Or maybe he was just being a coward. "What the fuck am I supposed to do?"

"Well," Marco hesitated. Danny was watching him expectantly. "You could patch."

Danny cocked his head in confusion. "I'm a Devil, Marco," he said flatly, after he remembered how to use words again. "My daddy was a Devil and his daddy before him. In case it fucking escaped your attention I'm not exactly part of the Santos-Diaz-Delgado-Calgano clan!"

"Hear me out—"

"Why?" Danny interrupted. "You and dad bought me my first bike when I was eighteen years old. It has the Devil's insignia etched into the fucking fiberglass!" Draining his second glass of whiskey, he coughed against the burning in his throat. "You want me to give it all up? For *what*? A woman who clearly doesn't love me and her idiot cousins?"

Marco slammed his fist against the table, causing the dogs to begin a cadence of angry barking. "Listen to me, Daniel!" he commanded. "Unless you want the next time you touch Cecelia's body to be when you're identifying her at the morgue, you need to take drastic action. Los Lobos have Rogelio out of the picture now and they're going to be gunning for Cece. And I don't have to tell you she's a tough bitch but those guys aren't going to stop for anything. At least Sofía Salma had a higher purpose. These guys have one goal: to get drugs on the streets and guns on every corner."

Danny's blood ran cold. He didn't know what to say to that and took to pacing the kitchen floor instead. Chip and Dale pranced at his feet and he sighed heavily, sinking down to pet Dale...or was it Chip? The little guy nudged his hand, jumping up on his thigh to lick at his face. At least the dog liked him. Danny didn't have anything else going for him at the moment. "I'm not going to let anything happen to her or Rogelio or any of them." He clenched his jaw. "Is patching the only way?"

"I don't see another alternative. If you keep trying to go in as a Devil, it could reopen old wounds," Marco replied grimly.

Cecelia had already threatened him once with war, and that was before she had the power to follow through. Now she was the President and Danny had no doubt she'd fight him every step of the way. That was Cece to the core. She'd rather go down in flames than concede to anyone, even a little bit. It was one of the many reasons he loved her...and the very reason he didn't *like* her all that much.

Danny stared down at his ragged fingernails, chewed to the quick. It was a nervous habit he'd never quite kicked, no matter how many times Lucy yelled at him to get his hand out of his mouth. His finger throbbed angrily as he bit down, tearing away the protective covering there and fresh droplets of crimson bubbled to the surface. The external pain was a welcome relief from the internal battle he was currently waging. "I need to call Archie and Lucy. I can't just defect without giving them a heads up."

"I think that's a great idea," Marco replied, "but you can't tell them about Los Lobos."

"Don't they have a right to know?" Danny huffed.

Marco shrugged. "Sure, if you want Archie and Lucy rushing down here to join the fray. Your sister is pregnant again and they're up to their eyeballs keeping the women's shelter running. The second they hear Cece's in trouble and Los Lobos are the cause, they're going to put it to a vote…I think you can figure out how the rest of that story goes." He stood and grabbed Danny a paper towel.

Staunching the flow of blood from his nail was only a temporary distraction. Danny's head was playing out the grim tale in his head: Lucy and Archie would come riding down here with the cavalry and take up arms against these ruthless bastards; violence would reign supreme, blood would be shed, and lives would be lost. Danny was Amelia's godfather; he was not fucking ready to take up the mantle of surrogate father when they got themselves killed. Plus, Lucy had a rough first trimester and had been following up very closely with her OBGYN. "Fine. I'll lie." Danny fished around for his phone with his opposite hand. He stared at it for a long time before he sighed. "I need to sober up."

Marco nodded in acquiescence. "I'll order a couple pizzas, that'll absorb some of the booze." He paused, his hand finding Danny's shoulder again. "You're doing the right thing, kid. It might be difficult right now but one day, everyone is going to talk about Daniel Harding, the hero who would do *anything* to protect the people he loves."

Danny really hoped that was true. Right now he was betraying his flesh and blood for a woman who couldn't stand to be in the same room as him. It wasn't a happy position to be in. He pinched the bridge of his nose and closed his eyes. Danny silently prayed he could find the right words to tell Lucy and Archie, and to get through to Cecelia. All of their lives depended on it.

God, he needed another drink.

Chapter Five

Lucy Archer rubbed the dark circles beneath her eyes and wiped away a smear she hoped was mushed peas from Amelia's dinner. Even though she was mentally and physically exhausted, she was filled with such an intense love for the toddling terror and her little brother or sister, who was currently giving Lucy horrible morning sickness. If not for her saintly husband taking pity on her and volunteering to do bath and bedtime, Lucy was sure she'd have lost her mind by now. The sound of Amelia splashing and Gabe griping about getting soaked to the bone caused a smile to tug at the corners of her lips.

The soft buzzing of her cell phone dragged Lucy out of a moment's peace and she sighed. This was the first opportunity she'd had today to simply sit down. She debated not answering, but she could see it was Danny. He was supposed to be riding home today and she sincerely hoped he wasn't having issues on the road. "Hello?" she answered. "Are you back in town yet?"

"Not...exactly..."

Lucy could already tell Danny had been drinking. His voice got huskier and noticeably precise as he tried not to show he had imbibed. "You better not be on your bike or it won't be an accident that puts you in the hospital!" He hesitated and Lucy sat straight up, her stomach churning. Danny was always quick with a retort; this wasn't like him at all. "What's the matter? Are you hurt? *Were* you in an accident?"

"No!" Danny huffed. "Luce, I'm fine. I'm at Marco's," he assured her. The sigh of relief from the other end of the telephone made Danny smile. His sister loved him deeply and made it her life's mission to protect him from the world. Ironically, she was his *little* sister, not that it ever mattered. "Is Archie there? I need to talk to the both of you."

"He's giving Amelia a bath right now. Let me see where we are in the process." Lucy dragged herself up with a little groan. The baby was screeching joyfully and slapping the water. Gabriel's jeans were soaked through and his grey t-shirt looked black from being saturated. "It's Danny."

Archie grabbed a towel off the rack and threw it over his shoulder. "We're done anyway, she's just playing." Leaning down, he pulled the plug on the water. Amelia wailed as the water began to recede but calmed instantly when daddy scooped her up into his arms. She snuggled right into his shoulder, pearly white teeth gnawing on the edge of the pink towel. "Can you put him on speaker?" Archie asked.

Danny tapped his foot, rolling his eyes impatiently while Lucy followed her husband into the bedroom and they worked together to get Amelia into a diaper and her pajamas before answering him. Several minutes passed before he heard the speaker function click on. "Finally!" Danny huffed.

"Hey, you know bath time is at seven every night." Archie warned. "Is everything okay? I know you mentioned

47

something was up with Rogelio…" The unspoken question was *'Is everything okay with Cece'* but he knew better than to come out and ask it that way. Danny was far too wrapped up in that woman and Archie felt responsible. He and Lucy had pushed Danny to make an effort with her. Cecelia seemed the perfect choice; they had similar values, strong personalities, and chemistry in spades. When the relationship blew up in his face, Archie was honestly worried Danny would never recover.

Lucy licked her lips, her hand sliding over Gabe's bicep as they waited in anticipation. Amelia seemed to understand and she occupied herself with the little make-believe cash register they'd gotten her for Christmas last year.

"I…" Danny cleared his throat half a dozen times. "I'm patching Los Santos." There was a long pause on the other end of the line. All Danny could hear was the cha-ching of his niece's toy. "Did you hear me?"

"I don't think so," Lucy squinted at the phone, as if it would give her some kind of clarity. "I thought I heard you say you were patching to another club…"

"Uh, yeah," Danny replied shakily. "That's what I said."

Archie swiped the phone from Lucy. He put his hand up in a vain attempt to keep his wife from working herself up. "I'll deal with this. Do you mind putting Amelia down? I know it's my turn." Danny caught the tail end of their muffled conversation before Archie was back on the line. "Look, man, you're the V.P. of this club. Our guys need to see that the original members are united. Not everyone loves the work we're doing in the community and we have a lot of new obstacles in our path. If they sense any dissent, it could be a real problem. I need you. We all do..." The man on the other line wasn't saying anything and Archie finally said what they were both waiting for. "If you abandon your patch, you'll be excommunicated."

A lump formed in Danny's throat. No matter how many times he tried to swallow, the emotion wouldn't go away. Of course he didn't want to leave his club or let Lucy or Archie down or be hundreds of miles from the only home he'd ever known, but the alternative was so very much worse. Los Lobos were bad news and if their reign of terror spread—or if Cecelia got hurt in any way—he'd never forgive himself.

Scrubbing a hand over his jaw, Danny gathered his strength. "I've thought this through. I'm asking you to pull my patch temporarily. Give the V.P. title to Kyle or Big Mike. We all know they deserve it more than I ever did."

"Danny, I'm not going to do that."

"Then I'm deserting, Archie. I'll burn my fucking cut, laser off my ink, and that'll be the end of it." Patience was a virtue Danny simply didn't possess. He didn't want to deal with this anymore; the longer he was on the phone with Archie, the greater risk of breaking down and spilling all his secrets. "I'm patching Los Santos and there's nothing you can do to stop me. Wipe my name off the charter." Archie hollering his name into the phone was the last thing Danny heard before he hung up. He didn't have to be in the room to know that his President and best friend was cursing his name right now.

Five minutes later he saw Lucy's name on his caller ID but sent it to voicemail. There was nothing they could say right now to change his mind. Hopefully, someday they would understand.

Lucy's teeth were gritted so tightly she was afraid her face would crack. She and Gabe had made a pact not to curse in front of the baby but she was practically foaming at the mouth. Instead, she threw herself into their usual bedtime routine by aggressively reading Goodnight Moon, rocking swiftly, and finally settling Amelia in the crib. Lucy took a moment, drawing in a deep breath and kissing her daughter with all the love and affection she had in her body. It wasn't Amelia's fault that her Uncle Danny was a fuck up of epic proportions.

Gabriel had his own responsibilities as President of the Devil's Own. Danny had been very clear he was abandoning his patch, and that meant a meeting had to be called. Lucy reluctantly handed over her proxy to her husband because one of them had to stay home with the baby. Besides, she still wasn't feeling well. All this upset was causing her stomach to churn. Lucy got herself a ginger ale and alternated sips of the fizzy beverage with little bites of cracker. With calmer nerves, she tried to call Danny again. This time, it went straight to voicemail.

If he wasn't going to answer her, she would just have to take a different approach.

"Hey, *mamacita*," Cecelia answered the telephone warmly. "*Qué pasa*? How are the little ones? Giving you hell, I hope." The smile in her voice was palpable. "You still puking your guts up day and night?"

"Mostly just at night now," Lucy chuckled. "I actually graduated to seeing my doctor every two weeks instead of every one." It had been quite a while since she called Cece and she ached to catch up on all that had changed during that time. Unfortunately, Lucy had much bigger problems to deal with at the moment. "I want to hear all about Atlanta and how Rogelio is doing but I've got a problem…"

"*Mira*, whatever it is, we'll fix it. What can I do?" Cece pressed.

"Danny called tonight and asked Gabe to rescind his patch."

Cecelia sobered. "Something is wrong with that fuckin' *cabrón*. He been huffin' paint or something?" She sighed.

"Danny's got it in his head that he's patching with Los Santos." Lucy huffed.

"*Qué?*"

"It wasn't even a subtle hint, he said it point blank. He's out of his fucking mind! This club is his family, his life!" Lucy was trembling. There was a long stretch of silence where she waited for Cecelia to chime in. She didn't. "Have you talked to him?"

"Yesterday I told him to get the fuck outta La Verdad and not to come back. *Hijo de puta*, I couldn't a' been clearer," she growled. "He musta got some stupid idea we need his help or some shit. Rogelio's out. I'm la Presidente de Los Santos now." Cecelia exhaled heavily. "Danny walked into some shit up here but I got it under control."

Lucy chose her words very carefully. "You know he's not going to rest until all the wrongs are righted. If he thinks there's something he can do to help you, he's going to do it. I never expected that would include giving up his own club though…" She chewed her bottom lip. "You know he's in love with you."

"It don't matter," Cecelia thundered. "I was all fucked up when I got outta the compound. Being locked up for a year screwed with my head and I shoulda told him sooner." She felt the familiar ache of pain rise up in her chest and muttered obscenities under her breath. "I'm married."

All the blood drained from Lucy's face and she sputtered, "I had no idea!" How could she have known someone so long and still know nothing about them? She'd practically thrown Danny into Cecelia's arms. Guilt speared through Lucy and rose like bile in her throat.

Cecelia shifted uncomfortably on the other end of the line. "I was still practically a kid when I married Ramón. Then he was in a terrible accident. I stayed the whole time by his side, I nursed him back to health…in sickness and in health, right?"

"*Ramón!*" Lucy gasped. "You're married to Ramón? Jesus fucking Christ, Cecelia!"

"It ain't none of Danielito's fuckin' business. Yours neither." Cecelia was raw and scared and tired and pissed. "Maybe spend a little more time worryin' about the Devils and less 'bout me." She scoffed. "Daniel and me aren't fuckin' anything to each other. You better find a way to keep him outta this territory because if I so much as see him around here. I'ma fuckin' kill him."

"Come on!" Lucy sputtered.

"I already warned him to stay the hell outta La Verdad. If he chooses to ignore me, it'll be *war*." Cecelia hated this. She didn't want to fight with Lucy, one of the few people on earth she considered close enough to call her friend. Then again, she had much bigger problems to deal with in La Verdad: Los Lobos, Rogelio's addictions, and Ramón. "Take care of yourself. Okay? *Te amo*. Bye."

Lucy barely had a moment to digest the full extent of the conversation before the meager dinner she'd managed to consume was in her throat. She darted to the bathroom, retching until nothing came up but bile. She must've been there a long time since Gabe returned from the meeting. He helped her up and carried her to bed then got her a cool washcloth and mopped at her brow. "What happened?" she croaked.

"Danny abandoned his patch, Lucy. What could I have done?" Archie whispered, bending down to kiss her forehead gently. "I had to black his name off the charter." Laying down beside her, he wrapped an arm around her waist and cradled her against him.

Tears streamed down her face and she sniffled plaintively. Gabe was murmuring comforting words into her ear but she couldn't let it rest. "I called Cecelia," she whispered, "whatever Danny is doing, it's for her." She could feel Gabe's discomfort through her skin.
"She's *married*, Gabe. I would never have pushed him to go after her if I had any clue. All I saw was two idiots so clearly in love with each other!" A cry lodged itself in her throat. "Now he's excommunicated and Cecelia said she's going to kill him if he returns to La Verdad."

"She's not going to kill him," Archie soothed. "Married or not, she *does* love him." Rubbing circles over the soft roundness of her belly, he smiled against the crook of her neck. "I asked Marco to talk some sense into Danny but either way, the decision has been made." He shook his head. "I don't know if Rogelio is going to let him patch—"

"*Cecelia's* their President, Gabriel," Lucy interrupted. "They voted yesterday." She cuddled closer against him, squeezing her eyes closed. "I know there's nothing we can do. I just hope Danny knows what he's doing."

Archie pulled the blankets up around them, tucking her in loosely. "I hope so too." He was rewarded with her lips brushing against his wrist and her warmth molded against his front. "I love you, Lucy. No matter what happens, we'll figure it out together." Whatever was going on with Danny would have to work itself out on its own. He couldn't let Lucy agonize over it; this was too much stress on her. Marco agreed to keep an eye out for Danny; that would allay her fears a little bit. It was the best they could do for now...

Marco Caraway finished putting away the leftover pizza. Danny was sprawled on the couch pretending to watch a stupid movie on television. "Well, at least they bought it. Keep your eye on the prize, Daniel." He folded his hands. "What do you think your dad would've done?"

Danny kept his eyes on the television, though his mind was elsewhere. "He'd have done anything for his club..."

"And that's exactly what you're doing," Marco replied. "He'd be proud of you."

There was a long silence and Danny sighed. "Thanks." Staring down at his phone, he chewed his bottom lip. Right now, all he wanted to do was forget this day had ever happened. "I'm tired. I'm going to crash. I'm leaving early tomorrow so if I don't see you, take care of yourself."

Marco didn't blame Danny for wanting to take some time to process. This was a lot to swallow and if not for the urgency of squashing Los Lobos before they gained even more territory, he'd never have pushed so hard. As it stood, this was larger than Los Santos and the Devils. It was about the safety and survival of everyone they knew; there was more at stake than Danny could even fathom.

"Alright, goodnight. Have a safe trip..." And he left it at that.

Danny grew tired of the television and flicked it off, tossing the remote onto the coffee table. Marco had a room made up for him but he didn't feel like going there. The couch was cozy and he didn't feel quite so out of place. When he closed his eyes, sleep came surprisingly quickly given the upset of the day. He wasn't thinking about Lucy and Archie, or the Devils, or even Cecelia. For the first time in a very long time, Danny dreamed of nothing.

Chapter Six

Cecelia had been unfolding and refolding the same clothes for the better part of an hour. Her suitcase was open on the raggedy black and grey striped comforter, still filled with her personal effects despite having been working at unpacking for most of the day.

The laundry had been done, sheets changed, and the towels folded with military precision. Even the microwave had been wiped out. Care had been taken to ensure every inch of the place sparkled. Ramón had clearly brought in a cleaning service because there was no way he had the wherewithal to wax the hardwood floors in the four bedroom bungalow she'd once called home.

Once upon a time, Cece hadn't hated this place. As a matter of fact, she had been the one to strong-arm Ramón into making an offer. He'd been very adamant that he wanted to live in one of the art deco condominiums in the middle of the city. Cece had made the argument that they would get more house for their money in a quieter, more suburban area. This charming little home in a cul-de-sac was what she used to dream of as a child.

It was funny how what people wanted in life changed as they got older...

A strong pair of arms slid around Cecelia's waist, dragging her out of her thoughts. The scent of Ramón's pungent cologne was overwhelming and she brushed him off as nonchalantly as possible. "I've still got a lot of shit to put away," she grunted at him.

"It can wait," Ramón whined. "We have the rest of our lives." A wry smile tipped up one corner of his mouth. Slipping to the other side of the bed, he flopped onto the covers, sending Cecelia's folded clothes tumbling over the side and onto the floor.

"*Qué coño*?" Cecelia barked at him. "I just folded those!"

Ramón's expression didn't change. "I made us a reservation at your favorite place." His mouth moved, trying to find the right words but failing each time. His frustration grew, building until he slammed his fist into the dresser, knocking it back into the wall. "The one, La...la..."

Cecelia flinched. "La Trattoria?" It wasn't uncommon for Ramón to have memory lapses; it was all part of the traumatic brain injury he'd sustained. For many years she'd stayed by his side, convincing herself that he really couldn't help it. On their wedding day, she had promised to love him in sickness and in health...but when sickness meant every part of the man she once loved had been wiped away, it made things extraordinarily difficult. Ramón smiled boyishly and batted his eyelashes at her; it only made her cringe. Cece hardly recognized the man before her anymore. He wasn't the man she married. He was the one she was stuck with for the low, low price of her soul.

Inhaling sharply, Cecelia picked up the clothes that had fallen and tossed them into the drawer, half-folded. "I'm tired," she lamented. "Can't we just eat at home?"

"This is a big night, Cece. I want to celebrate." Reaching for her, his hands cradled her hips. "Come on, Señora Presidente. *Vámanos!*"

Arguing about tonight's plans would've expended more energy than simply picking out an outfit and going along with it. Cecelia escaped to the bathroom, locking the door behind her. She threw on a pair of leather pants, a lacy black tank top, and tossed on her cut over the outfit. Spreading black eye shadow over her lids, she swiped mascara over her eyelashes, and applied a smear of balm to her lips. The shock of pink hair atop her head fell to her shoulders in soft waves. She didn't stand in front of the mirror very long because she could hear Ramón muttering obscenities outside the door.

Rolling her eyes skyward, Cecelia was just too tired to fight. After the vote yesterday, she drove Rogelio to the hospital and they admitted him. The brother she once thought walked on water had tested positive for cocaine, heroin, and PCP. It started to make sense as to why Los Lobos were so pissed. Rog wasn't just running their drugs anymore; he was diminishing their income by using their product.

It took a little leveraging but the hospital had helped Cecelia place Rogelio in a rehab where he could finish his detox and get the counseling and support he needed. It just so happened that she chose a facility way out of town. Gina and her son Raphael were on their way to Portland for some much needed rest, relaxation, and—in Rogelio's case—a reality check.

Ramón was already dressed and tapped his fingers impatiently on the dresser. When Cecelia stepped out of the bathroom, he grunted and stomped down the stairs. She didn't say anything in response. She got in the BMW and stared out the window as he headed down the busy avenue that led to La Trattoria.

As far as restaurants went, Cece had never been to a better one. They served simple Italian fare: pasta, chicken, veal, mariscos, all well prepared. But it wasn't the meals that kept her coming back. Jenna Dayton's cannoli cake was to die for. Cece *always* had a piece when they went out there and usually took another one home for later. It had been a few years since she'd been there and she was just praying that item was still on the menu.

La Trattoria symbolized more than just a good night out, though. The last few birthdays and anniversaries Cecelia and Ramón had spent together had been here. He wanted to remind her of their past. But Cecelia didn't just remember romantic dinners: there was also the night Ramón got wasted and abandoned her here, the night she'd gone to pick up takeout and came home to find another woman in her bed, and the tears she'd cried into a pan of cannoli cake after the doctor told her she would never have children.

Ramón didn't sense her discomfort at all as they headed in the front door—not that Cecelia expected him to. She'd come to terms with his apathy toward anything she was thinking or feeling a long time ago. At the very least, as la Presidente de los Santos, he couldn't ignore Cece's edicts for the club anymore. They weaved their way to the host station, slipping through young couples in love, older couples dressed in their Sunday best, and families waiting their turn.

"There's a forty-five minute wait," a young man with pearly white teeth called over the noise.

"Ay, no," Ramón snapped. "We have a reservation under Diaz."

"I'm sorry, sir, there's a private party tonight so we're a little bit backed up. If you'd like to head over to the bar-"

"I don't want to go to the bar, *asquero*! I want my table!" All pretense of being a gentleman disappeared and the monster was unleashed.

"Ramón, *cállate!*" Cecelia cuffed him by the collar. He reached upward, grabbing her wrist and holding tight enough to bruise. Murder rose in her eyes. "You got one second to let go of me or I'ma drop you..."

Every eye in the place seemed to be on the two of them. A buxom blonde in a white chef's coat bustled out of the kitchen, clearing her throat. "Sorry, folks, there must've been some kind of a mix-up...Mr. Diaz, your table is ready now." When Lacey had run back to tell her that the new President of the local MC was standing in her restaurant, Jenna had sprung into action. She grabbed the menus from the poor host and led Cecelia and Ramón over to a private booth near the back. It was already reserved, but she was willing to bet whoever had made that reservation would be easier to deal with than these two...

Jenna had been wrong before.

When she looked up, Daniel Harding was standing in the middle of the aisle, poised to sit down. She had to catch him before he settled in. As far as Jenna was concerned, he wasn't staying. Besides, Los Santos got priority here. This was *their* town and she had respect for the traditions here in La Verdad. Jenna was about to open her mouth to tell him so when Cecelia beat her to the punch.

"What the *fuck* are you doing here?" Reaching into her belt, Cece grabbed her pistol and whipped it out. Patrons began to scream, abandoning their food and drinks—and tabs— to take cover, and run for the door. Taking a menacing step forward, Cecelia pressed the barrel of the gun into his chest. "I told you to get the hell outta La Verdad."

Danny didn't flinch. He widened his stance, crossing his arms across his chest. Blue eyes narrowed dangerously. "You going to shoot me in the middle of a restaurant?" He cocked his head to the side. "There's a five year old kid over there, a woman celebrating her ninetieth birthday, and some weird bachelor party sipping fruity cocktails out of dick straws in the far corner...that'll make a great story for the ten o'clock news: Los Santos Presidente wastes handsome man in area restaurant while children,

62

gays, and old ladies watch in horror. What the fuck is the world coming to these days?"

Damn if Danny wasn't right. Cecelia couldn't kill him with so many people standing there watching her. If she was being really honest with herself, she didn't want to hurt him *period*. He smelled like soap and sandalwood, his reddish blonde hair flopping into crystal blue eyes, and that skilled mouth curved into a handsome grin. He took a step toward her and she punched him straight in the gut. There was a sick sense of pleasure as he crumpled, falling to his knees. He wasn't anticipating getting sucker punched, which made it all the more satisfying. "I talked to Lucy. She said you have some crazy idea that you're patching Los Santos. Well, I got news for you, *pendejo*. You ain't."

Tears sprang to Danny's eyes...from the blow, he told himself. "I'm not a Devil anymore. I can patch to any club I want."

"Yeah, so go fuckin' find one who wants you!" Cecelia fired back at him. "Los Santos are *familia*." She narrowed her eyes dangerously. "R*ogelio* is my brother, *Luis, Diego, y Martín* are my cousins...*entiendes*? You don't fit in!"

"What about Ramón?" Danny argued, pointing to the man standing behind her with the amused look on his face. Ramón seemed to love chaos, the more of it the better. It was no surprise he seemed to be getting off on the drama of arguing in the middle of a restaurant.

Cece's heart slammed into her ribs. "*Ramón es mi esposo.*" She waited for Danny to respond but there was nothing in his posture that gave her the impression he heard her, let alone understood. "He's my husband. You get it now, Danielito?" She rocked back on her heels, the back of her body connecting with Ramon's front; he instinctively slung his arm around her waist. Ever the dutiful husband, he kissed the curve of her neck and she had to steel her stomach from turning over.

Expression blank, Danny looked between the two of them. "How long have you been together?"

"Almost *diez años*," Ramón announced proudly. "We will have to have a big party to celebrate. Wouldn't that be good?" He grinned. Since he was speaking now, he decided it was as good a time as any to break in. His wife seemed irrationally angry and Danny had such a disheartened expression on his face. "Cecelia, I think we should give the man a chance. New blood would be good." He smirked. "I'd patch him."

Danny's brief moment of hope was overshadowed by the murderous look in Cecelia's eyes. Her gun was turned now toward the man who she'd promised to love, honor, and protect until death do them part. Right now, it seemed like the death part was coming sooner rather than later. If not for Ramón's hold on her, Danny had no doubt Cece would have set the gun down and wrung his neck instead. Danny had half a mind to let her...coming down here and helping Rogelio had been a shameless ploy to get her attention. He loved Cecelia with all his heart and soul. Finding out she was married was a crushing blow, made worse by the fact that now he had no choice but to bear witness to their joyful marriage.

Cecelia was thirty seconds away from a stroke. She dragged a hand over her face, feeling a headache pounding in her temples. Danny and Ramón ganging up on her was forcing her hand and she felt completely out of control. Before she had a chance to explode, she was saved by the owner of the restaurant clearing her throat. Jenna grabbed the nearest takeout order, pasted a smile on her face, and held it out to Cecelia and Ramón. "I can tell you two need some time alone. Take this, on me." She motioned for the host to clear a pathway. "Paul will make sure you get some cannoli cake on the way out. Just...*please*, go on home."

"*Gracias*," Cecelia replied before Ramón had a chance to argue. The last thing she wanted to do was sit down here trying to put food in her mouth. She was hurt and pissed. Worst of all, she felt like crying. Cecelia Santos was not some simpering little girl who broke down over the smallest insult or upset. Yes, she was trapped in a loveless marriage, pining for a man she could never have, her brother was in rehab, and a psycho had held her prisoner for a year...but she wasn't about to let that crush her. Reaching into her purse, Cece pulled out a wad of cash. "I ain't takin' nothin' for free though. You put up with our shit for too long."

"Oh I couldn't—" Jenna began, but being on the receiving end of one of Cecelia's death glares was just too much for her to handle. She took the money and shoved it into her apron with a forced smile. Cece stopped for her cake and ignored the stares as she headed back out the door.

Once Los Santos had pulled out of the parking lot, Jenna turned around. "We're closing up early tonight folks…" she announced.

Nobody needed to be told twice.

Patrons proceeded out and Jenna locked the door behind them. It didn't take her long to realize that there was one man who hadn't left. Daniel Harding wasn't just sitting at the booth in the back. He had his head buried in hands, big salty tears running down his face. She wanted to feel nothing. She wanted to throw him out with the same disdain she would a cockroach or a rat…but seeing him so disheartened hit her straight in the gut.

Jenna exhaled sharply. He reached for her before she had a chance to say a word, his face buried into her abdomen and his arms wrapped around her waist. She gripped his shoulders in an attempt to dislodge him but he held fast. "Come on," she huffed, "It can't be that bad."

"She's *married*." Danny wailed. He'd always worn his heart on his sleeve, even more so since he'd given his heart and soul to Cecelia. Finding out she was married was a crushing blow. The fact that he managed to hold onto his emotion while she was still in the room was a miracle. "I fucking love her. I came down here to protect her and she's been married to that asshole for *ten years*! She shouldn't be with him! She should be with me!"

Jenna's brows furrowed as she stared down at him. "Not to impinge on your little pity party but you had sex with me less than twenty-four hours ago."

Danny exhaled sharply, resting his forehead against her body. "How the fuck else am I supposed to cope with not having her, Jessa?"

"It's *Jenna*."

"Isn't that what I said?" he groused. Judging by her expression, he was guessing it wasn't. Danny sighed heavily. "I gave up my club, my family, my fucking life for this woman and she isn't mine to have." Shaking his head forcefully, he counted the tiles below Jenna's feet to try and calm himself. It was a trick his father had told him a long time ago. Harding men were notoriously emotional, which was a sharp contrast to the women they fell in love with. Cecelia was proof enough of that. "It doesn't matter," he said grimly, "The sooner I shut Los Lobos down, the sooner I can go home and forget this ever happened."

A gasp tore from Jenna's throat, catching Danny before he pulled away from her. Her heart pounded. "You're going after Los Lobos?"

Danny's eyebrow ticked up. "You know them?"

"*Everyone* knows them," Jenna scoffed. "They demand a monthly 'maintenance' fee for all the citizens in La Verdad now. If you don't pay what they ask, they come and trash your business, your home, they scare your family. They're ruthless!" She shook her head. "They have friends at the police station and eyes on every corner. The last guy who tried to turn them in ended up getting killed..." She licked her lips. "They made it look like a suicide but I knew Timothy well. He wasn't depressed."

"You ever tell Rogelio about this?" Danny probed.

Jenna chewed her bottom lip. "A year ago, I might have but we've all heard the rumors that he was in bed with them. I was too scared." She swallowed. "And Ramón is a little...unhinged. I don't want to gossip but I-I never thought I'd see the day Cecelia got back with him..." Pulling away from Danny, she wrapped her arms around herself. "You need to pack up and leave. I'll make you something to eat before you go."

Danny felt like a caged animal, blocked at every turn. He shook his head forcefully. "I ain't hungry." He was really trying not to be angry at Jenna. This wasn't her fault and he'd already dragged her in far too deep. "Is there a motel around here somewhere? I need something cheap." He looked down at his feet. He had very little money saved and was without the safety net the Devils usually provided him with. "Maybe a men's shelter?"

The thought of Danny sleeping at the YMCA made her feel so utterly guilty. Jenna wasn't sure if it was a ploy to garner her sympathy but she fell for it hook, line, and sinker. "Look, I have a spare bedroom—" Before she had a chance to get the rest of her words out, he was wrapped around her again. "It's not forever!" she clarified, but he was already thanking her.

"You are the best. I can't tell you how much it means to me," Danny gushed. "I promise I won't be a pain in the ass. You'll hardly even know I'm there!"

Somehow, Jenna doubted that. Either way, she smiled through her uncertainty. "I'm going to convince my staff not to quit while we clean up. Sit tight for a while, alright?"

Danny eagerly agreed. After everything that had transpired with Cecelia, he was going to need every friend he could find. At the very least, it seemed Ramón was on his side...but that could change if he ever found out Cecelia had cheated on him. It made more sense now why she'd always seemed so guilty.

While Jenna bustled around, Danny texted Marco to let him know about the developments he'd made. Even though the world around him had gone to shit, he was actually making progress. At least there was that.

Across town, Ramón was chattering away about something but Cecelia couldn't listen. Her anger was still white-hot and she was seconds away from violence. Grabbing her cannoli cake, she slid it into her saddlebag and headed for the door. "I need to go for a ride, clear my head," she announced. Ramón knew better than to argue; he was already on thin ice. She swiped her helmet off the countertop and practically ran outside.

Mounting her Harley, Cece kicked it into gear and sped off into the dark night. She found herself heading down the familiar road to her condo and its small private beach. She dragged her boots off and left them on the side of her bike, then pulled off her cut and settled it on the handlebars. Cece stalked toward the sand, obscured by the night and a moonless sky, she strode forward until she hit the water...and didn't stop. She closed her eyes as the icy spray engulfed her, clothes and all. She dunked herself under the waves and held her breath until her lungs hurt. Only then did she come up for air, dragging in that first lungful with all the joy of a newly baptized woman.

For almost an hour, she did laps until everything faded from her mind except the fatigue in her muscles. Cecelia stopped by her condo to change and eat her cake in silence. Ramón had left her several voicemails but she ignored them. She couldn't answer him tonight.

After a scalding hot shower and changing into clean clothes, she gathered her bearings before heading back to her bike. With the weight of the world slightly lighter upon her shoulders, she returned to the place she was supposed to call home. Cece fell into bed and the little house at the end of the cul-de-sac was silent once more.

Chapter Seven

Jenna was sick of Danny's moping.

She agreed to let him stay with the understanding that he would be a contributing member of the household. As it stood, he seemed to expect her to play housekeeper, hostess, and shrink. By the end of day two, she was done with it. Throwing open the door to the bedroom he'd claimed as his own, she waded through a pile of discarded clothes and rested her hands on her hips. "Enough!" she hollered at his motionless form. "You're not going to lay around here and take up space."

Danny blinked at her through bloodshot eyes. He hadn't slept in days. All he could do was lay there, staring up at the ceiling and wondering where he'd gone wrong. Cecelia burst into his life when he was vulnerable after Lucy had been abducted; Cece had been his rock. It probably wasn't fair, since she'd also been freed from the Black Jack compound, but she seemed eager to keep her mind off it.

While Lucy was lying unconscious in a hospital bed, Cece forced him to leave his sister's side and he'd cursed her up and down for it. Instead of smacking him upside the head—which he more than deserved—she allowed him to vent his frustrations in a controlled setting. Without her firm hand and sharp wit, he wasn't sure how he could've ever made it through. They hadn't made love that night or the morning he slipped away with a grunt of thanks and his number tucked into the pocket of her cut.

It wasn't until Cecelia showed up again a week later that everything changed.

Cece had been instrumental in dismantling the Black Jack compound and making sure no other tyrant could keep themselves locked behind fortress walls ever again. Once the structure came down, both Lucy and Cecelia seemed lost; they needed each other for support and it felt good to lean on one another. During that time, Danny sat down and listened to Cece's storm, he held her hand until she finally broke down. She told him everything Sofía had done to her while she was imprisoned and about how lost she'd been for so long. When she finally opened up, Danny felt such a deep love flare to life inside him...

But now he knew Cecelia hadn't been honest about everything. Not *once* had she mentioned she was married to Ramón Diaz, the most dangerous member of Los Santos. It wasn't that Ramón was particularly forbidding physically. He was medium height and muscled, sure, but he wasn't like Archie—who was a six foot four powerhouse of a man. Ramón was, to put it simply, unhinged. He was reckless, manic, and his actions were violent and brutal, often without provocation. Everyone knew the stories.

Jenna grabbed the blanket and ripped it from over Danny's prone form. "Are you even listening to me?"

"Not even a little bit," Danny admitted. He sat up, head cocked to the side. "You seem pissed. What's the matter?"

"*You* are the matter!" Jenna fumed. "Your shit is everywhere, you don't clean up after yourself, and you ate all my food!" She stomped her foot. "This is totally unacceptable! "

Danny crawled out of bed, his expression bewildered. "Oh…" He bent over, picking up clothes and throwing them into his bag. "Why didn't you just say so?"

Jenna was flabbergasted. "You're an adult, Danny. You should just *know*!" The expression on his face told her it may very well have been the first time anyone outside his family had been so blunt. Dutifully, he pulled on a pair of jeans and started making the bed. He looked so lost, she started to feel bad for being so harsh. "This is meant to be a temporary arrangement and…there are things I need taken care of."

"You want me to fuck you?" Danny's expression went from wounded to smug. "Come here—"

Just like that, she didn't feel bad for him anymore. "Not everything is about fucking!" Jenna hollered.

"Sheesh! Fine!" He raised his hands in mock surrender. "What do you want then?" Jenna whipped out a handwritten list and practically threw it at him. Danny stared down at it, back and front, his eyes sparkling with mirth. "This is it?"

Shifting uncomfortably on her feet, Jenna cleared her throat. "There hasn't been a man around here in a while…" She looked almost sheepish. "So, I need some help. If you can do that, you can stay."

Danny nodded eagerly. "Honey, I can finish all this up in a couple hours." They was mostly silly things: change the HVAC filter in the attic, fix the constantly running toilet in the guest bathroom, replace the light bulbs around the skylight in her bedroom, and look over her car which had recently begun to make a funny noise. "Whatever you need for me to do around here, I'm happy to help. And I'll buy groceries, alright?"

Jenna had obviously expected the conversation to go differently, since she was all wound up and ready for a fight. Gradually, the tension in her muscles eased and she nodded eagerly. "Expect a list like this every day. I have a lot of things that need doing." Honestly, she'd been deferring so much home maintenance and DIY projects because the restaurant monopolized her time. "Thank you, Danny."

"Thanks for letting me stay here," he replied cordially. Danny was dumb about a lot of things. He narrowly passed high school math, it had taken three attempts to get his driver's license, and his sister barely kept him from self-destructing more times than he cared to count. The only thing he'd been halfway decent at was keeping a woman happy. Unfortunately, Jenna wasn't going to be swayed by sex—that was a first for him. At least he could do chores. It would give him something to think about other than Cecelia.

Danny had to stay on Jenna's good side for a while. Los Santos had a protocol for new patches. When it came to outsiders, there was a weeklong waiting period where he made his intentions known. Then there was a vote. In order for Danny to get patched, he'd need a majority. Ramón was on his side, of course. Horatio, Diego, Martín, and Luis were going to swing one way or the other. At the very least, Ramón held Rogelio's proxy due to bylaws about la Presidente having too much power and influence over the club. It could still go either way, but Danny had a shot in the dark.

"I'm going to shower then get started." Danny pressed a gentle kiss to Jenna's cheek before bounding off to get ready for the day.

Jenna stood there, astonished by the turn of events. Daniel Harding wasn't at all the man she thought he was. When they met each other several years ago, she'd been young, wild, and her mother had just been diagnosed with breast cancer. Jenna wanted to soak up all the life she could as her mother's condition worsened and she began to slip away.

A weekend in Vegas had given her just the excuse she needed to make horrible decisions. She'd gotten shitfaced and very nearly ended up in bed with a handsome male prostitute. Danny was the one who saved her from a huge bill and they ended up exchanging numbers. A year after her mother died, he showed up out of the blue at the grand reopening of La Trattoria. She'd sent out a massive text inviting friends to the event and didn't regret including him. Danny had flirted, eaten a ton of free food, and really made a dent in the open bar. In spite of everything, Jenna found him charming. She always had a thing for the bad boys and Daniel Harding was the baddest of them all.

To be honest, that wasn't why she'd picked up the phone the other night...not entirely, anyway. Jenna was lonely. She had been living in this empty house for years. She dated a little bit but hadn't had a serious boyfriend since before her mastectomy, and as time went on, found it harder to find nice guys around. The men in La Verdad were either gangsters, gay, or married; online dating wasn't working, and she'd had her fill of blind dates set up by her blissfully married friends. The closer Jenna got to thirty, the thinner the herd seemed to get and the more disheartened she became. Enough was enough. She wanted her happily ever after...but happily right now was better than nothing.

Following Danny down the stairs, Jenna resumed her quest to make the perfect new appetizer to put on La Trattoria's menu. She'd gotten distracted after she discovered Danny had somehow eaten an entire jar of jam. It had been expensive to begin with and when she found out he ate it on stale crackers, she wasn't just offended as a host but also as a chef. Now that things were settled, Jenna felt a little better.

Danny whistled as he bustled around the house. He'd even managed to find a few tools stashed in a closet somewhere—not that she knew what any of them were for. For the first time in several days, he actually, genuinely smiled.

For the rest of the afternoon, Danny and Jenna fell into a comfortable routine. Sweat glistened on Danny's temples and his hair was slightly damp with it. Jenna chewed her bottom lip, unable to keep from staring at him as he traipsed around the house. His brow was furrowed with concentration as he finished her to-do list and started adding little projects of his own. He'd noticed the handle on the oven door was slightly loose and had taken it upon himself to tighten it. While he was doing that, he noticed there was a rip in the screen above the sink. Jenna was starting to remember why she had been attracted to Danny in the first place.

It was very lucky she'd set a timer for the oven, because she could easily have forgotten she'd put several delicate appetizers made with puff pastry. They'd have burned if not for the shattering buzz of her timer. Jenna gasped softly, hurrying to find her oven mitt and pull the pan out. She'd been shamelessly staring at Danny's ass while he was bent over, adjusting her table leg so it wouldn't wobble anymore.

"That smells good." He salivated as she transferred the little triangular appetizers onto a rack to cool.

"You're welcome to try them when they're—" Jenna stopped, her mouth falling open slightly as Danny rushed the counter and shoved two of the molten items into his mouth, "—*cool.*"

Danny let out a curse, his face turned beet red and tears gathered in his eyes. "Ow, ow, ow, ow, *owww!*" he whined, dancing around the kitchen.

Jenna sprang into action. "Here, take a drink and cool your mouth down," she commanded. He was still flailing around, as if his entire body was on fire...and she had to physically steel herself from rolling her eyes. His flair for the dramatic was alive and well, at the very least. "It's alright," she soothed, her hand sliding over the creamy skin of his back. He was lean and muscular, his warmth seeping into her palms as she leaned against him. "You're going to be okay."

Years of living life on the edge of a razor blade made Danny desperate for human companionship, especially from women. Although he'd legally been an adult when his parents were killed, losing his mother's guiding influence was a huge blow. His sister Lucy tried to fill in the gaps but he was surrounded by men who propagated the stereotype that women were simply conquests to be briefly courted, coupled with quickly, and then kicked curbside. His mantra had remained unchanged over the last ten years...until Cecelia Santos changed everything.

Suddenly realizing there was more to life than one night stands had given Danny a lot to think about. Losing Cece made him rethink his position and he'd gone to Jenna with the express purpose of meaningless sex. But maybe it could be more; maybe she could mend his broken heart.

What if he ignored his feelings and his passion? What if 'loving the one he was with' was a legitimate option? Jenna was pretty. She was sweet. She had a nice home and kept it clean. She paid her bills on time and was responsible about taking her birth control. No, she didn't make his blood boil with rage and love and lust but maybe she was good enough. Was it okay to settle for second best if the woman he loved was beyond his reach, out of his league, and married to a madman?

Danny leaned in, brushing a strand of platinum blond hair away from her neck. Just as he leaned in a curt cough from the doorway startled both of them.

"Hope we ain't interrupting." Cecelia's voice was honey-thick with poison as she stepped to the front of the group. "Your doorbell's broke."

Horatio awkwardly offered her the broken plastic box that had once been attached to the wall outside the front door with a sheepish grin. He had several teeth missing, which wouldn't have been readily noticeable beneath his bushy black beard except his lips were red and chapped.

Jenna accepted the wreckage, her entire body tensed as she turned to face the Los Santos Motorcycle Club as they amassed in her kitchen.

Danny tugged away from Jenna. He felt a surge of hope at how angry Cecelia was. But then her expression faded and it was back to business as usual. "Please tell me you're here with good news?"

"Depends on what ya' call good, *cabrón*," Cece fired back. "Luis!" Inclining her head, she watched her cousin walk forward with a fresh cut. The leather jacket itself was simple and black with the image of an angel crying stitched in blue thread below the 'Los Santos' embroidered across the top. Danny looked so happy; it made Cece burn with rage. She was stuck in this dead end town, married to a man she didn't love, and was being forced to take on a drug lord her brother had gotten in bed with. While she suffered and burned and toiled, Danny was shacking up in the nice end of town with a woman who was one nose job away from being Suburban Housewife Barbie.

"Fuck yes!" Danny jogged over, grabbing the leather cut from Luis as he held it out but his face fell when he read the back. "Prospect?" He glanced between them, his eyes settling on Ramón. "I'm not some fucking kid, green under the collar. I've been a patched member of the Devils since I was eighteen..."

"You ain't blood, you ain't family, and you ain't getting a free pass to the inner circle." Cecelia took a step toward him. "We voted, *pendejo*. Get ready for bitch work, because it's been a long fuckin' time since we had a prospect." Danny was clearly annoyed but didn't say anything. She was still holding out hope he'd be so offended by the offer he'd stomp back to Nevada where he belonged. "These are our terms. Take it or leave it."

Marco's words resonated with Danny about why this was so important. He had to protect his family, his friends, and the people he loved. Right now, none of them understood his motives but someday they would. For the first time in his life, Danny had to put someone else's needs before his own. It sucked, but he'd survive. "Well, what can I say?" Swiping the cut from Luis, he slid the slick new leather over his skin and inhaled deeply. "I'm honored."

Ramón had remained silent, watching the exchange between Cecelia and Danny with interest. It had been his idea to make Danny a prospect again, since Cecelia seemed so vehemently against adding a new member to their ranks. Ramón hadn't made the suggestion himself, of course. He wanted to keep his wife happy and that meant not rocking the boat. They were already on thin ice and arguing wasn't the way to get on her good side. Ramón didn't know why she was so vehemently against Danny joining Los Santos, but he'd never really understood the woman he married and probably never would.

Instead of being the one to bear the brunt of her ire, he called in a favor and had Martín make the suggestion to patch Danny. Horatio always voted with Martín and could sway Diego and Luis. Armed with Rogelio's proxy, Ramón was able to get the vote passed without Cecelia realizing his hand in it. She accepted that she'd been outvoted but it was clear she was still pissed.

Jenna cleared her throat, breaking the rising tension that rose like fog throughout the room. "I'm glad you stopped by but I'm sure there's some business you all have got to attend to?" She folded her arms tightly over her chest, trying to keep it from beating out of her chest.

Horatio had helped himself to the rest of the appetizers she'd made and she sighed at the crummy aftermath. At the very least, he seemed to have enjoyed them. She supposed she could do a limited run in the restaurant to determine if they'd do well on the menu.

"We're done here." Cecelia replied, inclining her head to the door to signal their departure.

Danny brushed off one more too-rough blow from Ramón and pasted a smile on his face. He'd never had beef with the man before, but knowing he was Cece's husband turned their mild friendship into full-blown hatred. As they mounted their bikes, Danny's eyes remained riveted on Cecelia. There was no question she was the leader, the sun rose and set on her edict. Danny was sure she loved every minute of it, but he hated how she'd built him up and left him broken in her wake. Right now, he could be home with his club, shooting the shit, and drinking away his sorrows. Instead, he was wearing a prospect cut, living with a woman who was using him for household chores, and protecting people who didn't think they needed him around. It was deeply frustrating.

When the roar of motorcycle engines finally faded, Danny turned to find Jenna still rooted to the spot. It wasn't until he looked at her face that he realized just how upset she was. "Hey," he reached for her, "I'll fix the doorbell."

"This isn't about the doorbell." Jenna's voice was oddly level. "Cecelia and her crew just walked it here like they owned the place." Even Danny's warm hands sliding over her shoulders didn't immediately snap her out of her thoughts. She was completely shell-shocked. "They could've killed me right here in my kitchen!"

Danny threw his head back and laughed until his stomach ached. He crushed Jenna to his chest, tenderly rubbing her back. "Don't worry. We're all on the same side."

Jenna shrugged him off. "There is no *we!*" she scoffed. "I've never even ridden on a motorcycle, let alone joined the MC. And I never thought I'd see the entire Los Santos Motorcycle Gang standing in my kitchen!"

Cupping her face, Danny smoothed his thumb over her cheek. "Nothing is going to happen to you, Jenna. I swear." It was one promise he was going to deeply regret making, sooner rather than later.

Chapter Eight

Cecelia was looking for reasons to avoid going home. Ramón was not the most astute but even he could work out she was dodging him. The moment they got to Black Ink after leaving Jenna Dayton's house, she barked a couple orders and then rode out into the dark. She didn't say where she was going or when she'd be back and it *infuriated* him.

Horatio suggested they hit the bar and Ramón went along to distract himself. Two shots of whiskey in, the little voice in the back of Ramón's head that reminded him not to fuck up had been put to sleep. "Hey boys, what do you say we give Danielito a little welcome to Los Santos?" He looked practically demonic in the fluorescent lights casting shadows across his face.

"Why?" Martín furrowed his brow. Daniel Harding wasn't a bad guy. Martín had met him briefly last summer when Los Santos rode to Nevada to negotiate the terms of the peace treaty that would temporarily suspend any bad blood between them for the purpose of taking down the Black Jacks. Danny had been distressed about his sister and not particularly social, but there wasn't anything specific that stood out in Martín's mind that would've pissed Ramón off.

"He's a prospect. What other fucking reason do we need?" Ramón growled menacingly. "You remember when you prospected, Martín?" The other man shifted uncomfortably, staring down at his hands. "That's what I thought," Ramón frowned.

Luis shook his head. "Danny's not some fucker off the street, Ramón. If not for Cece's vendetta against him, he'd be a full member and you know it," he countered. Luis opened his mouth to say more but he found all the air had left his lungs as Ramón's meaty hand wrapped around his windpipe and squeezed.

Diego wrenched Ramón away and put himself between the two men. "Are you off your fucking meds?" Diego was forced to duck to avoid the fist that flew at his face. He'd anticipated the reaction. Violence was Ramón's go-to response whenever he was angry or annoyed, or even when he was feeling happy and excited. "Calm down, *hombre!*" Ramón made another grab for Luis but Diego grabbed him by the cut and pressed him against the bar.

Ramón continued to struggle but Diego had half a foot and a hundred pounds on him. He was outclassed and sorely outnumbered, since Horatio and Luis were at Diego's side, fists tight and expressions dark. "Alright," Ramón grunted. "I'm cool." He twisted, spitting the bitter taste of regret from his mouth before popping the collar on his cut. He brushed away invisible dirt and turned to face the bar again.

"Christ," Horatio grumbled. "How the fuck are we supposed to fight Los Lobos if we can't even get along with each other?" He glanced between them, finishing off the last warm sips of his beer before throwing a bill onto the bar. "I thought you *liked* Danny!"

85

"He ain't a bad kid!" Ramón admonished, "But when the fuck did we forget our traditions?" There was a long silence as the five men loitered around the bar, thinking over what he'd said.

Los Santos hadn't prospected anyone in a while. Usually they kept things in the family, meaning acceptance was cemented by either blood or marriage. The problem occurred when none of them had a legacy to call their own. Only Rogelio had a child and Raphael was five years old—he was not yet ready to take up the mantle of his father. Ramón and Cecelia were still legally married, but it had been in name only for years now. Horatio was a strange little man who mostly kept to himself; he seemed more interested in his lizard than a woman or a family. Diego's current girlfriend wasn't going to last. Martín was a widower with no interest in marrying again and, as he rapidly approached his sixties, didn't have the patience for kids. Luis had a new boyfriend every other week. It certainly didn't lend itself to growing their ranks.

Ramón took another shot. "You fuckers are no fun. I'm going home."

Luis narrowed his eyes. "Why don't you stay a while and sober up? We can get something to eat."

"Nah."

"It ain't a request," Luis retorted and herded Ramón toward the exit. La Trattoria was a block away and the perfect place to get pasta to soak up the booze. Besides, Luis couldn't shake Horatio bragging about how delicious the appetizers Jenna had made were. They sure smelled good and he was hoping they'd be on the menu tonight. Ramón clearly wasn't happy but something told Luis if Cecelia found out her husband had been drinking and driving, the law would be the least of his worries. His wife would rip out his heart and serve it to him stone cold.

Martín, Diego, and Horatio followed a ways behind them, making small talk to avoid awkward silence. La Trattoria appeared before them, the sandy colored façade warm and red tiled roof warm and inviting. There wasn't much of a crowd tonight, which worked out well.

A nervous hostess hurriedly grabbed a handful of menus. "Right this way, gentlemen," she offered. Ushering them over to the restaurant's best table, she narrowly avoided getting her ass slapped by Ramón as she skittered into the kitchen.

"I'm never going to escape these guys," Jenna muttered and pinched the bridge of her nose. Pasting a smile on her face, she stepped out and greeted them personally. "Twice in one day! I must be lucky." Or decidedly unlucky.

"You're Danny's old lady, ain'cha?" Horatio leaned in, baring his ragged teeth at her.

Jenna flinched. "We're just friends. Danny sleeps in the guest room."

"I could use a new friend, specially if she's got a *guest room* like yours," Diego chuckled.

Horatio made a slurping noise and Jenna folded her arms across her body to hold in some of her dignity. "Do you want to order something?" she demanded, her voice rising nearly an octave.

Ramón grinned. "Hey, *chica*, you seem a little tense. Why not let my boy Diego take care of that for you. Since you're not Danny's old lady, you're more than welcome to one of *mis amigos*. You look like you got a wild side…"

Luis shifted in his seat and Jenna nearly jumped out of her skin. She took a step back, connecting with the lean, lithe form of a man who smelled like he'd just chopped down an evergreen tree. Her nameless savior tugged her behind him, his mercury eyes flashing dangerously. "That's no way to speak to a lady." His voice was low and dangerous, thrumming with energy that seemed to fill the room. Without moving a hair, every eye in the place was on him.

"Don't get bent outta shape. We were just having a little fun," Ramón broke in. He rose from his chair, cracking his knuckles menacingly. "We gonna have a problem here?"

The man turned away from Ramón as if he hadn't spoken at all. "Are you alright, miss?"

Jenna's mouth fell open slightly, wondering if maybe she'd stroked out, died, and gone to heaven. Slightly shaggy blonde hair, chiseled cheekbones, a dimpled chin, rough hands, and a shy smile coupled with his warm friendliness made her go instantly weak in the knees. "Oh," she fumbled her words, "I'm fine, thanks. I'm, um…" She had to think about it for a moment. "I'm Jenna Dayton."

Without missing a beat, he leaned down, brushing a gentle kiss to her knuckles. "Lazarus Caine," he spoke softly. "It's a pleasure to meet you, Ms. Dayton."

"*Lazarus Caine*," Ramón taunted, "Your mama gave you that name? You sound like the evil boss on one of those telenovelas on Univisión!" His friends sniggered, except Luis who was staring at his phone. Ramón stood up. "We ain't here to cause any trouble. Jenna's our little *chiquita*." Holding his hand out to her, he inclined his head. "Tell him you're part of our crew."

Jenna shook her head. "I own this restaurant, I live in this city, and I keep my head down. I'm not looking for trouble from anybody." Pulling a couple of menus off another table, she placed them in front of Horatio. "Why don't you just order something and we can put all this behind us?"

If it were anyone else, they'd likely have accepted Jenna's offer with grace. Ramón, on the other hand, advanced menacingly. "You might wanna rethink your answer, *puta*," he warned. Whenever Ramón Diaz got on a power trip, it was likely to last for a while. He loved his soliloquies; truly, he loved hearing the sound of his own voice. "If you ain't with us, you're against us."

Lazarus's jaw ticked but before he had a chance to come to Jenna's rescue, the front door blew open and Cecelia stormed in like the whole world was on fire. "Ramón!" she thundered. He shrank away from her and the rest of the boys scattered to the far corners of the room, shaking. "You run and it'll be worse," she advised each of them. "This is how you treat girls when I ain't around? You would treat your *madre* like this?" she accused. "You should be ashamed of yourselves."

Ramón didn't move for a full minute, as if waiting for her to crush him like the bug he was. Lazarus was staring at her like he'd just found his new savior and Jenna...well, she looked like she was going to throw up.

"I asked you a fuckin' question!" Cecelia raged. "You..." she pointed at Ramón menacingly. "Call yourself a taxi and get your ass home." She turned to Diego then. "Make sure the rest of these *cabrones* get home in one piece or you'll be lucky if they ever find your skinny ass body. *Entiendes*?"

Los Santos scattered like dust in the wind, leaving her alone with Jenna and Lazarus. Cecelia frowned deeply, her heart and head still pounding painfully. It took her a long moment to compose herself, but when she finally was able to manage it, she turned fully to Jenna and her eyes were full of concern. "Are you alright?" She scrubbed a hand over her scarred face. "This shit isn't what Los Santos are about and I want you to know, you ain't got nothing to fear from *mi familia.*"

"How am I supposed to believe that when you come barging in my home unannounced then your *familia* busts into my restaurant and makes lewd gestures at me? They started accusing me of being Danny's old lady and when I set the record straight, it was like I'd given them a free invitation to make me their personal, private sex slave!" Jenna exploded. "I've been afraid all day but if I ask Danny to leave, then I lose the only person who can possibly protect me!"

Cecelia grimaced. On the one hand, she wanted to be sensitive to Jenna's position and her feelings...but on the other hand, she wanted to beat the woman over the head for thinking she couldn't protect herself. It was this mindset that made women like Sofía Salma go from being victims to being the victimizer. It was a vicious cycle that she wasn't going to allow to repeat again. Not ever again. "I ain't gonna let anything happen to you, Jenna. You can take my word on that."

The more Jenna's tantrum escalated, the louder her voice got. "Your *word*? Your word means nothing to me! Every time I see you, the shit hits the fan. It's keeping me awake at night!" She was shaking like a leaf. "You waltz back into town and everything goes to hell in a hand basket. I'm not going to turn a blind eye anymore. I don't care if you *personally* kill every last one of Los Lobos and return every dime they've taken from me. I don't want to see you in this restaurant again!"

Lazarus, who had been conspicuously silent for the duration of the conversation, suddenly laughed. It wasn't just a little chuckle, but a thunderous roar. The earth itself seemed to stop on its axis as Cecelia and Jenna turned to look at him. "Ah, Señora Santos..." Lazarus turned to face her, his handsome face looking about to crack with his grin. "We meet at last." He stepped forward, extending his hand to her. "Lazarus Caine: Chancellor of Los Lobos."

Nobody moved. Jenna, who had been initially standing closer to Lazarus, suddenly shifted alliances and skittered behind Cecelia.

To her credit, Cecelia didn't even blink. She refused to shake his hand and tightened her posture in response. Hazel eyes met grey as they engaged in a silent battle of wills. "You got some fuckin' nerve coming into my town and trying to lay down roots," she said, after a long stretch of silence. "Rogelio may have fallen for your tricks and empty promises but I ain't so easily swayed. Los Santos aren't going to be cutting you any more slack."

Lazarus's smile never faded from his face. "I'm sorry you feel that way but there's nothing you can do about it. We have an ironclad contract." Reaching into the pocket of his brown leather jacket and pulling out a manila folder, he continued, "Since Rogelio is indisposed, I've brought a new copy for you. Feel free to bring it to your finest lawyer. You'll see it's very well done."

"What kinda fuckin' gangster has a contract?" Cecelia fumed, swiping the document from him.

"A smart one," Lazarus replied, without missing a beat.

Opening it, she stared down at the words but couldn't seem to make heads or tails of it. It was in the most ridiculous verbiage she'd ever read. Holding it up to him, she ripped it in half and then half again, throwing the shreds back at him. "If I see you slinking around my fuckin' town again, I will shoot to kill. And I'm a really fuckin' good shot. You hear me?"

Lazarus beamed. "I am not slinking anywhere, Cecelia. I was having a quiet dinner with close friends when I noticed several lewd gentleman attacking poor Ms. Dayton. I felt it was my duty to step in and assist in her hour of need." He stepped back. "Now that we've settled the issue, you're more than welcome to join us for dinner. The new brie and jam appetizers are scrumptious."

Cecelia realized very quickly that she was outmanned and outgunned. Not one man sitting at the Chancellor's table had drawn a weapon, but she was not stupid. There were guns and knives and other assorted items they could use to rip her to shreds hidden in plain sight. "Not a chance in hell."

"Suit yourself. Allow me to make introductions, then. Petrik Villeneuve, my second in command," Lazarus gestured to a lean, pale-skinned man with a handsome face and dead eyes. "Sven Villeneuve, Petrik's twin brother." They were identical, except for something decidedly less deadly in the second man's dark orbs. "Lucian Musgrave and, of course, his charming companion, Madame Harriet Fleming."

What the fuck kind of people were they dealing with? Cecelia had gotten the impression Los Lobos were a band of hood rats tearing up her neighborhoods. Instead, she found a cohort of European gentlemen and women sitting around eating pasta like they were the fucking mafia. "As you already know, I'm Cecelia Santos, la Presdiente de Los Santos. I own this town and don't you fucking forget it." She curtseyed for dramatic effect...but she got the impression the group thought she was being serious. It only annoyed her more. Cece turned to Jenna. "Let's go. We're blowing this shithole."

Jenna balked. "This is *my* restaurant!"

"Oh, right..." Cecelia looked appropriately sheepish. "Well, I think it's time you close down for the evening then?"

"I have a business to run here!"

Lazarus cleared his throat. "We were just finishing up anyway." Reaching into his pocket, he grabbed out a wad of bills and handed it over. It was clearly a lot more than what was owed. "Excellent food and service. I'm sorry the company wasn't as sparkling but that won't be an issue for very much longer..." Lazarus let the threat linger in the air as he and his cohorts followed him out of the front door.

Head in hand, Jenna inhaled sharply. Tears replaced the rage roiling in her gut and when she turned to face Cecelia again, she found herself to face to face with a very different woman.

"Aye, *niña*," Cece soothed, brushing blonde hair away from her neck. She wasn't a touchy-feely person by nature but she knew when someone needed to be comforted. Jenna melted into her, tears soaking her shoulder. Cecelia patted her back until the hiccupping sobs dissolved into whimpering cries. "Come on, I'll take you home. You ever ridden before?"

Shaking her head, Jenna followed Cece outside to where her Harley was parked alongside the restaurant. "Is it safe?" Jenna whispered.

"If you hold on tight and don't make any sudden moves," Cece explained and handed over the helmet from the back of her bike.

Glancing back at the restaurant where her staff was cleaning the place up, Jenna chewed her bottom lip. She was tired and just wanted to go home. Settling the heavy helmet over her hair, she inched closer to the bike. Cece threw her leg over like a pro but Jenna's hips were slimmer and she needed a few tries to get it right. Once she was on, she grabbed Jenna's arms and threaded them around her waist. The Harley roared to life and they took off like a shot. At first, Jenna was terrified and shut her eyes tightly against the onslaught. Wind ghosted over her skin like a lover's caress, the hum of the engine between her thighs was no longer jarring but oddly pleasant. Opening her eyes, she stared at the starry sky all around them and suddenly all was right with the world.

"Take the long way around," Jenna begged. "This is fun."

Cecelia didn't answer, but did as requested nonetheless. They finally made their way back to Jenna's house and she idled in the driveway. "Look, I'm sorry about this mess. I ain't gonna let anyone hurt you."

Jenna's legs were like jelly as she stepped away from the bike; she barely trusted her own body. "I don't want to be part of your club, I don't want to be involved with Los Lobos. I just want to run my restaurant in this beautiful little town I've always called home."

"And you're gonna get that. It'll just take time," Cecelia exhaled sharply. "I didn't realize how bad shit had gotten around here." Reaching into her pocket, she pulled out a card and placed it in the blonde woman's hands. "That's my cell phone number. Call me anytime, day or night, if you need something."

"Thanks." Jenna stared at the card for a long moment before turning and jogging up the steps.

Cece waited for Jenna to get inside before she took off. She didn't notice Danny standing on the second floor balcony, watching her like a hawk. Even if she had, she had far bigger problems to deal with right now: like how she was going to deal with Lazarus Caine and his companions, what she could do to help Rogelio in his hour of need, and where she could hide her stupid husband's body after she got through with him.

Before things got better, they were going to get a lot worse.

Chapter Nine

July 11, 2013
Reno, Nevada

Cecelia rolled to the side, her stomach heaving violently as the room twisted into view. The back of her hair was somehow soggy and crunchy at the same time. When she slid her hand up to assess the area, she gasped at the flash of pain that burned through her skull. Vision swimming, Cece closed her eyes and slid back into unconsciousness.

When she awoke again, the darkness had been shattered by a halogen light bulb. At first, Cecelia was disoriented and she attempted to reach up and wipe away the crust around her eyes. It didn't take long to realize her arms and legs were tethered to metal railings. She was laying in a twin-sized bed, unable to do anything more than turn her head from left to right. There were rows of similar beds filled with bodies but she couldn't immediately decipher if they were living or dead.

A feral cry ripped from her chest as thrashed, ignoring the pain simmering in her veins. Cecelia's only focus was on getting free. The more the restraints held her back, the more she fought until her entire skeleton rattled with the force of her efforts.

"Stop!" a voice hollered from across the room, heavy with an accent she wanted to say was Irish. "You're going to hurt yourself!"

"Get me outta these fuckin' chains!" Cecelia gasped. She wanted to scream but her throat was bone dry and scratchy as sandpaper. A face appeared over her and she paused to take in the sight of her captor.

Blonde stringy hair was tied up in a messy bun, and flecks of blood speckled her cheek. "I'm running low on Ativan and I'd rather we don't have to bring in the big guns." Cecelia spat at her, and the woman sighed; Cece didn't have enough saliva to make any great mess, but the hatred emanating off her was palpable. "You may be the one in restraints but I'm a prisoner here too. I don't want them to come in and hurt you. I've seen them do it before and they don't care how fragile you are."

Cece didn't immediately stop trying to buck her tethers, but she was at least listening. "What the fuck are you talking about? Who are *they*?"

"The Black Jacks…" The woman's voice was a low whisper. "They brought you here. They brought me too."

"Why?"

A shadow crossed the Irish woman's face and she seemed to sag under the weight of her own body. "I don't know. I was—*am*—an ER nurse. I think they brought me here to keep this medical wing running." She chewed her bottom lip. "There are others, though: Jane Does who don't seem to know who they are, girls not even old enough to be called women, and a building full of bitches who will stab you in the back in a hot second." She glanced over her shoulder, as if expecting someone to appear behind her. "I'm only telling you this because I think you're different. You've been in and out of consciousness but you've been talking. You've been fighting."

Cecelia was completely calm now, hazel eyes boring right down to the soul of her guardian angel. There was no malice in the nurse's voice or her eyes, only fear. Cece also got the impression this woman was unused to feeling such emotion. Glancing around, her eyes caught the IV bag pouring fluids into her veins and the machine monitoring the beating of her heart. "Can you let me outta these?" She rattled the leather straps holding her down.

"If you promise not to go running out of here. You're weak and you'll fall. You'll also be captured by the guard and brought right back here, and this time I'm not sure I'll be able to put you back together again," the blonde tsked. "Do you understand?"

"I ain't stupid," Cecelia snapped at her. "I won't go anywhere, alright?"

Gently, she undid the buckle on the straps, first on Cece's feet and then her wrists. The nurse grasped her hand, shaking her head. "You rubbed the skin raw. Let me put some salve on there so you don't get an infection."

Cecelia pushed herself up, blinking rapidly as she finally took stock of the room around her. Her savior bustled over to a cabinet and pulled out some ointment, handing it to her to smear over her numb hands. "I'm Cecelia Santos."

"I know."

"And you are?"

"Oh!" The woman gasped at the oversight. "Sorry, I'm forgetting my manners. Beatrice Patton, but my friends call me Bea." Reaching for a cup by the bedside, she poured some fresh ice water and handed it to Cecelia with a straw. "Small sips to start," she urged.

The first swallow was like heaven in her mouth as it put out the fire currently raging in her belly. An exhaustion beyond any she'd ever known was creeping over her, but she didn't want to succumb to it again. "How long've I been out?"

Bea grabbed a blood pressure cuff from the crash cart and unwound her stethoscope from her neck. She slid it over Cecelia's arm, taking a quick reading before shaking her head. "Your blood pressure is through the roof, not that I blame you. Waking up in this hellhole every morning gives me the vapours."

"Is that shit contagious? I don't need nothin' else to heal from." Cecelia eyeballed her skeptically before she began to explore the damage to her skull. Most of the blue dye was still in place but a huge chunk of her hair had been shaved away and her head stapled shut. "What the fuck happened?"

"I'm not sure. Sofía brought you here with your head bashed in and informed me I was to use every resource to save you." She cleared her throat. "I'm sorry, I'm not a plastic surgeon. The staples aren't pretty, but they haven't gotten infected yet and that's a big win for the both of us." Bea took care to assess Cecelia's neurological status, took her temperature, listened to her heart and lungs, then sat back. "You're going to survive...but it'll take a while for your hair to grow back."

Cecelia shrugged her off. "I don't care about that." Bea's lip ticked upward in a smile but it faded slightly when she leaned in. "What I do care about is figuring out how the fuck to get out of here."

"Keep your voice down," Bea warned. "There's always somebody listening in."

And that's when Cecelia found out just how true that statement was. Guards stormed like Herod's army coming to drag Jesus to Pontius Pilate. They were women of all ages, shapes, sizes, and colors but they all wore the darkest, vilest expressions she'd ever seen. Cecelia scrambled for the side of the bed, ripping the IV out of her arm in the process and more of the crimson liquid that ran in her veins spurted onto the bed. She knocked into another bed where a comatose woman with skin the color of sour milk was laying, not breathing or flinching. Cece let out a cry, her legs failing her as she tried and failed to get up off the tiled floor. The more she tried to get away, the more the guards seemed to laugh at her plight. They surrounded her, pulling her up off the floor and dragging her to the door.

"She's not clear yet!" Cecelia heard Bea scream. "Let her go!" Her pleas fell on deaf ears, because they hauled the blue-haired woman down the hall, legs half dragging behind her as she tried in vain to buck her captors. They wound their way down through dark hallways and thickly paneled metal doorways, to an elevator that didn't look like it would hold her weight, let alone that of six other women.

Cecelia held her breath, stilling only as long as it took to get up to the main floor. When the door opened blinding white light bounced off every surface, burning the eyes that had been adjusted to darkness for so long. As her body slumped onto the pristinely kept floor, she brought her hand up to shield against the stinging glare.

"*Bienvenidos a mi casa.*" A venomous voice seemed to echo throughout the entire room. This was the first time Cecelia ever heard the voice of Sofía Salma, but she knew instantly this woman was pure evil. "I am glad you are improving, *mija.*" The demon's painted lips never seemed to move even as she spoke. "I have been waiting some time to speak to you. You have done amazing work with the project I hired you for. You are just as skilled as your references indicate, which is why I've brought you here." She perched on the edge of a bench, staring upward at a massive oil painting lit by natural sunlight. When she turned to Cecelia again, Sofía was frowning. "This place is secluded and well protected, but it cannot suit all my needs. I intend to make it a haven for the new Black Jacks. I have an architect and a contractor, now all I need is an engineer."

Cecelia laughed bitterly. "Go ahead and kill me, I ain't going to do shit for you."

"Kill you?" Sofía chuckled. "No, of course not...but I will kill that darling little nephew of yours." She slid her phone out of her pocket. "How sweet he looks at his preschool graduation. He looks just like his papa, don't you think?" She flipped through several more pictures of Rogelio and Raphael snuggling together at a booth at the boy's favorite restaurant. "It would be a shame if something were to happen, especially if there was something you could've done to save him..."

Descending into a violent string of curses in Spanish, Cecelia grew angrier when Sofía just laughed. Mustering up all the strength in her body, she took a flying leap with murder on her mind. Her body connected with Sofía's and she dragged the bitch to the floor. "Don't you touch them!" Cecelia screamed.

There was a brief moment where panic flashed in the older woman's eyes and then suddenly, Cece's world went black again...

Cecelia didn't wake for three more days and when she did, she had several broken ribs, a stab wound centimeters from her kidney, and two horribly blackened eyes. It took quite a while to regain her strength but Cece had to fight for Rog, Raphael, Gina, and Los Santos. No harm would come to the people she loved while she had breath in her body...even if it meant working for the enemy.

Chapter Ten

Cecelia awoke drenched in a cold sweat. Her heart pounded in her chest and her throat was tight with fear. This night—just like many nights before—she forgot where she was and panicked. A year held hostage made her very squirrelly, especially after a nightmare like that one. Cece glanced around the room expecting Ramón to be lurking somewhere nearby. After their tiff last night, he'd slunk to the far corner of the house to avoid her for the rest of the night.

Ramón wanted to make their marriage work; it was all he'd talked about since they separated. But it didn't change the fact that Cecelia hadn't been happy in a long time. They had been young and stupid when she agreed to marry him. At nineteen years old, she'd been looking for the stability she hadn't had growing up. Cecelia's mother had always been more interested in partying than in the welfare of her two children; her dad left before Cece was even a year old. It had been her "*Tío*" Angelo who had filled that paternal role in her life. He had never allowed Cece to believe she was any less just because she was outnumbered in the club ten to one.

Angelo Diaz was a lifetime member of Los Santos. He had a son who lived with his ex-wife in Reseda and split his time between visiting there and hanging out with Cecelia and Rogelio. Cece had met Angelo's son Ramón a few times at picnics and family events, but she was always more focused on her schoolwork than boys. Angelo told her she could be anything she wanted and she took the bait: hook, line, and sinker. At the age of thirteen, Cecelia applied to a magnet school that focused on applied sciences and math to help students get a leg up in the college process. There had been an interview and a home visit, and Angelo had been there for all of it. Cecelia got into the private academy on a full scholarship and it certainly paved the way to a full ride at UCLA. Angelo had never been prouder.

In between her freshman and sophomore year, Cecelia returned home for summer break and found herself smack in the middle of a turf war. The Devils of California were encroaching on La Verdad's territory and things were getting rough. Rogelio's priority wasn't protecting Cecelia but Angelo wanted to make sure she was safe. When Ramón showed up at her house that evening, it was lust at first sight. He was lean and handsome, with long dark hair that he braided to keep out of his warm brown eyes. He was a perfect gentleman...at least for the first few minutes.

They went at it like animals for weeks. Even after the threat had passed, Ramón and Cecelia were inseparable. As the time ticked closer to her returning to school, it felt like her heart was going to break. Ramón must've felt the same way, because he proposed to her two days before she was set to return to her dorm at UCLA. They were married in Vegas the following afternoon. To say that the family was shocked was an understatement. Angelo congratulated them but there was something in his demeanor that told Cecelia he disapproved. Her mother was ecstatic, of course; Cece had landed a man who was willing to put his ring on her finger and offer her the protection of his name...but Cecelia never wanted to be a

Diaz. She wanted to keep the same name as her club and her family; Ramón always respected that.

For two years, Ramón and Cece lived for her time away from school. Although he visited on weekends, it wasn't the marriage either of them had anticipated. Terrible fights were smoothed over with booze and sex and then by distance. Neither of them realized how toxic the relationship truly was. They were young and stupid and in love. It wasn't until a month before Cecelia was set to receive her degree in electrical engineering, Ramón gave her a graduation present she'd never forget.

At first, Cece thought it was just the stress of finals but lingering nausea, fatigue, and a positive pregnancy test changed her perspective. Ramón was over the moon when she told him. Pushing aside everything else, the two of them returned to La Verdad and immediately started looking at real estate. On the very first day, Cecelia found her dream home. It had taken some convincing, since Ramón hadn't wanted something so traditional, but eventually he capitulated to whatever his pregnant wife wanted. They hadn't even closed on the house when the unthinkable happened...

Ramón had been out celebrating his impending fatherhood and new homeownership. Not wanting to spend the night away from his wife, he got on his bike while intoxicated and wrecked hard.

Cecelia still had nightmares about receiving that call at three in the morning informing her a motorcyclist had been brought in. He was so mangled in the accident he couldn't be identified and all his teeth were shattered so they could not even check dentals. The wallet found at the scene contained her phone number. It could have belonged to anyone, really...but Cecelia already knew it was her husband's. She'd had a sick feeling in the pit of her stomach the whole night.

Having to identify a man being kept alive on life support, not knowing if he had any brain function or any ability to heal, was devastating. It was even worse when three days into her vigil at Ramón's bedside she had excruciating back and abdominal pain that resulted in her being rushed to surgery herself. Her pregnancy had been ectopic and had caused a life threatening rupture. The hits kept coming when the doctor who had done her surgery told her they'd had to take her left ovary and fallopian tube, which meant conceiving would be more difficult. Not only was Ramón's life hanging in the balance but Cecelia had lost his child as well.

Angelo stayed by Cece's side day and night. When she was discharged from the hospital, he got the administration to put her up in a special suite for family members of critically ill patients. Ramón still hadn't woken up but he was breathing through a tracheostomy and was getting nutrition through a feeding tube. There were hundreds of conversations about medical decisions, power of attorney paperwork, disability insurance, and the grieving process. Cecelia was so numb, she wasn't sure if she would feel anything ever again.

Then, three weeks into Ramón's hospitalization, he began to spontaneously open his eyes.

It wasn't necessarily a sign that her husband was in there, but it was the first shred of hope they'd had so far. Test after test followed a slew of repeated surgeries on his bones, his spine, and his face. There were so many therapists: physical, occupational, speech, psychiatrists, physiatrists... Cecelia couldn't keep them straight anymore. She sat at Ramón's side, waiting for those minutes a day he could focus solely on her, and tried not to crumble.

It was another month before Ramón began to make strides. He was able to support his respiratory status enough that they could placed a cap over the breathing tube and he could speak—not that anything he said made sense. Shortly thereafter the tracheostomy was removed and replaced with a bandage over the stoma. The only thing that didn't seem to be improving was Ramón's cognition. He was angry, often violent and agitated. He had to be physically and chemically restrained on many, many occasions. Cecelia hated when he spit and kicked and clawed. She was deeply embarrassed when he sent a perfectly lovely nurse to the emergency room with a nasty bruise. No matter how many times Cece apologized on Ramón's behalf, it didn't seem to be enough. The doctors told her it was related to the injury and he would hopefully regain some semblance of control but they couldn't make any promises.

Finally, it came time to be discharged from the hospital but Ramón's recovery was far from over. The rehabilitation facility they'd selected was the best in the state, but it was a haul from La Verdad. Angelo found her an apartment close by so their commute wouldn't be so awful. Cecelia focused on her husband's care, spending hours in therapy with him and learning how to do his exercise regimen. After being bedridden for so long, Ramón took his first few steps and hope was renewed once more. Cecelia still hadn't shed a single tear. In fact, it took her another six months before Ramón began to improve and the pain finally overwhelmed her.

On the eve of his discharge home, Cecelia returned to their little house on the quiet street to prepare. Los Santos had dipped into club funds to pay for the house; they'd also taken a collection to furnish the entire place. That night, as Cece lay in bed and stared up at the ceiling, the tears began to fall and she was certain they'd never ever stop. She cried for the child she lost, the husband she once knew, and for a life that should've been perfect. Cece was afraid she might drown in the river of tears that poured out of her...

It took all she had to hide her sadness from Angelo and the home health nurse that came to visit Ramón several times a week. Her husband had no idea how to process his own feelings, let alone hers, so she didn't need to worry about bothering him. There were long periods of time now when Cece was alone with her husband and she realized how truly damaged he was. He was no longer affectionate, he got angry over the stupidest things, and his regimen of medications required more than her engineering degree to manage. There were still so many doctor's appointments and follow-ups and repeat scans. Bills were mounting and the insurance company was calling every day...

Cecelia had to go to work. Honestly, it was a blessed relief. Angelo came to stay with Ramón while she searched for jobs. She started freelancing which led to a steady stream of income that at least kept the creditors at bay. They finally found a routine that worked. Cecelia began to realize Ramón wasn't ever going to be the same...but neither was she. She wasn't warm and funny anymore; she was cold and callous and brutality was her only defense.

Time no longer seemed to ebb and flow the way it once had. Years passed before Ramón was able to acclimate to a normal daily routine. He got his driver's license back, was able to help around the house, and get involved with the club again. Prior to his injury, he had been the club's treasurer but he couldn't focus or concentrate long enough to be accurate with the daily financials of Black Ink and Los Santos anymore. Diego stepped in to provide assistance and Cecelia breathed a little easier.

When it really started to go to shit was when Ramón started pressuring Cecelia to have kids. Memory loss was a huge part of his injury and it didn't seem to matter how matter how many times she reminded him about the loss of her first pregnancy. He just kept pressing her and the onslaught never ceased. There were several occasions Cecelia was afraid of what he would do to her if she didn't acquiesce and '*try*' again. She could barely keep her husband in line. Even if she had wanted it, how could she work and raise a child too?

One night, during one of Ramón's rages, he laid his hands on Cecelia and any hope of reconciliation was gone. She had been living in a loveless marriage for years and she couldn't do it anymore. After hiring a lawyer to draft up the divorce papers, she decided to kick off their separation by taking an engineering gig out of state. They both needed some space and a chance to heal. It crushed her when she had to tell Angelo. He understood, of course, and encouraged her to do what was right for her. He gave his blessing before he moved to Florida with his girlfriend and they started a new life together. Cecelia hadn't talked to him since. It wasn't her place...but maybe she needed him now.

Ramón had never stopped trying to get them back together. It was one of the reasons he'd never signed the divorce papers. He sat on them for almost a year of separation before she started getting tough. Then Sofía abducted her and she returned even harder and more violent than ever before. It wasn't until Cecelia met Daniel Harding that she realized how very wrong she'd been about Ramón even from the day she met him. She had been obsessed with his power and strength, she ached to be protected...but she didn't need that anymore. What Cece wanted was a partner, an equal, and Ramón could never offer that to her.

The taste of freedom and passion and love was equal parts exciting and frightening for Cecelia. She wasn't sure how to process it but she sure knew how to keep herself busy. Going to Georgia was enough to slake her thirst for a time but she missed home.

Rogelio's descent into depravity was just the opportunity she needed to get back.

Everything had spiraled from there and now, Cecelia was torn. On the one hand, Ramón's behavior with Jenna Dayton gave Cecelia the out she was looking for. He'd been crude, rude, and—left unchecked—likely would have become violent. Receiving that text from Diego about what her own club was doing to the locals made her skin burn. After rescuing Jenna, she returned home to find Ramón waiting. It wasn't anger he threw at her feet. As usual, it was tears and apologies. She should've cut him off at the knees and left. Instead, she'd brushed him off and told him to find somewhere else to sleep tonight.

Ramón was still passed out on the couch in the den when she slipped out of bed. Cecelia rubbed the exhaustion from her eyes, blinking blearily at the numbers on the stove. It wasn't even four in the morning yet but she hadn't eaten since breakfast yesterday. She thought about making herself something to eat but that would likely wake Ramón and she couldn't face him yet.

Slipping on her jacket and her shoes, Cece snuck out the side door with the car keys in hand. It was too early for her bike; she'd wake up the whole neighborhood. At least with Ramón's car, she was able ease the car out and head to the twenty-four hour diner without disturbing anyone. Hopefully she wouldn't run into Lazarus Caine or Los Lobos. Wouldn't that be the icing on her shit sundae?

The bell above the door jangled as Cece stepped inside the diner and found her way to a booth. She hunched over, resting her head in her hands. The shuffling sound of footsteps made the hair on the back of her neck stand straight up. It wasn't in fear this time but recognition.

Daniel Harding stood in front of the table with his hands jammed in his pockets and his expression grim. "I know it's not what you want but we need to talk…"

"Yeah," Cecelia heaved a sigh. "But first? I need coffee."

Danny nodded and plopped into the seat opposite her.

It was the first thing they'd agreed upon all year.

Chapter Eleven

Cecelia had made a valiant effort to avoid Daniel Harding and all the feelings he dredged up in her over the last few months. She'd almost convinced herself she felt something for him only because she was coming out of a horrific year being held prisoner inside an impenetrable fortress. Seeing him now, she knew it all a lie. Cece sat across from him, sipping coffee and picking at chicken fingers, while trying to ignore the feelings welling back to the surface. The time they'd spent together in Errol had been the happiest in her life...she couldn't ignore it anymore.

"How'd you know I'd be here?" Cece finally asked.

"I didn't." Danny scratched the back of his neck. "You told me you came here when you needed to get away." He licked his lips. "I needed to get away tonight."

Cecelia stared at him incredulously. "I said that?" It was the truth; she just couldn't fathom a version of herself that would've revealed something so personal about herself.

"You said a lot of things," he muttered.

Cecelia had shared quite a bit during their brief relationship but so had Danny. She knew how deeply he regretted not being the man his sister needed growing up and how he was lost without a father's guiding influence. He'd broken down when he realized just how much he'd been relying on Lucy and the toll it had taken on her.

Cecelia held him for a long time as he confessed every stupid conquest he'd undertaken in a vain attempt to stave off loneliness and how it had crashed and burned every single time. At the end of the day, he swore there wasn't anyone he wanted but her. And he stayed true to his word; he really was going to do anything to win her.

Danny pushed around the fruit that had come with his order of pancakes. He didn't understand Cecelia or her obsession with keeping him at arm's length. She'd never officially said *'I love you'* but Danny knew in his soul she did. Nobody had ever given him as much shit as Cecelia—except for Lucy, and his sister was obligated by Jesus or the law or some other higher force bullshit to love him. When Cece treated him with the same angry passion, he knew she cared about him deeply. Sitting across from her now was enough to break his heart all over again. The best he could do was change the subject. Danny cleared his throat, "Jenna told me what happened—"

"I wasn't gonna let anything happen to her. You gotta know that. And I made sure Ramón and the boys understand that ain't appropriate behavior," Cece interrupted. "I don't know what the fuck kinda club Rog was runnin' while I was away but it ain't gonna be the same now that I'm in charge."

"I get it, Cece." Danny pushed his plate away and started to play with sugar packets instead. "What I don't get is why you won't let me help you. I ain't some fuckin' thug who's new to MC life." He let out a shuddering breath. "I broke my allegiance to the Devils so I could be here.

I want to help you with Los Lobos and you're punishing me for it."

Cecelia couldn't look him in the eye. "Los Santos is a *family* club."

"Fuck that!" Danny snorted in annoyance. "Family is more than blood. You are part of me and I'm part of you, like it or not." He leaned in closer, keeping his voice low. "Do you remember the night you cried in my arms, Cecelia?"

It felt as if she'd been burned with an electric shock: her insides clenched and she felt nauseated. "It meant nothing."

"Like hell it did! I was there for you because I wanted to be. I'd have followed you to the ends of the earth." Danny's expression darkened. "Except you left out the part where Ramón was your *husband*. It wouldn't have mattered to me, you know. I didn't think I was the first guy to fall in love with you and it occurred to me you might've loved one back before you met me!" He scoffed. "I ain't as stupid as you seem to think!" If looks could kill, Danny would've been laid out right there.

Cecelia lashed out. "You *are* stupid! And the worst part is you don't even seem to understand how fuckin' stupid you really are!" She slammed her fist against the table, rattling the plates and napkin dispenser. The few people milling around the diner knew better than to look up at la Presidente de Los Santos and her doomed companion. "You ain't one of us and you never will be."

"Oh really? Because the Prospect patch I'm wearing says different." Danny argued. "I know Sofía and her crew made you feel unstable. You might've already been fucked because of everything you went through with Ramón and the baby." He flinched at the pain that crossed her features, but he had long ago realized brutal honesty was the most effective way of making her listen. "All the things that led up to this point made you who you are. And maybe I'm going about helping you the wrong way. But you know what I ain't wrong about? You loving me. You can front all you want but I don't believe you for a fucking second. You're trying to push me away and I'm not letting it happen."

"I ain't lookin' for some overgrown man child to come poking around my town, stirring up trouble." Cecelia fired back. She took a sip of water to try and calm the rage bubbling in her gut. "You wanna be part of this club for real? Well, you better get on Luis' good side because he's the only member of this club you got a chance with."

Danny rested his palm on the table. "I am *not* going away. I am going to keep going until you see this for what it is. I'm here to protect the people I love. So, I'm not going to leave here until Los Lobos have been run out of La Verdad. Even if you never admit that you love me, I'm not backing down." Inching his hand over, his fingertips traced the knuckles of her fist. "You think you're stubborn? I fuckin' invented that."

Cecelia's eyes locked on Danny's. His touch should've been unwelcome but it instantly made her feel warm inside. Suddenly, she was transported to Errol as they settled into the house he'd grown up in. Lucy was wrapped up in Archie and their love...Cecelia was honestly jealous. She decided picking up with the club's biggest player would mean she wouldn't lose her heart. Oh, how wrong she'd been. "You might be used to getting your way but you ain't ever played with me before."

"I'm not playing with you, Cecelia. I'm dead fucking serious about all of this. All I want is a shot..." Danny pressed. "If for no reason other than there's a greater chance of beating these fuckwads if we work together. Jenna told me these aren't some hoodlums in a gang. They're sophisticated, educated guys and they are rich as sin. They have the people in this town running scared...and you know what? That's exactly what the Devils had with the Blackjacks. They were smart, they were growing in numbers, and it took all our clubs to put those fuckers down!" He gripped her hand tighter. "Let's nip this in the bud before they start doing what Sofía did to you!"

There was a whole minute where Cecelia simply stared. Danny's blue eyes were filled with passion and fire. His posture was tight, his heartbeat thrumming steadily in his veins, and his breathing was ragged. She reached into her pocket and palmed the item she'd been carrying around since they'd handed over that prospect cut; it was just small piece of fabric but its significance was paramount. Cece chewed her bottom lip. Danny was right...she was at the very beginning of this thing and if she couldn't accept help now, she might end up in a situation where people she loved and cared about would be hurt or worse. Rogelio was already hundreds of miles away at a rehab because of what Los Lobos had done to him...who would it be next?

"You got one chance at this, Danielito," Cecelia warned as she pulled out the patch and slid it across the table to him. "If you fuck up in any way, you're gonna be turfed back to the Devils in ashes. You got it?"

"Sí madame!" Danny saluted.

Cecelia laughed despite herself. "We gotta work on your Spanish for sure, *gringo*, but that's for another day." The sun was starting to rise in the East, casting a warm glow over the diner around them. Sitting here with Danny reminded her of everything she'd been trying to forget. When she got home, Ramón would likely want to debrief about the blowout fight they had last night. Needless to say, she wasn't looking forward to it.

Danny wisely decided not to bring up the fact that he had actually won an argument with Cecelia Santos. He was much too happy ripping away the little fabric square that said 'Prospect' on it and trying to decide where to put his 'Miembro' badge. "You aren't going to regret this."

"See that I don't." She licked her lips. "I've got to get going. Thanks for breakfast." Before he had a chance to answer, she was gone.

Tipping his head, Danny reached into his pocket to check for change before he signaled the waitress. Once the bill was settled, Danny headed out to where his bike was parked and inhaled the cool morning air deep into his lungs. As he jetted down the street, avoiding most of the crush of rush hour traffic, he stared up at Jenna's house and smiled sadly. Jenna had been exhausted after she returned home from the restaurant last night and he had carefully tucked her into bed. She deserved better than her lot in life. When all of this was over, he was going to make it up to her...somehow.

Slipping into the house, he found half a cup of coffee spilled on the counter and her powder pink bathrobe on the floor. That wasn't like Jenna. She was a neat freak and any clutter threw her into a tailspin. "Jen?" he called out, sliding through the house. His hand was resting on the firearm sitting against his hip. "Jenna?" He called again. He hoped she had rushed off to attend to some business, but a full lap of the house didn't give him any clues.

Danny stepped onto the front porch to see if she had gone outside when he saw something that made his heart stop...

Sitting on the doorstep was an envelope of yellowed parchment with the image of a wolf ghosting over the paper in ash. A handwritten letter inside announced Jenna had been taken and if Los Santos wanted her back alive, they would have to meet all of Los Lobos' demands.

Dragging a hand over his face, Danny cursed bitterly.

He was starting to get really fucking sick of bad guys abducting people he cared about. Slipping his phone out of his pocket, he stabbed the speed dial for Cece and pulled the phone to his ear. "We were too late," he explained to her voicemail. "Those fuckers took Jenna. I'll be at Black Ink in ten minutes. Get the boys together." And with that, he fled the house and rode for his new clubhouse. Time was of the essence.

Chapter Twelve

Jenna's eyes rolled open slowly, as if there was an invisible film over them. At first she was certain she was still in bed and being abducted by Lazarus Caine was nothing but a nightmare. Jenna moved to sit up and nearly screamed when she started to slide against the satin sheets. She grabbed the other side of the mattress for leverage, swimming against the slippery fabric. The movement propelled her forward and she bumped her head against a side table. A warm, luxurious bed was not the kind of torture chamber she was expecting to wake up in...but it also wasn't home. "Ouch!"

"Not used to such finery?" A sly voice chuckled from the other side of the room.

"Oh!" she gasped in surprise, pulling up the comforter to cover herself. She must've lost her bathrobe in the shuffle and was left in a tank top and pair of shorts. "I didn't realize satin sheets would be so, well, *silky*. I used to think they were romantic but they seem dangerous. You start moving around too much during sex and someone's going to end up in the hospital!" There was a bottle of water on the table and she grabbed it, taking a drink to soothe her. Jenna's throat was bone dry, her head aching, and her body still feeling weak and limp. "You drugged me." It was more of an observation than an accusation.

"I assure you, nothing untoward happened while you were slumbering," Lazarus replied coolly.

"*Slumbering*?" Jenna huffed. "You mean *passed out cold*?" Glaring at him was making her head pound and she rubbed her temples. "Why was it necessary to kidnap me anyway? I already told you, I'm not involved with Los Santos business or Daniel Harding. I'm just a chef trying to make my business work in a struggling economy."

Lazarus leaned forward, resting elbows against his knees. "That's the thing, Jenna dear. You were involved the moment you let that Neanderthal stay with you, whether you like it or not. " A glint in his grey eyes seemed to catch the dull light filling the room. "As long as Los Santos cooperate, you have nothing to fear."

A lump lodged itself in Jenna's throat and she gripped tighter to the bed sheets in terror. "And if they don't?"

Without warning, Lazarus stood to his full height. "You should hope they do. I would hate to harm a hair on your pretty little head…" He headed for the door, pausing to glance behind him. "You must be hungry after all the commotion this morning. May I offer you something? Coffee? Tea? A pastry?"

"I'm not hungry." Jenna replied fiercely. "I would like to freshen up, though."

"Of course," Lazarus bowed. His touch was gentle against her back as he helped her to stand. Jenna didn't realize how weak she was until she tested her legs and nearly went ass over teakettle. Lazarus caught her waist, supporting her slight weight easily.

Shepherding her into the bathroom, he made sure she had something before loosening his grasp.

Jenna's visage was ghastly. There were dark purple stains beneath her eyes and her makeup had smeared terribly. Her hair was sticking up and frizzy from the friction of the satin sheets. In the reflection she could see the man staring at her as if he could see into her very soul. Goosebumps rose over her skin equal parts lust and disgust. What was wrong with her? She couldn't be attracted to this monster who had drugged her and dragged her God only knew where...it wasn't right.

As she peeked out the bathroom window, Jenna's heart seized. They were in a rustic cabin surrounded by dense trees. The sky was vibrant and blue, puffy clouds dulling the rays of the sun. It must have been late morning by now and the lack of caffeine only fueled the headache that simmered in her veins. Soft, fluffy towels were hung on a handcrafted wooden towel rack. Everything around her smelled earthy and pure. It struck her as odd. Lazarus seemed to be made of steel and mercurochrome, but he was as staunch and steadfast as a tree.

Turning the shower on full blast, Jenna stepped under the scalding spray and practically melted. If not for the little lip at the edge of the tub, she could've honestly flopped over and been unable to get up. Steam rose around her, clearing her senses and the cobwebs in her vision. For a long time she sat there, weak and quiet until there was a knock on the door.

"Jenna? Are you alright?"

"I don't know," she answered honestly. The door slid open and she wrapped her arms around her breasts. Pink, puckered scars still livid after all these years marred her once perfect skin. Lazarus bent, dragging her into his arms. He brought her over to the chair he'd been sitting in before settling her down and going back for a towel. He slipped it around her shoulders and knelt beside her. Jenna cleared her throat weakly. "Whatever you gave me is still in my system..."

Lazarus honestly looked remorseful. "I should perhaps have given you a smaller dose. I did not think it would affect you so profoundly."

Jenna dragged her fingers through her soggy hair in an attempt to comb it. "It's something I've dealt with for a long time. I'm very sensitive to medication." She chewed her bottom lip. "Speaking of, did you manage to grab mine when you kidnapped me? It's kind of a matter of life and death..."

"Where is it?" Lazarus queried.

Shifting uncomfortably in her seat, Jenna wrapped the towel tighter around herself. "In the upstairs bathroom there are three bottles: my birth control pill, the nausea pill that keeps me from throwing up all day, and my Tamoxifen which I take so my cancer doesn't come back..." She waited for him to recoil from her. They all did. Anytime someone found out about her illness, they immediately began to treat her as if she were damaged and diseased.

But Lazarus didn't pull away. He reached out and his thumb brushed over her collarbone. "I will return to your home and obtain your medications."

Gooseflesh erupted over every inch of Jenna's body and she shuddered. "I wouldn't mind a few pairs of clean underwear, a bra, and some clothes," she urged, "if you're already going."

Lazarus nodded his assent. "You are the first house guest I've had. It would not do to tarnish my reputation as a host." He gathered her into his arms again and carried her to bed. Once he was sure she was alright, he tucked her in as tenderly as if she were a babe. "Rest now and I will also return with something more than water for sustenance."

Jenna murmured, blinking at him blearily. "Why are you being so nice to me? I'm a hostage you're probably going to have to kill." Her stomach ached. "Los Santos don't care about me and neither does Danny. You got yourself a useless bargaining chip."

A single finger soothed over her rosy cheek. "Do not underestimate your power, Jenna. You are worth more than you know." He grew serious once more. "Before you go getting any ideas about escaping, we are hundreds of miles from civilization. These woods are chock full of rabbits, deer, coyotes, bears, and mountain lions that will tear you limb from limb. And that's if my dog doesn't get you first…"

"Dog?" Jenna swallowed hard.

"Just rest...don't worry about escaping and everything will be fine." Lazarus soothed.

Jenna she wasn't so sure. As she hunkered down in bed, she was certain nightmares would plague her, but when the darkness descended it was nothing but merciful.

Lazarus jogged down the stairs, glancing around the living area, kitchen, and hearth. A decrepit old mutt cocked his head to the side, one ear flopping over. "Keep an eye on our guest, McGruff." The old man wheezed and plopped his head back on his paws. Lazarus knelt to scratch his head before heading out of the house and rearming the security system. McGruff had been his constant companion and best friend since he was a boy; he was also far too old to be any danger to Jenna. Slipping into the Jeep, Lazarus threw the car into drive and headed out into the wilderness.

It was an hour-long drive back to La Verdad. Lazarus pulled up to Jenna's house, slipping the keys out of his pocket and unlocking the front door. The house was eerily silent as he searched through her closets. There was a floral suitcase inside one and he tugged it out. He found underwear, bras, shoes, pants, socks, and shirts, and then went in search of her pills. The Tamoxifen and Ondansetron were sitting on the sink beside a bottle of water. He placed them in the front pouch with her toiletries. Once they were acquired, he slipped them into the suitcase and paused to glance at several frames on the nightstand.

There were pictures of a younger Jenna wrapped up in the arms of a woman who could've been her twin. Lazarus picked up a photograph, the corner of his lips ticking upward as he settled it in the suitcase. Behind it was a picture of the same woman, bald and sickly, smiling even though her eyes were half closed. Jenna looked drawn, scared, and pale; even though she faked a smile, it didn't quite reach her eyes. He debated leaving that one behind, but decided to pack it as well.

On his way out one of Jenna's neighbor's gave Lazarus a wave and he stopped, smiling and waving back. He was already back on the road when he saw Los Santos heading for their clubhouse. Lazarus couldn't help but smile. This world was made for men like him; the monsters always won out in the end.

Cranking up the radio, Lazarus let a concerto carry him the long way home. On the way back he stopped off at the store outside of town. It was a family run place that catered mostly to the hillbilly crowd, but he made it work. Lazarus picked up a couple of steaks and vegetables, a bag of dog food for McGruff, and a couple bottles of wine before heading back to the cabin. Jenna was still asleep when he arrived but quickly roused when he brought her the bag and then headed into the kitchen to make dinner.

She brushed the tangles out of her hair and braided it to keep it out of her face. With new, clean clothes she felt like a whole new woman. The lingering traces of drug in her system seemed to have vanished with the nap and the Ondansetron helped with the nausea that had been left in its wake. Twenty minutes later she took her Tamoxifen then followed her nose downstairs. Someone was cooking and it smelled amazing. The minute she stepped down the stairs, Jenna let out a cry of fear. The dog Lazarus had warned her against came skittering toward her, barking and whining.

Lazarus darted out of the kitchen, his face molded into a mask of fear. "What's the matter?" He realized quickly he'd made her worry about the dog for nothing and began to laugh. "McGruff, heel!" he commanded, but the deaf old man paid no attention. McGruff licked at Jenna's hands before flopping over and exposing his belly for a rub.

"This is the *vicious* animal you keep on the premises?" Jenna was suddenly fighting a smile. "And his name is McGruff, as in the crime fighting 'don't do drugs' dog from the eighties?" She scoffed at him. "You must see the irony in that..."

"I named him when I was a boy," Lazarus countered. "The only danger you are truly in is being licked to death. Or perhaps he may get a bit too excited and becomes incontinent. He is almost fifteen years old, after all."

Jenna crouched down, rubbing the dog's belly. His leg began to twitch and he rolled over to kiss her face. "You're just a big love, huh?" she laughed, grinning. Suddenly, another sense kicked in. "Are you cooking?"

"*Schieße!*" Lazarus had been so engrossed in watching Jenna and the dog getting acquainted he'd nearly burned dinner. Running back into the kitchen, he pulled the cast iron skillet from the burner and coughed at the black smoke rising from the pan. "I hope you like your steak well done."

Always a chef, Jenna jumped in to save the meal. She tossed the potatoes he was roasting in the oven and gave the mushroom sauce he had tried to make a quick stir and some seasoning. Lazarus took a step back, allowing her full range in the kitchen. "I'm guessing you don't cook much?"

Lazarus cleared his throat. "Not for others. I am not used to having so many irons in the fire, if you will." He padded to the window, opening it up to clear the air.

Jenna walked over to the blackened little steaks in the pan and cut into one. "Black and blue, just as I suspected...but I can fix it." Grabbing some butter and a bit of the mushroom sauce, she added both to the skillet before placing it into the oven under a medium heat. "You can set the table if you want," she offered. Lazarus looked like he needed some direction and she was more than happy to give him some.

Nodding curtly, he grabbed plates from the cabinet and carried them over to the table. Lazarus was the leader of a criminal organization was unused to taking orders. But Jenna wasn't actually demanding anything of him; she made a suggestion and he took it. He collected silverware next, settling it beside the plates. "Would you care for some wine?"

"Oh," Jenna hesitated, "I usually don't, because of the medicine but...why not?" She was going to die anyway when Lazarus realized Los Santos weren't going to capitulate, she might as well enjoy her time left. He held up two bottles for her to choose from and she pointed at the merlot. "It'll complement dinner well."

Lazarus poured them heavy-handed portions. Jenna was almost finished plating up the food when he pressed a glass into her hand, clinking his own against hers. "Life is wonderful when you see it through the right glasses. *Zum Wohl*!"

"Cheers," Jenna replied, clinking her glass against his before she took a sip. She carried over the food and then settled in the seat across from him. Her stomach was growling fiercely and she was looking forward to the meal. She dug in and when she glanced up, she realized that Lazarus was staring at her. "Is something the matter?"

"No."

"Okay," Jenna replied, returning her attention to her plate. When she glanced up again, he was still staring. She furrowed her eyebrows. "*What*?"

Lazarus took another long swallow of wine and ignored her steely gaze. He'd noticed she was attractive before but seeing her now, sitting across from him at dinner in her casual clothing, posture relaxed, she was truly beautiful. Feelings he hadn't felt in years welled to the surface and it scared the hell out of him.

Appetite suddenly gone, Lazarus refilled his wine and took a long drink. Of course he didn't want any harm to come to Jenna...he didn't get into this business to hurt people. He wanted to provide his clients with enough drugs to keep their addictions fed and make a little money in the process. Hurting this woman went against his moral code...but he would do what he had to.

After the meal was over, he cleaned up and she retired to the living room. McGruff cuddled against her side as they watched the news. Jenna had been scouring every channel for almost an hour but her picture never showed up. She wasn't even sure anyone knew she was missing yet. Her family was gone, her friends were scattered all over the country, and Danny couldn't be counted on to manage his own fly, let alone another human being. How long was it going to take before anyone realized she was gone?

Lazarus settled casually across the room, reading a book. He looked so calm. Jenna sighed...she wasn't tired, she wasn't hungry, she was just bored. For now, she settled on watching whatever stupid show was on and thinking up ways to keep herself sane. Eventually, she'd get out of this, but for now, she had to bide her time. If Jenna could just get Lazarus to trust her, maybe he'd let down his guard and she could finally be free.

Chapter Thirteen

Danny paced the length of Black Ink's tiled floor for what felt like the millionth time. He could do little else. Jenna had been missing for three days now and they hadn't heard a single word from Los Lobos. What the hell kind of people took a hostage and then didn't make demands in a timely manner? Danny had never given much thought to abducting somebody but *Christ*, if he was going to, he'd at least let their family know what he wanted ASAP. It was common decency!

Cecelia was sitting with her legs up, her short fingernails tapping against the desk. Ramón, Luis, Martín, and Horatio were huddled in the break room playing poker while Diego took care of some paperwork out front. There wasn't a big pool of clients looking for tattoos in the middle of the afternoon on a Wednesday, which was why everyone was on edge when a shiny black car pulled into the driveway and idled.

Weapons at the ready, Los Santos didn't immediately move from their positions. The door swung open, revealing the Chancellor himself in a charcoal grey suit. Petrik was at his side in all black. There was a woman on his arm who looked like she'd been ripped off the pages of a 1930s fashion magazine; her lips were painted a shiny, apple red and she walked like she was ice skating. All of them did, in fact. They practically walked in slow motion. Lazarus inclined his head cordially. "Good afternoon."

"What's so fuckin' good about it?" There was a stark contrast between Cecelia's scarred face, her hair that was finally back to blue, and leather getup. Cece looked the other woman up and down, frowning deeper. "Where'd you find Norma Bates in this part of Cali?"

A wheezing laugh was covered not-very-convincingly with cough. "*Lo siento*," Horatio grinned, "Allergies."

"Of course," Lazarus inclined his head. It was not a friendly gesture, but it wasn't overtly rude either. "I believe I have something that belongs to the lot of you." He smiled. "Ms. Dayton is quite an interesting woman and an excellent cook. I fear if I don't return her to you soon, I may no longer fit in my trousers." He smiled grimly. "Are you ready to meet our demands?"

Danny clenched his teeth and his fists. "How do we know she's even still alive?"

"I don't make it a habit of torturing my houseguests, but if you insist..." Reaching into his pocket, Lazarus pulled out his cellphone and handed it over to Danny without fanfare. There was a camera in the room at the lodge. Jenna was sitting on the couch with McGruff, her fingers gently stroking the dog's floppy ears while she read today's paper. Every once in a while she'd lean over and take a sip from delicate teacup.

It was a huge weight off Danny's shoulders that Jenna wasn't in some kind of pit or warehouse or tied up in a basement somewhere. She looked peaceful, despite her captivity.

Cecelia pushed Danny away and grabbed the phone out of his hand to see for herself. Her hazel eyes darted back and forth, glancing around the house as if looking for any sign of torture devices. "I don't get it," she huffed. "Girl's got a wide open shot at getting out of there and she's fuckin' sittin' on a couch with an old ass dog. What did you threaten her with?"

Lazarus returned his arms to his sides. "Perhaps it is because she knows she is not in danger, unless you decide to cross me. I've been treating her very well. No bodily harm has come to her *yet* but I am not a patient man. I have drafted a list that I expect will be followed to the letter." He smirked. "I assure you, our requests are very simple."

Ramón appeared out of nowhere and grabbed the letter from Lazarus' hand. He couldn't read it without his glasses, but he handed it over to Cecelia without fanfare. Winging Lazarus' phone at his lackey freed up her hands to figure out what these people wanted. She read silently at first, a cold snort of disdain ripping through her. "So you want me to give up my fuckin' town, pack up my life, and get the fuck outta Dodge so you can flood the place with drugs and guns?" She frowned. "It ain't gonna happen, *cabrón*. This is Los Santos territory and always will be."

"I suppose you won't miss one resident then," Lazarus shrugged casually and headed for the door with Petrik on his heels.

"Stop!" Cecelia growled. "There has to be some kind of compromise here. I ain't leaving my home but I also ain't going to let you slice and dice one of my people either." Lazarus had her by the ovaries but there was something that made her wonder. Calling his bluff was a dangerous move but she was out of options. "You return Jenna to us and I'll consider honoring the contract my brother signed."

Lazarus raised an eyebrow at her. "You're obligated to do that either way, Señora Santos." He smirked at her. "It's time to accept that and hand over the reins to a man who can actually *do* something with this town." He pushed open the door, holding it for his associates. "You have until the end of the month to clear out. You will be compensated for your homes and Black Ink. I believe this to be far more generous than you deserve."

"Generous?" Danny snapped. "You're a dirty fucking crook." He growled. "You aren't going to get away with this!"

"On the contrary," Lazarus replied coolly. "I have already gotten away with it. You can either accept defeat gracefully or I can make this harder on you. As it stands, I believe I've been more than fair."

"Fair!?"

"Danny," Cecelia warned, pulling Danny behind her. "This ain't over, Lazarus."

The Chancellor did not dignify that with a response. He bowed and headed back out of the tattoo parlor.

Los Santos were left staring at one another. They lived by a code of ethics and valued human life. How could they compete with a man who was willing to break all the rules to get what he wanted? The one thing Lazarus did not have, though, was a staunch family to stand at his side through thick and thin. "I got an idea," Cece said finally. "I'm not sure it's gonna work, but it's the best shot we got. We've got three weeks and we need to make the most of them. We've got to make it look like we're cooperating."

Ramón nodded in agreement. "My dad's got a property in Florida I told him I'd look at. I'll leave town under the pretense of visiting and setting up shop down there."

"Rogelio's supposed to get out of rehab next week and Gina wants me to drive up to help out," Cecelia replied.

Danny nodded eagerly. "Marco Caraway is like an uncle to me. Even if I'm not a Devil anymore, he'll still help out." He turned to face Cecelia. "But I don't want this getting back to Lucy and Archie, they've got enough on their plate." The point of this whole charade was to keep them out of this fight. He didn't want his pregnant sister and best friend/brother in law in the line of fire.

Cecelia huffed. "I thought that went without saying. We don't want too many people to know. That being said, Narayan Bosko owes me a favor. I don't need the whole club, but I think having a little bit of extra muscle around here wouldn't hurt. We beef up our numbers for a while, come up with a clever way to draw Lazarus and Los Lobos out. In the meantime, we need to figure out where the fuck he's keeping Jenna." She glanced at Horatio. "You think you can trace his phone?"

"I'm not sure," the mustachioed man admitted. "I mostly use my hacking powers to get free porn. Something like that takes real skill...but I'll try."

"The place is fairly wooded, the house faces east, and would be someplace secluded where there isn't a ton of traffic." Cece glanced at the men assembled and frowned. "Cali is a big state but he can't be too far from La Verdad. It's got to be within a reasonable driving distance." She folded her arms. "I want surveillance on any cars Los Lobos are driving so get their plates. I think I know somebody else who can help us out." Standing up straighter, she cleared her throat. "We all on board with this? I don't want there to be any fucking around. A girl's life is at stake."

"We're with you, Cece," Luis spoke up. The sentiment was echoed amongst her cousins, and Ramón and Danny as well.

Cece rocked back on her heels. "Right now we gotta make our departure look authentic. Book your flight, Ramón, and I'll let Gina know we're coming up for Rog's discharge." It was an action plan...though not a very well thought out one. It hinged on the assumption that Horatio could stop jerking off long enough to ping a signal off Lazarus' phone to find out where he was holding Jenna. It meant that Ramón had to be apart from his club during all this, though that was Cece's intention all along. And then there was Danny. He was going to be tapping into Devil resources to save Los Santos and as reluctant as she was initially, she definitely was thankful now. How could she have managed without him?

Danny called Marco immediately. The man was quite surprised Cece had allowed him to pull the Devils of California into this fight. Los Lobos wouldn't be expecting that. Club unity had worked once...why couldn't it work another time? The only real problem was keeping word of it from spreading to the mother charter. Lucy was still not over Danny defecting to Los Santos and she probably never would be. It had taken Archie and Anita working nonstop to keep Lucy from storming down there and dragging Danny back up by his earlobe.

Mounting his bike, Danny headed back to Jenna's place. It felt strange staying there without her but it was also too concerning not to be there. If she got free, it was the place she was most likely to return to and he needed to be there to protect her if she did. Dragging a hand over his face, he stared down at his reflection in the marble tile of the countertop. It wasn't like him to keep things so neat but he wanted everything to be perfect if Jenna returned...*when* she returned.

* * *

The scraping click of a lock sent dread spearing through Jenna's belly and she scrambled toward the other side of the couch. McGruff whined and pawed at her, annoyed at his nap being disturbed. Lazarus had gotten up this morning and instead of putting on a pair of jeans and a button down, he'd gone right for the power suit. Petrik came by the house and they spoke in hushed tones. Jenna tried to listen in but she didn't speak German; her eavesdropping was in vain but it hardly mattered. She knew what they were discussing: her fate.

Petrik stared at her nastily and threw her the newspaper, impolitely suggesting she read it in its entirety. There was something dark and malicious in him and she decided to do as he asked rather than take a risk. As the men collected themselves and headed out, she settled on the couch with a cup of tea and pored over the newspaper.

The world was a truly terrifying place. Jenna wanted to be sympathetic to refugees and the families of innocents killed in the streets but she wasn't exactly safe with Lazarus either. As she thumbed through the crinkly pages, it was hard not to think about where her own story would go. Jena was a single woman with no real family to claim her. It was unlikely there would be a giant outpouring of support when Los Lobos eventually killed her. She'd be another page thirteen blurb about a woman murdered in La Verdad. Of course it wasn't headline news. Worst of all, Los Lobos had enough influence to get away with her death. Lazarus Caine would never see a day of jail time for any of this.

Jenna kept her arms wrapped around herself as Lazarus stepped through the door, tugging the tie away from his throat. He glanced at her before heading into the kitchen to put on the kettle. Usually McGruff would half-flop off the couch and follow him around but the traitor had clearly taken her side. Ever since Jenna arrived, he'd hardly seen his dog. McGruff was always cuddled up beside her, begging for affection. To Jenna's credit, she always gave it without question. Despite the rocky start they'd endured, she was infinitely tender with the half-deaf, mostly blind, somewhat incontinent beast Lazarus had loved for nearly half his life.

When the water boiled, Lazarus filled two cups and headed back into the living area. He held one out to Jenna, his face grimly set. Surprisingly, she didn't immediately reach for the cup and he furrowed his eyebrows. "Take the tea," he demanded. Jenna's eyes were suddenly glassy as she accepted his offering. Before he realized what was happening, tears were rolling down her cheeks and creating ripples in the amber liquid. "Jenna, what is ailing you?"

Choking back a soft sob, she shook her head. "It's nothing," she whispered past the lump in her throat and took a shaky sip. It didn't taste any different from a normal cup of tea; though she hadn't noticed the last time he poisoned her either. "I was afraid you were going to make my death painful or draw it out. I'm relieved, in a lot of ways you decided to do it this way." Jenna grasped his wrist and gently squeezed. "Thank you..."

Lazarus's stared at her trembling fingers warming his skin. Her other hand was wrapped around the mug of tea she thought would seal her fate. Instead of fighting and raging against him, she succumbed...and the horror that rose up inside him was more frightening than anything

141

he'd ever experienced. How could she give herself up so easily? Jenna was kind and sweet, bright and talented. She lit up a room when she walked in, not only because she was beautiful on the outside but because the grace inside of her radiated outward. The tears burning down her rosy cheeks turned his stomach to lead. Jenna's eyes closed as she brought the cup to her lips again. Lazarus couldn't stand it. Wrenching it away, he grasped her chin so she could watch as he drained the scalding liquid. When it was empty, he threw the useless vessel into the fire. "Why would you not fight? You do not value your life?"

Jenna ached to look away but Lazarus was holding her, forcing her to stare into his mercury eyes. He smelled like the woods and soft summer rain, confusing her senses. The warmth of his body bled through his clothes and onto her skin, and his hot breath teased the hair on her neck.

"I am expecting an answer, Jenna."

"I don't have one, Lazarus," she replied miserably. "If you're asking me if I want to die, the answer is no." It wasn't just Jenna's hands that were trembling now, but her entire body. A fresh set of tears worked their way to the surface and the salty pools dripped over Lazarus's fingers. "But what does it matter? Even if Los Santos meet your demands, will you let me go back to my life, knowing all I do?" She shook her head. "I've observed a few things in my time here and I know you don't trust anyone. You have people you work with and tolerate, but at the end of the day you're a lone wolf... that's why you choose to live so far away from them." Dragging in a ragged breath, Jenna felt the fear begin to sweep over her again. "How can I expect you'll trust *me* to keep quiet about all this when you don't even trust *them*?"

Lazarus was eerily silent.

A bitter laugh passed Jenna's lips. "I'm as good as dead, either way." She licked her lips. "Every night I lay in bed wondering if it will be the night you come in with a knife or a gun to torture me until I finally give up my life." Her entire body jerked with the weight of her fear. "So yes, poison seems infinitely preferable. I would just go to sleep like the last time and...not wake up. At least I wouldn't suffer." Jenna gazed into his soul. "You know I'm right."

Lazarus *hated* that she was right.

Against all odds, he was genuinely starting to care for Jenna. When Lazarus first walked into La Trattoria, he was not immediately distressed by his primal reaction to her. He was a man and she was a very attractive woman. Wanting to bed her was normal, healthy even. Lazarus ignored the impulse, of course. Contrary to popular belief, he was not an animal. Jenna Dayton was a means to an end; she had taken Daniel Harding into her home, which meant Lazarus could exploit the connection. The jealousy that raged in him when he thought of Jenna in that cretin's bed was better left ignored.

Los Lobos had been unevenly divided about taking Jenna in the first place. Getting their hands dirty was distasteful; they preferred to hire young, uneducated goons with guns to perpetuate the violence they were known for. But Lazarus could not fathom leaving Jenna in the hands of a sadist or a sociopath or, god forbid, a rapist. The thought of any harm coming to her made him sick to his stomach. So, then what exactly was he going to do now?

Lazarus looked so stricken Jenna briefly felt a zip of compassion but she quickly brushed it away. "I'm tired," she lied, "I'm going to bed."

McGruff let out a simpering cry when she stood and fled up the stairs. He wormed his way to the edge of the couch, shoving his wizened grey and brown muzzle beneath Lazarus' hand. He smoothed the mutt's floppy ears, whispering soothing words in his native tongue. Lazarus knew exactly how the dog felt; he was just as empty when Jenna left the room. There were exactly three weeks until Los Santos's time ran out and he would be forced to act. Lazarus didn't like any of his options when it came to Jenna. The predator inside him had already accepted her as one of his own. He couldn't let her get caught in the crossfire...but he also couldn't betray Los Lobos.

Needless to say, Lazarus had some thinking to do.

Chapter Fourteen

La Verdad was in crisis.

People weren't running or screaming. There were no buildings on fire or hail raining from the sky. The sea had not yet turned to blood, nor were they overrun with pestilence but there was something dark that permeated the air. The town's residents skittered around like frightened mice. La Trattoria had closed down since Jenna Dayton was not there to give the orders. Other local businesses soon followed suit. Grocery store shelves were bare from residents stocking up on bread, milk, eggs, and liquor. Even the birds were suspiciously silent...

La Verdad had always looked to Los Santos for guidance. Over the course of forty-eight hours Ramón Diaz got on a plane and headed out of the state, Horatio had not been seen at any of the local bars or strip clubs in just as long, and Cecelia Santos—who they knew to be tough as nails—was packing for a trip. Needless to say, the community was unnerved.

Daniel Harding stood at Cecelia's side, never wavering through the upheaval. It might've been enough to quell the fear, but the citizens of La Verdad didn't know Danny from Adam. He walked with a loping gait, smiled a little too wide, and was clearly an outsider. His presence did nothing to calm them.

"You don't need all that fuckin' shit. They got snacks all over California," Cece chastised as she went in search of the pack she had wanted to bring on their trip. "Couple pairs of pants, shirts, and socks is all you need. And *underwear.* You forgot those the last time."

"That wasn't an accident, sweetheart," Danny retorted cheekily. He was shoving things into a cloth backpack, not bothering to fold anything. If Lucy could see him now, she'd be rolling her eyes for sure; but since she wasn't around, the task fell to Cece—and she clearly took the responsibility very seriously. Pausing to hastily fold the rest of his clothing, he made an exaggerated display when he got to his boxers. Cece didn't praise him but it was the first time in two days she hadn't looked completely pissed. It was a start.

Cecelia found the item she was looking for under a laundry basket in the garage. She grabbed a plastic poncho from a hook behind the basement door and rolled it up for transport. Although there was no rain in the forecast in their neck of the woods, their final destination was Portland, where Rogelio was finishing up his rehab program. They had three days to get up there, which was the perfect setup for a powwow with Marco Caraway. Cece had met him a couple times and he didn't seem like a bad guy; she just hoped Danny hadn't oversold the man's willingness to assist them. "Get your dick in gear, we ride out in twenty." She knelt, giving her bike a once over before the long trip.

"My dick's in top shape," Danny fired back, his expression never changing. He threw a rag over the handlebar of his bike and stalked back into the house. Cecelia was driving him out of his mind. He might've been a full member of

Los Santos now but she was still treating him as if he were lower than a prospect. Horatio, Luis, Diego, and Martín all had important jobs protecting the town. He was basically a mealticket getting her an audience with Marco and she didn't let him forget it.

"*Ey ese, qué te pasó?*" Luis called to Danny from his position on the couch. He had one hand down his pants and the other one tucked behind his head. "You look like somebody pissed in your corn flakes." He glanced over his shoulder. Cecelia was checked the oil level and wiped off the bottom of her bike before hoisting herself up to finish packing. She brushed past the two of them in the living room and jogged up the stairs. Luis smirked. "Ah yeah...I get it."

"You think you do, but you really fuckin' don't." Danny murmured obscenities under his breath before flopping down beside the man. "Was she always like this? I mean, growing up."

Luis suddenly grew somber. "Nah, not at all. Cece was kinda a free spirit, not all uptight like she is now." Reaching into his pocket, he pulled out his wallet and pulled out a wad of chintzy plastic film. He had a couple photos of himself smiling and cuddling a handsome blonde, just behind that was one of him and his grandmother on her eightieth birthday, and then there was one of all the cousins. Cecelia was standing in the middle of all the boys in a soft blue dress trimmed in lace and shimmering red shoes that looked like it had been ripped out of the Wizard of Oz. She was smiling and wrapped up in Rogelio's arms. "This was her ninth birthday. She wanted to be Dorothy. We painted paper yellow and made a yellow brick road up to the house, she had this huge pink cake, and she made us pretend to be the scarecrow, the tin man, and the lion."

Staring down at the bright eyed, happy little girl in the photo, Danny felt his heart twist. "What happened?"

"Life, I guess," Luis shrugged. "She grew up with us boys and I guess we must've rubbed off on her. Then she met Ramón and everything that happened seemed to suck the life out of her…" he ran a hand over his perfectly manicured stubble and licked his lips. "Then she got taken by the Black Jacks and…it was like her soul was scrubbed away. Every once in a while I'll see flashes of the girl I knew a long time ago but mostly, I'm just fuckin' terrified of her."

Exhaling sharply, Danny closed his eyes to take in everything Luis was saying. Then suddenly there was a shift on the couch and Luis was half on top of him, lips crushed to his. "What the—" Danny pushed the man off. "What the fuck was that?"

"Come on, I can't be the only one who was feeling the tension here!"

"Yes! You were!" Danny wiped his mouth on the back of his arm. "I'm all about the titties, if you haven't noticed." He frowned deeper. "Shit, man, your lips are so soft! How the hell do you do that?"

Luis whipped out his organic lip balm, showing it off to Danny enthusiastically.

Cecelia traipsed down the stairs, folding her arms, "If you two *pendejos* are done making out, we need to hit the road."

Scrambling up from the couch, Danny jogged after her, his cheeks flaming. Luis winked at him and he huffed in annoyance. Throwing his leg over his bike, he kicked it into gear. The only saving grace was that Cecelia was hiding her mirth beneath her bike helmet. It was the first time in a long time Danny had actually seen that facial expression. A little humiliation and an impromptu make out session with her cousin were more than worth it to see her smile.

* * *

Danny and Cece arrived in Fresno shortly before dark. They'd had a fairly uneventful trip, except for a squabble at a rest stop outside Delano that very nearly gotten both of them thrown in jail. It was only by the grace of God they managed to ride off before the state trooper glaring daggers at them got out his badge and gun. The rest of the ride was completed in stony silence.

Marco, as usual, was standing out on his front lawn when they arrived. Just like last time, he was wearing a pair of khaki shorts and a button down shirt. He smiled and waved, excited to have guests at home. The only difference was the dogs had already been let out, fed, and herded into the basement so they could play freely without being a barrier to the ongoing negotiations.

Cecelia stretched, her back aching from the long ride. The injuries she'd sustained at the hands of Sofía Salma were severe and had lingering side effects. Cece rubbed a sore area above her kidney, remaining quiet as the two men embraced and clasped each other on the back. Marco turned toward her and she gave him an overly firm handshake and a smile that didn't quite reach her eyes. "I appreciate you taking the time to see us."

"Of course," Marco replied cordially and ushered them up the steps to his house. There was a table of appetizers and drinks for far more than three people. He cleared his throat. "I hope you don't mind I invited some of my guys to join us. After all, this is a decision that involves more than just the three of us." He smiled. "The treaty allows a lot of leeway but I want to make sure we're all on the same page…"

Danny gritted his teeth when he felt Cecelia tense beside him. Of course he knew they were not in any danger but this was a betrayal to the woman who he'd encouraged to come along. As they entered the living room, Los Santos were suddenly outnumbered three to one by Devils. If not for the presence of a familiar face, she likely would've dragged him outside and made sure there was nothing left for the state trooper to find.

"Cecelia!" A familiar voice gasped.

"Shit, girl, you look fuckin' amazing!" Cecelia rushed to embrace Candace Rey—her sister in arms and one of the only people who had kept her sane while being locked up. "Life on the outside looks good on you, chica." The last time Cece had seen the woman, she had been pale and drawn and desperately missing her seventeen year old son. Now, she was sun kissed, glowing, and happier than Cece had ever seen her. "I didn't expect to see you with this crowd. Ain't your sister still living with that FBI guy? What's his name? Stewart?"

"Steve," Candy replied with a chuckle. "Yeah, she's living in quite a fantasy world. Not that it's very different than how she usually is. They're still telling everyone they're just roommates. Last I talked to her, she hadn't even screwed him." Candy snorted. "I guess that's the real difference between us."

Cece smirked. "Well, you *are* half-sisters." She wrapped an arm around Candy's waist and turned to the rest of the group. "Who're these *vaqueros*?"

"Well, you know my son Matthew," she grinned. "He turned eighteen a week ago and he thinks he's a hot little dog."

"Mom!" The man-child groaned and covered his face with his hands. "*Stop!*"

Cecelia and Candy both shared a look before they laughed again. "I'm not sure if you've met Callum Murdoch, he's been part of the Devils of California since before I was born. Then there's his son Greg, and grandson William who's Matty's age." She licked her lips. "Don't be too mad at Marco. I really wanted to be here when I heard you were coming down and that meant bringing some extra security. I kind of stepped in something recently..."

"You alright?" Cecelia asked, her expression darkening again. "Whatever you need, I'm here for you, chica."

Candy hugged Cece tighter. "I'm well taken care of, I assure you. Besides, I overheard you have some trouble of your own. Los Lobos have a reputation far beyond what they're doing in La Verdad and it's very scary. There were two overdose related deaths in Matthew's graduating class this past May that have been traced to this cartel. We need to get the situation under control before the epidemic starts to spread."

"That's exactly why we're here," Danny cut in.

Candy moved toward Danny and threaded her arms around him. "It's so good to see you." It was clear by the look on her face that she'd recently talked to Lucy and had gotten an earful.

Danny reminded himself he had to be careful, especially in the presence of two women Lucy counted as surrogate sisters. Turning to face Marco again, he inclined his head and decided it was safer to change the subject. "Well, I'm starving and I need a drink. Let's see what we've got." Danny used it as an excuse to drag Marco into the kitchen. "What the fuck is this? You know Candy is just going to go blabbing to Lucy and everything we've been trying to do will be for shit!" he snapped. "The point of all this was to make sure my sister stayed out of it."

"Relax," Marco warned, his posture tight. "Candy's not going to tell Lucy anything. She doesn't want your sister getting caught in this any more than we do. They're friends and Candy cares deeply about her." He patted Danny on the back. "Trust me, I would never do something to put Lucy's life in jeopardy." He sighed. "I promised Candy I would never lie to her again and that means sometimes telling her things I would've kept to myself before..." Glancing back into the living room, Cecelia and Candy had settled on the couch to get the full rundown on what had changed since they last saw each other. "Total honesty isn't always easy but it got me my son and the love of my life back, and I won't mess that up."

Danny no longer had a leg to stand on and continuing to be angry with someone who refused to rise to the challenge was unsatisfying. "As long as you know what you're doing, I trust you. Lazarus Caine is bad news. He's smart, he's rich, and very well connected. He knows how to get shit done without dirtying his hands and he's got Jenna."

Leaning up against the doorjamb, Marco crossed his arms. "How'd this girl get involved?"

Danny dragged a hand through his helmet-flattened hair and sighed heavily. "I met her a while ago, I knew she was living in La Verdad..."

"So, you used her?"

"No!" Danny cried. "Yes? Maybe..." Then he sagged. "If you're asking if I fucked her then yes, I did. *Once*. It was before I patched Los Santos." Somehow, that didn't make it seem any better. "She's sweet. I respect her a lot." He couldn't stop the aching in his chest. "I can't let anything happen to her."

Marco slid a comforting palm over Danny's shoulder. "I'm sorry, son. We're going to do everything in our power to get her back. I had the Devils vote before you and Cecelia even left La Verdad this morning. They are in full agreement: Los Lobos need to be put down like the rabid dogs they are." He cracked open a beer and handed it to Danny. "You've had a long trip. Why don't you go sit down and relax? These are just the appetizers. I'm going to cook tonight."

"You *cook*?"

Candy stepped into the kitchen, laughing softly.
"You *can* teach an old dog new tricks. He's making pasta bake with cheese, I'm making a salad, and Matty whipped up a bunch of meatballs. We wanted to make sure you got a home cooked meal before heading up to Portland."

Cecelia's presence behind Danny did not go unnoticed. "This is great. I gotta say, this wasn't at all what I was expecting."

"We're allies, Cecelia. The Devils, Los Santos, the Nightriders, and the Redhawks have really done a great job of keeping this thing going. It's a new era for the MC and I, for one, think it was a long time coming." Marco grinned. "You're my honored guests, and I want to make sure you enjoy yourselves. If there's anything I can do to make you two more comfortable, let me know." He clasped his hands together, "Why don't you freshen up while we get dinner ready? I'm sure you want to wash the road off you."

"*Gracias*," Cecelia replied, her lips curled up in a smile. She really was impressed. Danny led her toward the stairs and to the guest rooms.

Candy turned to Marco, shifting uncomfortably. "Are you sure this is going to work?"

"Of course it will, babydoll," Marco leaned down, kissing her sweetly on the mouth. "Wait and see." He tugged her closer, ignoring Matty groaning and rolling his eyes. Candy leaned against Marco, not quite convinced this was the right way to go about things, but she wanted Cecelia to be happy and Danny needed a push. At the very least, this would force them to work out some of their differences. They could finally clear the air and start fresh...either that or both of them would end up dead.

Candy was really hoping for the former.

Chapter Fifteen

Cecelia found her way to an open room and tossed her bag on the bed. Danny, on the other hand, couldn't seem to find a single place unoccupied or unlocked. He followed Cece into her bedroom, his brows furrowed. "I'm not sure what's going on but this may be the only spot left?"

"Well looks like yer sleepin' with the dogs then." Cece grabbed a towel from the armoire and headed toward the bathroom. She was dusty from the trip and was pretty sure she'd swallowed a bug somewhere near Bakersfield. She felt dirty, inside and out.

Danny pouted. "Fine, but can I at least change in here? I don't want to show up to dinner all grimy. Marco will tell Luce and I'll never hear the end of it."

"Yeah, whatever," Cece replied and headed into the bathroom and turned on the shower full blast. Ignoring Danny's presence on the other side of a very thin door, she took her sweet time. She lathered with luxurious soap, washed her hair and then conditioned it. When she was done, she stood there and let the water run until some of the knots had eased in her lower back. Finally, she knew she had to get out. A rush of steam followed her into the bedroom. It didn't surprise her to find Danny still there, sitting on the bed cross-legged when she returned. "Out."

"I'd love to, sweetheart, except the door's locked from the outside."

Danny raised his hand to silence her before she got on his case. "Yes, I tried calling Marco. His phone's off. And I tried yelling but they put on music downstairs. We're stuck in here."

Cecelia wasn't about to take that for an answer and vigorously jiggled the handle. When that method inevitably failed, she pounded on the door and yelled for someone but nothing happened. Finally, she called Candy and it went straight to voicemail. "What the fuck?" she scoffed.

Danny was somewhat vindicated by the fact that she hadn't been able to free them either. "Told you," he said smugly. Danny immediately regretted it, because Cecelia turned her death glare on him and he shrank away. "Eventually they're going to realize when we don't come down for dinner or someone will turn their phone on." He leaned back on the bed. "It's not like we're in any imminent danger. We're in a comfy bedroom, we have a bathroom, and..." He poured out his bag, grinning like a fool as candy bars and beef jerky rained down on the bed. "I didn't listen to you about those snacks so we aren't going to starve to death either!" Despite his reasoning with her, she still looked oddly panicked. "What's wrong?"

"I just don't like being locked up, alright?" Cecelia growled. She paced the floor like a caged animal, posture tight and eyes wild.

Cursing softly, Danny stood and unleashed a furious attack against the door. It rattled on the hinges and he continued to slam against it until he grabbed his shoulder in pain. It would take a whole lot more strength, and violence—not to mention damage to Danny and the house—to get anywhere.

"Stop!" Cece ordered. "You're right. We ain't gonna die in here. I'm sure someone will be up sooner or later."

Boy, was Cecelia wrong.

She took her time getting dressed, opting for a pair of black yoga pants and a t-shirt. She braided her blue hair and applied a bit of makeup over the scarred area. They were guests here; she didn't want to walk around looking like the Phantom of the Opera. When Cece headed back into the main bedroom area, Danny was laying there on the bed with his arms behind his head, yawning and scratching his belly. As usual, his pants were just a little too big and his boxers were showing. She could see the delightful band of reddish hair that trailed from his belly button down much, *much* lower.

A bead of desire dripped through Cecelia and raced through her blood. She had to force herself to look away, turning her attention to the door again. She was an engineer, for God's sake, she could figure out how to unlock a door. Hazel eyes swept over the hinges and she licked her lips. Maybe she could remove the pin, pull the door off the hinges, and then reattach it once she was free—preferably with Danny still on the other side, so she wouldn't have to deal with him for a few hours. The only problem with that plan was she'd definitely need a screwdriver or some kind of tool to make it happen. Cece turned to face Danny, "You got your knife?"

Danny felt around his pockets but came up with a flimsy Swiss Army knife. He shrugged and slipped off the bed. "This is the best I can do." Handing it over to her, he glanced between her and the door. "So what's the plan here, boss?"

"Try and loosen the hinges..." But it was never going to work with such a little knife. She would be better off with a nail file, honestly. Perhaps if she was the type to get her nails done, she'd have something like that. Sliding the small knife along the hinge, she shook her head when the blade nearly snapped. The doorknob was obviously professionally installed because she couldn't find a single nail to loosen. "We really are fucked."

Danny didn't blink when she closed up the Swiss Army knife and threw it at him. She seemed irritated, but hadn't reached the point of true rage yet. That wasn't like her. She could usually muster at least burning fury over the slightest insult. Cocking his head to the side, he tried to read her but kept coming up empty. Cecelia's posture was slightly crooked, there were dark circles under her eyes and she looked exhausted. "Why don't you lay down and close your eyes for a while?"

Cecelia brushed him off, walking around to the other side of the room to look out the window. There was no way she could get out that way without breaking her legs. They were directly above a lovely brick-laid patio with no bushes or flora to break her fall. She'd likely kill

herself just trying to get away from Danny and—
although she considered it for a moment—decided that
wasn't a viable solution. "Don't worry about me."

"I'll always worry about you," Danny's voice was soft and
tender, not at all the forceful tone he'd used in the past
with her. "You're under a lot of stress. Los Lobos, Rogelio,
Jenna being taken, and even Ramón. He mentioned you
two have been fighting..."

"My marriage is none of your fuckin' business, Daniel."

"Don't you think you made it my business when you
fucked my brains out?" Danny pressed. He didn't have
anything to lose at this point. Cecelia was stuck in this
room with him, nowhere to run or hide. He might as well
use this time to try and clear the air. "I'm not trying to
start a fight. I'm just trying to figure out why you'd do
that to me. You're not cruel. And you're no fuckin' whore.
So *why*?"

Cecelia rounded on him, "Why are you bringing this shit
up now?"

"I've been trying to bring up this shit for *months*, Cece. I
was happy. I wanted to start a life with you then just
when I thought it could happen, you ran back to La
Verdad. Then I find out you're *married*!" Danny sighed.
"Was anything we shared real or were you just looking to
get off after a long lockup?" He raised his palms in mock
surrender. "Look, if that's the case, I would never judge
you for it. I get it. You were kept against your will and
you were lonely and you were looking for something. I'm

happy to be that for you, believe me. I just...I've agonized over this. I need to know if it meant as much to you as it meant to me."

A heavy silence hung in the room. Cecelia was seriously considering busting out the bedroom window, even if it dumped out onto a concrete patio. She wouldn't have died...*probably*. Sure, she could've gone into the bathroom and slammed the door, but that wouldn't put enough distance between them. Dragging a hand through blue locks, she settled on the edge of the bed. "Of course our time meant something to me. More than it should have...more than *anything* has in a long time." Cece picked at a wayward string on the edge of the comforter and sighed heavily. "Being with you made me realize I wanted more out of life than what I'd been dealing with for so long."

Danny frowned. "After everything you went through with Ramón, why go back?"

"It was a stipulation of my becoming la Presidente. He'd vote in my favor if I gave our marriage one more chance," Cece admitted. "But it ain't working. He's the same as he was before. Maybe worse..." She licked her lips. "He doesn't respect me. He doesn't understand. After *everything* that happened, he still thinks we can just get pregnant everything will go back to the way it was before the accident."

"How could he do that to you?" Danny breathed.

"Does it matter?"

"Are you fuckin' kidding me, Cecelia?" He jammed a hand through his shaggy reddish blonde hair and settled down beside her. "It's the *only* thing that matters!"

Cece swallowed hard. "He's all scrambled. He doesn't even remember when I was pregnant...which makes it even harder on me when he tries to push the subject." She shifted uncomfortably. "It's always been about starting a family with Ramón. I still think he got me pregnant on purpose the first time."

Danny watched her cradle her empty belly as she stared up at the ceiling. "Is it something you want?"

"I don't know," Cecelia grimaced. "The doctor said my chances aren't good for conceiving naturally and why the fuck am I going to go on all the hormones and the treatments when I'm not sure I'd be a good mother. I'm not even sure I like kids." She shook her head. "Maybe it's better I can't..."

"That's bullshit."

Darkness tainted her features, her anger radiating outward like thunder rolling in the night. "Did you have a seizure or something? You can't call bullshit on my fuckin' feelings. It doesn't work like that."

Sitting up over her, Danny shook his head. "I've seen the way you look at Amelia. You adore that little girl!"

"Just because I love my goddaughter don't mean I want to run out and get myself knocked up the first chance I get!"

Cecelia fired back at him. "There was a time I thought having a baby was everything I ever wanted. I was looking forward to it...but then I lost the kid and I realized how many ways I could've fucked it up!" She fisted her hands in the bedspread as hurt crawled in her chest. "How would it have worked anyway? Ramón was injured and needed me; I was trying to keep my life from crumbling. What would I have done with a kid? Honestly!"

"That was the past, Cece. This is the present," Danny replied somberly. "I know you don't want to hear it, especially from me, but you've been living on autopilot for so long, waiting for something to go wrong, waiting for the other shoe to drop. I am *not* Ramón...and you're not the same woman you were years ago either. Things can be different with us." Cecelia wasn't screaming and she hadn't yet stabbed him with something; she just looked tired and sad. Reaching out, Danny slid his hand over her shoulder and was surprised when she didn't pull away. "When you first got out of Reno, you were so tightly wound I was afraid you might snap. Then you started to relax." Danny's fingers brushed over her scarred cheek. "You let me see underneath your armor and I fell in love with you. I wanted it all with you, the family, the responsibility..."

Cecelia's face was a mask of pain and anger. "You know, Danielito, I ain't even sure how you survived this long being as fucking stupid as you are. I give your sister a lot of credit for putting up with you," she growled. "I'm my own woman. I make the decision who I love and who I don't. Just because you love me don't mean I'm obligated to love you back or make you feel better about casting your lot with somebody who ain't interested."

Danny snorted at her. "What I lack in book smarts, I more than make up for in knowing what people want." He didn't let her get away from him, moving in front of her. "You're pissed and closed off and damn mean, but you love me."

"No, I don't!"

"Then prove it!" Danny challenged. Their bodies were mere inches from each other. Cecelia tensed, but she didn't move away. Closing the distance between them, he cradled the back of her head as he pressed his lips to hers. At first, she was cool and unwavering...but then something amazing happened. A sigh tumbled from her lips and she widened her posture, melting against him. "Tell me you feel nothing, Cece, and I'll never touch you again."

Fire ignited in Cecelia's veins the moment Danny touched her. The stupid boy was infuriating but when he wasn't speaking, she really was putty in his hands. She had spent so much of the last few months trying to forget what it felt like when he poured all of himself into her. It wasn't even about sex, although she couldn't deny he knew what he was doing. They were connected on a spiritual level. When they made love, she was carried far away from the pain, heartache, and horror that had been her constant companions since she was far too young.

Just like magic, Danny's shirt was gone and he was kicking off his jeans. Cecelia's blue hair had been pulled from its plait and the locks—still wet from the shower—fanned out over the bedspread. Warm, rough fingertips trailed over her flesh. He kissed across her collarbone and suckled the tender spot he knew drove her out of her mind. A punctuated breath exploded from her lungs as he nudged open her thighs, trailing kisses downward until he reached the overflowing space between her thighs.

Danny was aching to join himself with Cece, but he knew she needed convincing. It wasn't just about the act of mutually getting off, though they both enjoyed that very much. He needed to show her there was more here than just a quick roll in the hay. Hooking his finger in the scrap of fabric she wore as panties, he dragged them down her hips and let them drop to the ground. She'd had a tough few months. She wasn't eating well and he could tell she wasn't sleeping from the purple stains of exhaustion beneath her eyes barely hidden with concealer. Perhaps the most obvious sign of all was the hollowness of her stomach. As he drank in the sight of her, Cece looked about ready to snap from tension and intended to release it.

Kneeling before her, Danny pressed soft kisses to her creamy thighs. Cecelia's fingers fisted in his hair as he turned his attention to the core of her. Starting with light licks, his nose bumped against the little bead that ached for his attention the most. Soft Spanish curses tumbled from her lips as he increased the pressure and the pace. Nails dug into his scalp as he felt her begin to tremble around him and then sweet honey overflowed his mouth as she gasped for breath. Danny kissed up her belly, then paused at the heaviness of her breasts. Cecelia's warm hazel eyes were glazed and she was flushed but he was hardly done with her.

Danny leaned down, kissing her hard. She could taste herself on his lips, an oddly erotic experience. He was rock hard and throbbed against her as his chest dragged across her diamond hard nipples. Although she'd fought him for so long, Cecelia was powerless to stop the rush of need that burned inside of her. Pushing Danny back against the bed, she threw her leg over him. There was no protest, only joy as his hands slid up to cradle her hips. He helped her seat herself over him. His entire body seemed to tighten as she took him inside of her with a grunt of pleasure.

Danny and Cecelia fit together like puzzle pieces, two halves of a whole, yin and yang. She swiveled her hips and he gripped her tighter, surging upward to match her movement. Months of deprivation and his deep love for her heightened the experience. He wished he could've held on longer but after only a few thrusts, he poured his soul deep inside of her as she continued to grind atop him. Cecelia came again moments later, limp and breathless as she rested on top of him. Danny pressed soft kisses to her lips and face, his arms wrapped around her.

Perhaps it was the trip or the lack of sleep, but it wasn't long after until Cecelia was out cold. Danny smiled sweetly, gently rolling her and tucking her under the covers. He pulled them up to her chin before pressing a soft kiss to her forehead. Cece sighed and burrowed against him. It was one of those subtle declarations of love Danny had been clinging to ever since she left. Maybe she didn't realize it yet or perhaps she'd just forgotten what it felt like but he held her heart the same way she held his. True love like this only came around once in a lifetime and Danny would be damned if he let stubbornness get away again.

Chapter Sixteen

Marco Caraway stretched out on the couch, glancing down at the gorgeous woman asleep at his side. His expression was smug, not only because they'd managed an entire night without sniping at each other but they'd also pulled off the biggest con of all time. The two of them had put Cecelia Santos and Daniel Harding into a room together, sealed it so even an engineer couldn't get through, and helped them to work through their issues. And— if the squeaking of the bed had been any indication—Cece and Danny had done a lot more than talk.

Candy had turned on her phone shortly thereafter but she got no calls or texts. Eventually they decided Danny and Cecelia were engaged in far more important activities and shouldn't be disturbed. Candy had sent Marco upstairs to unlock the door without arousing suspicion and the rest of them tucked into a quiet meal followed by a movie.

Matty had decided to hang out in the basement with the dogs, leaving his parents alone for a while. Candy actually felt like she was living in a happier time when they were young and stupid and in love. It was almost like the years apart had never happened at all. Sometime in the course of the evening, Candy must've dozed off. Marco's gentle movements woke her up and she glanced over at him, her cheeks glowing red as she realized the intimate position they were in. She cleared her throat. "What time is it?"

"Almost five." Marco's voice was husky and thick with sleep. "I don't know what time I passed out."

Candy snuggled against him, legs tucked beneath her body. "I'm not sure either but I slept well." She glanced around the house, looking for an escape. Thankfully, she found one fairly quickly. "It's a mess in here. I should get to cleaning before Danny and Cece get up."

"Leave it," Marco begged. "This is why I have a housekeeper."

"I thought you had a housekeeper because she's a gorgeous woman who you get to screw whenever you want," Candy fired back.

Marco looked properly horrified. "I've never slept with Magdalena! Even if I wanted to, she's strictly my employee. Besides, she's taking classes at the local community college and working on getting her visa. I'm not in the habit of screwing young women trying to make their way in the world." He frowned. "Candy, she's a child. What could possibly entice me about a girl who doesn't know anything about the world?"

Candy flushed. "I was young when *we* met..."

"That's completely different," Marco replied tersely. "I always knew I wanted to spend the rest of my life with you and it wasn't because you were young. It's because you are smart and funny and you don't ever let me get away with giving you anything less than my best. And did I mention you're gorgeous?" He nudged her playfully.

"The only reason we broke up was because I was an idiot." He glanced down at his hands. "I drove you away because I didn't want to rush you into anything." Marco's thumb brushed her cheek. "I still lay awake at night thinking about how it must've been for you and it kills me, Candy. If I had any idea you were carrying my child, there is absolutely nothing that would've stopped me from making you my wife and raising our son together."

Hurt clawed its way through Candy's chest and she was forced to look away. "There was a part of me that always knew that, Marco. You're still the man I want to go to bed with every night..." She leaned in and kissed him sweetly on the lips. "I know things are still weird, especially with our son being part of the MC but I think we can really make it this time..."

"I've been waiting so long for you to say that," Marco murmured. "I love you, Candy, so, so much."

"I love you too, Marco."

A loud cough from the doorway broke both of them out of their reverie. Cecelia and Danny were standing in the hall, fully dressed and their packs slung over their shoulders. "We weren't sure anyone would be up at this time. I guess I was wrong..." Cece snorted. "Thanks for the hospitality but we gotta get going."

Marco and Candy scrambled, looking guilty—as if they were a couple of young kids caught canoodling. "Are you sure you don't want some breakfast? I can at least make some coffee before you go," Marco offered.

170

Danny shook his head and moved toward the door. "Nah, we really need to get going if we want to get to Portland in time." Cecelia had been acting very strange this morning. She didn't push him away physically but he got the impression she needed her space and he was happy to give her some time to figure everything out.

Cecelia hugged Candy tightly. "Take care of yourself."

"I will," Candy smiled broadly. "You two have a safe trip."

Although it was nice to visit, it was also a relief to get out of there. Cece and Danny mounted their bikes and headed out into the brisk morning. The sun began to rise in the East, bathing them in soft orange light. The closer they got to Portland, the cooler it seemed to get.

Late in the morning they stopped for breakfast at a restaurant off the highway. Cecelia caved and bought a sweatshirt. Danny couldn't help but smile. The item of clothing was bubblegum pink and read *'Cali Girl'* in swirling white letters. She put her cut on over it, but it made her look cute nonetheless. They ate in relative silence, both very hungry from their activities last night and not having had much to eat the day before. Danny devoured the lumberjack special and Cecelia took down an omelet the size of her forearm, hash browns, toast, and at least half a pound of bacon.

They got back on the road full and happy. Thankfully the chill kept them awake as they continued their journey. The rest of the trip was relatively uneventful. Utopia Rehabilitation truly lived up to its name. They drove up a perfectly paved road, winding through manicured trees until a large wooden lodge came into view. Gina's dusty jalopy stood out like a sore thumb among a sea of shiny Jeeps, Jaguars, and BMWs.

Cecelia and Danny parked their bikes in a spot near the back. It didn't take him long to realize Cecelia was holding back. He could sense her fear and it churned in his gut. "Hey," he murmured, "I'm right here. You don't need to worry."

"Yeah, I'm just stiff." It was a baldfaced lie. Cecelia was reliving the day she picked up Ramón from rehab. That program had been for physical rehab and relearning the skills to walk and function as an independent person. Rogelio needed drug and alcohol detox. The places just looked similar and it evoked a sea of bad memories inside of her. Cece wondered if Rogelio would ever be the brother she knew or if she'd now have two men in her life that were irrevocably changed. Before she realized what was happening, she was shaking.

"Shit," Danny jogged over, dragging her into his arm. "Honey, it's going to be fine. They wouldn't be letting Rog out if he wasn't doing better." He tried to be soothing but the more he spoke, the harder she seemed to struggle. He smoothed her blue hair and pressed a soft kiss to the top of her head. Watching her hold back her pain and sadness was like a knife to his chest. "You don't need to be strong for me, Cece. I can take it."

Cecelia's eyes fluttered closed. "Now ain't the time to be fallin' apart." She dragged a breath deep into her lungs and was suddenly reminded why being with Danny was so appealing. He let her be herself. With him, she didn't feel she needed to hide anything. Forcing a smile, she gathered her courage and forged ahead.

Danny was forever in awe of this woman. Pressing his luck, he rested his hand at the small of her back; if Cecelia minded, she certainly didn't say anything. Once they signed in with the soft-spoken secretary, Danny and Cece were admitted through a heavy metal door. Neither were carrying bags, but they were made to go through a basic search before they were allowed into the patient care area. The procedure and technique put Cecelia at ease; obviously Utopia Rehab worked hard to keep patients safe.

Rogelio's room was on the second floor, up a set of well-crafted wooden stairs. It was fairly stark, only a simple twin sized bed with a blue flannel comforter. There were twin dressers and nightstands, as well as two closets. Although it was set up much like her prison cell at the Black Jack's compound, this one had a warm feel to it. Gina and Raphael were sitting on the bed while Rogelio packed When Cecelia and Danny walked into the room, he rushed to his sister's side.

"Cecelia," Rogelio cried against her shoulder as he held her close. "*Lo siento, hermanita.*" His chocolate brown eyes were bright and shimmering with tears, he was attuned to her posture and body language. "If you want to kick my ass, take your shot. I don't blame you."

"Shut up," Cecelia replied gruffly, hugging him tighter. "I'm just glad you're okay." She glanced at Danny out of the corner of her eye and smiled. He was kneeling beside Raphael, giving him a high five and talking about how his trip to Portland had been. They were hundreds of miles from home and very much out of their element, but somehow Danny made it feel natural. She rested her head against her brother's shoulder. "I was worried about you."

Rogelio smiled gently. "You don't need to worry anymore. I'm clean and sober and I don't plan on that changing any time soon." He exhaled sharply. "I made a lot of mistakes and I'm just...I'm grateful you got my back." He turned around, facing Gina. "I'm a lucky man to have such amazing women in my life."

"You gotta thank *her* more than me," Cecelia inclined her head in Gina's direction. "She put up with your shit a lot more than I did." She grinned and slapped Rog on the back. "Finish packing. We got to get back to La Verdad early tomorrow." She opened up his closet, pulling out clothes and folding them while he emptied the drawers. Raphael crawled around and made sure nothing had gotten kicked underneath the bed.

Once everything was packed, they regrouped downstairs. Rogelio's treatment team was waiting for him there, smiling and congratulating him on completing the program. They went over his discharge paperwork and the providers they'd set up in La Verdad to aid in relapse prevention. Everything seemed to be in order for

Rogelio's continued success and they left Utopia Rehab with hope in their hearts.

Gina led the way to the apartment she'd been staying at for the last few weeks and they settled in for a celebratory dinner of pizza and root beer. Cecelia kept glancing over at Danny, expecting him to look awkward and worried. Instead, he seemed to fit in perfectly with the group. Raphael already worshipped the ground he walked on; the five-year-old thought *Tío Danny* was the coolest man ever. They played dinosaurs, raced cars, and ran around the house until poor Raphael passed out on the couch.

Conversation flowed pleasantly, Cecelia purposefully steering it away from Los Lobos and the state of the MC. Rogelio hadn't even had a full day out of rehab, there was no need to stress him out so soon. Of course, that didn't mean he didn't ask but Gina played the perfect partner in crime. Rogelio was ordered to wash the dishes while Danny took the pizza boxes out to the trashcan. The two women sat on the couch, put up their feet, and talked about nothing. It was peaceful.

Before long, Gina was yawning and Rogelio was eager to get some time alone with his decidedly on-again girlfriend, leaving Danny and Cece alone again. She turned to face him, her expression blank.

"What're you thinking about?" Danny asked finally, taking another long swig of root beer.

"About how this club used to be about family and now…I don't even know." Cece sighed heavily. "When I was a kid, I always wanted to be a part of Los Santos. It's my legacy, for fuck's sake." She smiled sadly. "Over the years it's become more about infamy and being tough than about blood." Cecelia leaned back. "Once Los Lobos are over, I'm getting this club back to its roots."

Danny nodded. "That's the way it was with the Devils too. My parents got murdered and we were all a bit too obsessed with revenge. Don't get me wrong, the Black Jacks needed to be taken down, but it was an all-consuming need. Things are very different now. With Archie and Lucy running things, working on the shelter, and focusing on their family, the Devil's Own works. It makes the guys in the group a little nuts sometimes because they're used to the old way but I like it."

"So why'd you leave?" Cece frowned when the man before her peered down at his hands, conspicuously silent. She wasn't going to let him off that easily. "Don't lie to me, Danny."

He hadn't been intending to. "I love you, Cecelia. When I came to La Verdad and saw everything that was happening, I had to do something. The best way to do that was to become a part of Los Santos. Treaty or not, you needed a deeper commitment and this was the way to do it." Danny brushed a strand of blue hair away from her shoulder. "I need to see this through. I need to be part of this. You're my heart, Cecelia…and that's a bond deeper than blood."

Of all the answers Cece anticipated, such a tender truth was not among them. She expected Danny to flounder and eventually lie through his teeth; then she could get angry at him and push him away again. He didn't give her the chance. Cecelia kissed him sweetly before she wrapped her hand around his wrist. "It's time for bed," she announced.

Danny scrambled to his feet, following her to the spare room. Although they didn't make love that night, he held her close until they were both sound asleep. Taking things slow was definitely not easy, but Danny was making headway. A future with Cecelia was within his reach and for now, that had to be enough.

Chapter Seventeen

Jenna wasn't sure exactly how much time had passed since the Chancellor had taken her but it felt like a hundred years. Lazarus was in and out, frequently leaving her alone with her thoughts and her fears. McGruff was her constant companion and only solace. She'd taken to sleeping on the couch because the dog had a hard time getting up the stairs because of arthritis in his hips. If Lazarus minded, he didn't say anything. As a matter of fact, after their misunderstanding a few days ago, he had barely spoken to her at all. It was terrible how badly she missed human interaction.

Jenna had taken to spending most of the day in the kitchen, whipping up enough food to feed an army. Homemade, fresh pasta was drying on racks all around the counter, and Jenna had a big pot of Bolognese bubbling away. She liked to let it simmer all day to let the flavors meld and mingle. Nobody could beat her sauce and they knew better than to try. She also made chocolate chip cookies, used the rest of the eggs to do mini-quiches they could pull out of the freezer for breakfast, and started baking some homemade bread for supper tonight...

Lazarus walked in to a house that smelled like a restaurant and a woman covered in flour from head to toe. Arousal flooded him, his mouth watering with animal hunger. "Are we expecting company?" His voice was husky with desire.

Startled by the sound of his voice, Jenna whirled around. McGruff scooted over to flop on her feet protectively. "I didn't hear you come in." There was something predatory in Lazarus's gaze. She grew tense, words tumbling quickly in an attempt to dampen some of the tension. "You're going to need to pick up some more groceries. We're out of flour, butter, sugar, eggs, and basil. We're running low on paper towels and a couple dozen other things."

"I'll see that they are acquired immediately," Lazarus inclined his head. Grey eyes locked onto the pulse pounding at Jenna's throat. "I was not expecting you to cook."

"What else am I supposed to do with myself?" Jenna asked irritably. She'd tried all the doors and windows to see if one of them was loose; she probably could've busted one open and escaped but then she wondered. Who would feed McGruff? She didn't like the idea of the dog being alone for long periods of time and, if she was being honest, escaping and not knowing where she was or who she could go to for help was more terrifying than staying put. "I've watched about a thousand hours of crap television, I've nearly paced a hole in the floor, and I am bored out of my damn mind."

Lazarus let out a curt laugh. "I'm terribly sorry I haven't provided enough for you to do, sweetheart."

"Don't call me that," Jenna snapped at him. "I can't be your sweetheart and your prisoner at the same time."

The mirth he had been feeling died away as quickly as it had flared to life. "I am not in the mood to play games this evening," Lazarus frowned at her.

"Oh, don't tell me you're exhausted from torturing and killing innocents?" Sarcasm laced her words as she rounded on him. "You poor, poor man. Sit down and let me rub your feet."

Lazarus took a menacing step toward her. "In case you've forgotten, you are a hostage. I am more than happy to drag you down to the basement and tether you to a chair in the dark. I have been more than lenient with you, Jenna. Do not tempt me."

Muttering obscenities under her breath, Jenna added salt to the large pot of boiling water on the stove. She gathered up the pasta she'd cut by hand. It only took a few minutes before she had two bowls of pasta with homemade sauce and the loaf of fresh baked bread sitting on the table. She plopped one of the portions in front of him before sitting across from him, her expression murderous.

With a roll of his eyes, Lazarus settled and took a bite. Jenna had clearly spent the day slaving in the kitchen to make all of this for them and it took some of the wind out of his sails. "This is delicious."

"Thanks." Jenna only picked at her meal; the fight had caused her to lose her appetite. Lazarus continued to eat but she sat back, glancing over at where McGruff was snoozing. "Am I allowed to clean up before you tie me in the dungeon?"

Lazarus froze. "Have I done something to offend you?" She didn't answer and it prompted him to take action. Standing straight up, he walked around the table and closed the distance between them. "I am speaking to you, Jenna." She skittered to the far side of the kitchen but he grabbed her arm, forcing her to face him.

Jenna tried to shrink away but he held tighter until his fingers were digging into her skin. "I'm sick and tired of waiting to die, Lazarus!"

He was already far more enamored of her than he should be. Jenna was everything he'd ever wanted in a woman and never thought he'd find. Watching her sink into depression was deeply painful. "Focusing on an unknown future helps no one. You do not know what will be…"

"Haven't we established I do?" Jenna scoffed. "This only ends one of two ways and either way, one of us is going to die."

"I won't have this conversation again," Lazarus barked. He turned on his heel and walked away from her. Jenna took a step toward him and he whipped around, finger raised. "If you push me, I will not be held responsible for my actions." Storming out the front door, he slammed it behind him with such force that the windows rattled.

Jenna stomped her foot in anger before turning her attention to the dishes. She cursed, threw things around.

McGruff whined but she was too angry to temper herself. Once the kitchen was immaculate, she headed upstairs and took a hot shower before changing into a pair of old sweatpants and a tank top. Lazarus must've returned to take McGruff out since the dog was nowhere to be found. For some reason, that made Jenna feel a little better. She went to make a cup of tea, setting the kettle onto the stove. Just as the water boiled, she heard the front door burst open and McGruff hobbled in to greet her. Jenna kept her back turned as she dunked her tea bag into the hot water. She felt a presence behind her and her eyes fluttered closed. "Loom all you want, I'm not going to apologize."

"You may want to rethink your position..."

Jenna's stomach tightened when she realized it wasn't Lazarus standing behind her. Petrik was the opposite of Lazarus in every way. Lazarus was calm and controlled, Petrik was fury and chaos. Petrik's posture was low and tight, as if he were waiting to pounce at any moment; Lazarus stood straight and tall, gliding whenever he moved.

Jenna felt safe with Lazarus...she was terrified of Petrik.

Before Jenna could open her mouth to scream, she found herself crushed against the counter and the breath knocked out of her chest. McGruff let out a warning bark, but it didn't faze the violent offender.

Petrik looked right through her, not seeing the woman but a vessel to unleash his violence within. "I am unsure what you have done to annoy Lazarus but he has been insufferable for days." Petrik frowned deeper. "He canceled our meeting after I drove all the way to this filthy pit. I wondered what was making him so miserable and now I think I've found the source. You haven't been broken in properly yet but I think I can do something about that."

Jenna was as far back as she could go but Petrik was right there, his body flush against hers now. Ice ran in her veins. "Don't," she begged.

"You're lucky you're still alive, you little bitch. Lazarus has afforded you every luxury and still you are ungrateful..." Slamming her against the cabinets, Petrik jerked her by the strands of damp blonde hair, nearly ripping a handful from her head with one hand while the other fumbled with his belt and zipper.

Panic clawed through Jenna's chest as she raged against him fruitlessly. Petrik was stronger than she was by far. Clawing at him with nails and teeth only seemed to incite his excitement. Jenna managed to grab the hot tea and she threw it at him, crying out at the blowback of hot water as it burned the skin between them. Petrik momentarily let her go but he wasn't giving up the chase so easily. He let her scramble across the kitchen floor and make it into the living room before he grabbed her by the ankle and watched her fall to the ground.

The blow to Jenna's face knocked her head back and her vision swam. Petrik pushed her down again and the taste of copper filled her mouth. "Stop, please!" It didn't seem to matter how she pled, he ripped off her sweatpants and laughed wheezingly, his fingernails biting into her hips as he tried to keep her still. Tears burned down her cheeks as she turned her head away and tried to block out his violation.

Something caught Jenna's eye as she stared beneath the couch. She half-rolled, reaching for a piece of metal pipe that must've been left behind during a renovation. There was a split second of opportunity and she swung it with all her might. Petrik was only momentarily dazed but it gave her enough time to squirm away from him again. She hurtled forward, focused solely on getting away but her whole body was trembling. Jenna would've fallen again except the door opened and she crashed into Lazarus.

Time ground to a screeching halt. Lazarus's rage billowed outward and exploded with such a fury that Jenna was afraid she would burn with the heat of it. He caught her around the waist and practically threw her behind him. Petrik was breathing heavily, the side of his head trickled blood. "The bitch just came at me out of nowhere!"

Jenna opened her mouth to argue but Lazarus didn't let her get a word in edgewise. He pulled his gun from its holster and fired six shots point blank into Petrik. The first bullet shredded the penis hanging out of his zipper, the next two hit him straight in both his legs, then one blasted through his windpipe...Petrik gurgled and choked on his own screams, eyes bulging wide. The last two bullets blew his head wide open, leaving a mess of sinew and bone sprayed all over the floor. Petrik was dead but Lazarus was hardly done. He turned to Jenna, his expression murderous. "Go upstairs and do come down until I say so."

Standing on shaky legs, Jenna managed to get into the bedroom without tripping. Lazarus followed behind her, carrying McGruff as he couldn't walk himself. The Chancellor paused, opening his mouth as if he was going to say something but words failed him. He turned and slammed the door behind him.

Falling to her knees, Jenna wept bitterly into McGruff's warm brown fur. The sun was starting to set and she moved toward the window. Lazarus was in the backyard standing over a pyre that most definitely contained the remains of Petrik's body. He thundered upstairs hours later. When the door to the bedroom opened, Jenna pulled the blanket around herself. Lazarus slipped into the bathroom and showered for what felt like hours.

When he finally left the bathroom, Lazarus's eyes were bloodshot and his body half-crumpled with grief. He inched toward the bed and crawled in beside her. Reaching out, his warm palm cupped her cheek and he shuddered. She had a livid purple bruise on her cheek and blood was crusted around her mouth from where her lip had split. "Jenna, I'm so sorry..." His breath hitched in his throat, as if he were fighting the urge to cry, "This is my fault."

A fresh set of tears filled Jenna's eyes and spilled down her cheeks. Lazarus dragged her against his chest.

"I will never allow anyone to hurt you. Not now, not ever," he murmured into her golden blonde hair. Lazarus tried to comfort her but Jenna only cried harder. He held her against him until her harsh sobs were nothing but hiccups and her breathing was soft and even. Guilt unlike anything Lazarus had ever known burned through him. Walking into the house and seeing Jenna fighting for her life, while a man who was once his closest friend tried to violate her, was horrifying.

Lazarus did not sleep that night. He kept vigil over her the entire night, his mind turning with all the possibilities. What if he had not decided to return when he did? What would he have done if Petrik hurt Jenna in some way? Lazarus wanted only good things for this brave, beautiful woman...and yet it was his actions that had put her in danger. It had been his idea to hold her as leverage against Los Santos.

Lazarus wanted this territory and to grow his business but at what cost? Had he fallen so far from grace that it no longer mattered if people lived or died? It was certainly a question Lazarus had to ask himself and something he would eventually have to explain to his crew—especially Petrik's twin brother, Sven. Tomorrow would be a day of reckoning, but for now, he could do nothing but succumb to the depth of his exhaustion.

Chapter Eighteen

Jenna awoke before Lazarus the next morning. She slipped out of bed and nimbly dressed for the day. The light of the morning cast a warm glow and illuminated the mess that was her face. Her eyes were bruised, her lip was swollen and split on the side, and dried blood flaked off her in several spots. Running her hand down her body, she traced the old mastectomy scars and then covered the new, livid wounds made by fingernails and the wooden floor as Petrik had dragged her along it. The memory made her blood turn to ice.

Hurrying into the bedroom, Jenna went in search of a sweater. McGruff was sprawled at the foot of the bed, unmoving. That wasn't so unusual for him as he was an old dog and didn't like getting up in the morning. Most of the time when he wasn't in the kitchen, he was on the little flannel bed that sat beside the couch, snoring away. Except this morning, there was no snoring…

"Lazarus?" Jenna hissed. He didn't immediately move and she hopped on the bed, pressing his shoulder. "Laz, I think there's something wrong with McGruff." She gripped his arm in terror, watching as one of his bloodshot mercury eyes peeked open.

Lazarus had been in the middle of a terrible dream where he had to drag Petrik off Jenna. In his rage he'd promptly mangled Petrik's corpse and burned him to charred remains. The smell of cauterized flesh filled his nostrils and burned all the way to his lungs. Being startled awake made him realize it wasn't a nightmare...he was simply remembering yesterday's events. Jenna's broken face appeared over him as she shook him awake. He lay helplessly in her bed, a place he didn't belong. The moment he realized why she woke him, he panicked and leapt from the bed.

Rationally, Lazarus understood his dog was extremely elderly and would not be around forever. McGruff had been failing for the better part of five years; his arthritis inhibited his ability to get around, the incontinence got progressively worse, and he slept more often than he was awake. Unfortunately, the reality losing the dog Lazarus had grown up with was too much to bear. McGruff had comforted him when he was small and afraid; he had been the only constant in Lazarus's dark life...

Sliding off the bed, Laz crawled toward the animal. His beloved friend was resting on his side, quiet and still. Pain clawed at his chest as he knelt, caressing the dog's brown and grey fur. He checked for breath, for a pulse...any sign of life, and came up empty. A horrible cry of pain filled the room and it took Lazarus several moments to realize that the noise was being dragged from deep inside his own soul.

Jenna fell to her knees beside McGruff and wept bitterly over the friend they had both lost today. Lazarus crumpled over his childhood companion, resting his head on the dog's chest and fisting his hands in his fur. Jenna threw herself over him, sliding her fingers through Lazarus's hair as he cried. She was aware this was the man who took her from her home and had nearly allowed her to be torn apart by a madman...but seeing him flayed bare, weeping openly for this poor wretched creature, it tore something open inside of her.

Pulling Lazarus against her body, Jenna whispered soothing words into his ear. He shifted and pressed his face into the crook of her neck. As she rubbed his back, she peppered gentle kisses to the top of his head as if she were soothing a small child. They stayed like this for an inordinate amount of time. Jenna's hips had begun to cramp and she could tell Lazarus was stiff from sitting on the floor. "We need to make some preparations."

Lazarus nodded, his eyes red and gritty from crying. He pulled himself up and grabbed the sheet off the bed; he settled McGruff's body on top of it and wrapped him up tenderly. Jenna went into the bathroom and found some clips to keep the fabric clasped as they began their trip downstairs.

Reverently carrying his beloved friend, Lazarus paused to let Jenna open the door. He didn't have on any shoes, only jeans and a button down shirt. His hair was wild and his five o'clock shadow shaded his powerful jaw. He looked more beast than man as he stepped out into the dewy morning grass and headed for the trees. Jenna trailed behind him, glancing around the yard. She'd never been outside the front doors of the house and was stunned at how beautiful the landscape was.

There was thick tree cover on all sides, woods all around except the dirt path that led into yet another dense copse down the lane. Large boulders punctuated the pathway, subtly marking the entrance to the driveway. They went further down, winding through paths that were more mud than grass, but Lazarus didn't stop. He didn't seem to feel the stones under his feet or the brambles that tore at their legs. Jenna's breathing was heavy and uneven as they traversed a hill and came to a giant tree that looked like it had been growing since the dawn of time.

The reddish brown bark reminded her of the pictures of McGruff's fur when he had been a puppy in his prime. Grass around the tree was soft and green, the perfect spot for a burial. Lazarus sank to his knees and dragged in a deep breath. They hadn't brought a shovel out here, which was no barrier as he began to dig with his hands. Jenna knelt beside him, joining in. They pushed aside the moist brown dirt, dirtying themselves from head to toe as they worked to create a space for the body of a beloved friend.

Sweat beaded on Jenna's upper lip and it stung fiercely against her injuries. The sun beat down against their bodies, warming the earth and their skin. Jenna didn't stop until Lazarus finally grasped her arm, his expression unwavering. Stepping back, he eased McGruff into the fresh grave. Jenna pushed herself up, standing beside him as they gazed at the hole in the ground. Fresh emotion burned in her eyes and she turned, burying her face against Lazarus's chest. The dirt all over them turned tears to mud as they clung to each other for support.

"Should we say something?" Jenna glanced up at him.

Lazarus stared down at his feet, his throat tight and painful. "I am not sure where to begin...will you go first?"

Nodding her assent, Jenna took a deep breath. "Um," she hesitated, "I only met McGruff a short time ago but he was an amazing soul. He was always happy to see me, no matter what. There was always a sloppy kiss and a wagging tail waiting when I was feeling sad. He loved stealing table scraps and cuddling...and even though he's gone, there will be a special place in my heart for him forever. Rest in peace, little buddy."

It was a touching tribute, Lazarus had to admit. Jenna had a way of seeing the essence of a person—or a dog, in this case—and truly understanding who they were. It was how she could read him so perfectly from the moment they first met and how easy it was for her to get under his skin. Honestly, he was in awe of her. Her arms wrapped around his waist made him feel strong, even though he was moments away from tumbling over again and folding in grief. "I..." he choked on his tears again. It was too hard to look down at the sheet-clad body of the dog he had raised from an eight-week-old puppy.

Lazarus grasped a handful of dirt and gently spread it over the body. "McGruff was more than simply a pet to me. He was my heart, my soul, and my very best friend..." He was trembling again, unable to see through the deluge of tears. "My father never wanted a pet. He was just another mouth to feed he said, but I begged and pleaded and he told me if I could afford to feed the mongrel myself, I could keep him." Lazarus looked down at his past. "We were very poor, barely surviving on scraps of food tossed our way. My mother was in Belgium working in a factory, separated from us. My father worked eighty hours a week to run his business and it was all we could do to keep the hovel from falling down around us. I had three sisters. My brother had died of pneumonia when he was just a few weeks old. My father refused to buy the medicine for him. A funeral was a far cheaper expense than another mouth to feed."

Jenna held tighter as Lazarus continued his story. "I took a job running packages for a wealthy man in the city, Frick Dedvylder. He liked me, said I was bright. I learned to speak English from him and his associates and it opened up more doors for me." He licked his lips. "The man had no children of his own and doted on me like I was his own son. I wished to leave school to work for him but he insisted that I did not. He made sure I graduated school and went to college…it was only after I graduated that he brought me into the fold." He let out a rumbling sigh. "Powders and drugs of all kinds were his trade. It was how he made his money and he offered me a partnership. With his help I helped my family move out of the ghetto and into a nice house, my sisters had clothes and shoes and finished their schooling. Louisa became a nurse, Ella a botanist, and my little Kayla married a wealthy man and has half a dozen beautiful children she is happy to raise." He swallowed. "Most importantly, I could feed my dog…"

Lazarus pulled away from Jenna, moving to the side of the pit and scooping handfuls of dirt. She knelt to help him but he stopped her with a shake of his head. "When Frick passed, he left the empire to me. Over time I lost sight of simply surviving and learned what the finer things in life were. I wanted more money, more power, and I gave up my soul."

Jenna listened quietly...but she was also distracted by the fact she knew *exactly* where he'd taken her now. Castaic Lake was just about an hour away from La Verdad and was home to many quiet cabins tucked around the periphery. She wasn't sure what side of the park they were on, but she knew there was a bus that ran fairly regularly just a few miles away from the main inlet. When her mother was still living, they used to get away from the bustle of the city and enjoy each other's company. Sure, there were wild animals around her...bunnies, turtles, and more squirrels than she could count, but there weren't wolves or anything that would tear her apart. Just as Lazarus had trumped up McGruff's threat to her, he had done the same with the woods surrounding the cabin.

Once the dog was buried, Lazarus offered his arm to her and they headed along the path to the house. Jenna made sure she kept a close eye out for landmarks that would guide her along her way. If she could find her way back to this tree, she'd be able to find use it as a vantage point to guide her where she needed to go. It wasn't going to be easy terrain but at least she was sure she wouldn't die in the wilderness.

They got back to the house and dirt caked their bodies and souls. As they stepped into the house, she cleared her throat. "Lazarus, you're bleeding," she called. He must've cut his foot on a rock or a thorn on the trip back, or perhaps reopened a wound he'd sustained on the trip up to the tree. He glanced down at it, as if he was unsure what to do. "Come on," she urged. "You need to wash up."

Guiding him up the stairs, she led him into the bathroom and turned on the water. Lazarus was staring at her, his expression suddenly going from stony and sad to something altogether more recognizable. Jenna felt a bead of heat sing through her veins as he leaned into her, arm threading around her waist. It was a blissful moment when he bent and kissed her. The stinging of her lip only lasted a moment, adding to the depth of feeling as he poured his heart and soul into that one stunning kiss.

Jenna melted against him, and he pushed harder. Lazarus was desperate to feel something other than pain and heartache. The moment he touched her, she succumbed and he felt power beyond anything he'd ever gotten from running Los Lobos. Tugging off her dirty clothes, he pulled her beneath the hot spray of the shower, reveling in the heat that burned inside and out. "You do not know how long I have wanted to touch you like this," he whispered.

If Jenna was being honest with herself, she'd fantasized about being with Lazarus for just as long. His kidnapping her and holding her as collateral against Los Santos clouded her feelings. Knowing how he'd grown up didn't quite change her opinion of his tactics but it certainly made her more sympathetic to his plight. He had once been a boy willing to do anything for his family and those he loved, but on the way to his endgame, he'd lost his way. Jenna could see how it could happen. She could also see how amazing Lazarus looked without his shirt and all rational thought left her brain...

Jenna was more animal than woman when their lips met again beneath the water. It flowed over her skin, baptizing her a new woman, tainted by only her baser urges. As she let him take her over, Jenna learned what it was to be fully open. Lazarus touched her in ways she didn't think were humanly possible. They first made love in the shower, then in the kitchen, on the couch, and finally in the bed. When Lazarus was inside her, Jenna felt as if her entire life suddenly made sense. As he slept beside her that night, she fought her exhaustion as she wrapped herself around him. Jenna had the opportunity to escape. She could take the keys that Lazarus dropped in his haste to please her and flee into the night...but as he breathed and cuddled her closer, she couldn't bear the thought.

Tomorrow was a new day. Jenna had a chance to figure out what she needed to do to survive. It would be up to Lazarus the role he played in her new life, but for tonight she would simply let sleeping dogs lie.

Chapter Nineteen

March 15, 2014
Reno, Nevada

Cecelia leaned over her Bible, searching out the linear patterns and sequences she would need to forge a sustainable code. Bea was on board and had been able to obtain the books under the guise of starting a prayer group. Sofía didn't see any harm in prayer and the Bibles were released the next day. Since then, the group had doubled in size when Candice Rey and her half-sister Julia Amos arrived and were immediately thrown into the fray.

It burned in Cece's gut when a terrified girl, barely seventeen years old showed up and was expected to do Sofía's bidding. Cece immediately took her under her wing. She learned the girl's name was Adela—not from the girl herself, since she couldn't stop crying long enough to speak—but from the name stenciled on her sketchbook. Cecelia was honestly concerned the girl was going to die of dehydration and asked Bea to keep a close eye on her.

The longer they waited, the more dangerous escape became and the more potential for breakdown. If the group continued to increase there was a greater risk of someone spilling the beans. Cecelia needed to come up with a plan, but that was easier said than done.

Sofía had insisted Cece upgrade the electrical circuits and HVAC system. It was honestly outside of her scope as an electrical engineer; she understood the mechanism of action and had a natural inclination for figuring out complex systems, but she was not an electrician. Cecelia couldn't exactly tell Sofía that. After all, her day job gave her full access to all the ductwork, panels, and machinery she needed to figure a way out. Under the guise of knowing how to calculate the wattage they'd need to keep the lights on and what areas to target, Cece managed to get ahold of the blueprints. Sofía wasn't completely stupid and made sure she only got a little piece at a time and was never allowed to look at the full plans for the building. Even so, after a few weeks Cece had nearly figured a way out of here. The next step was to test her hypothesis. If she was able to make it to the exit, she would return and let the girls know through the code she'd devised and they'd make a plan.

Today was the day.

Tugging on a pair of black jeans and a tank top, Cece threw on a sweatshirt over the outfit. The air was hot in the ducts, but Cecelia needed to protect her skin from insulation and irritants. She also tucked her jeans into her work boots and made sure her they were laced up tight. Grabbing her tool belt from the side of the bed, she headed down the usual path she took to the compound's basement. The stink of musty pipes and a faint chemical smell assaulted her senses. Cecelia swallowed hard, steeling her nerves and banishing the nervous butterflies in her belly.

She was supposed to be checking some of the wiring for the foyer this morning. Sofía wanted some special lightning and a temperature controlled zone for a couple paintings she'd recently acquired and it would require some changes to the grid. Cecelia promised she could get it done today. She had plenty of time to search for the exit and get back in time to complete her task.

Instead of going straight to the electrical panel, Cece squeezed through the ductwork until she reached the end of the shafting that led out into an exhaust system. Tying a bandana around her mouth and nose in case dust flew up, she used her screwdriver to pop off the vent cover. Pausing for a moment, she glanced skyward and said a silent prayer before she tugged herself up into the space. Keeping her eyes forward, she gave her full attention to remembering all of the details in the blueprints Sofía had given her access to. Cece still wasn't entirely sure how the system connected or where she'd dump out, but hoped this little excursion would clarify things.

Most of the pipes were much larger than a human being and Cecelia moved easily through them, yet the closer she got to the outside, the tighter things got. Several times she had to stop to catch her breath in fear she might be crushed to death. She'd never considered herself claustrophobic before, but this whole experience was enough to make it so. The only thing that carried her through was the smell of fresh air. A whirring—soft at first and then louder as she got closer— filled the space around her. Straight ahead was a massive fan...and behind it, her freedom.

Wiping a bead of sweat from her face, Cecelia pulled away the bandana and inhaled the fresh air deep into her lungs. The fan itself was industrial size and the blades were moving too quickly for her to assess the situation. It was going to be difficult to work around and would slice her apart if she wasn't careful. Cece undid the screws holding the grate and set it aside. Taking infinite care, she stepped back to take stock.

Cecelia had to be pretty high up, which didn't make it easy. She'd have to devise some kind of ladder or rope to climb down. Bed sheets tied and then lowered would have to do, and they'd have to find some way to anchor it for when the last person came down. As an engineer, she was confident in her ability to come up with something that would work. Thankfully, the ground beneath the drop was grassy, which would hopefully ease the blow a little bit.

Stepping back to make a few notes, Cecelia's stomach tightened when she heard something coming from just beyond the entrance to where she was standing. It didn't take a mechanical prodigy to figure out she'd been caught. The woman that came through the door like a wild dog on a rampage was Sofía's little pet. "You bitch!" Angie screeched and lunged for Cecelia. "Sofía has given you *everything*!"

The theatrics were lost on Cecelia. She gritted her teeth and braced for the impact. Cece narrowly avoided the fan's whirring blades and instead of it taking her apart, it just took a chunk out of the sleeve of her sweatshirt and nicked her arm. Dragging herself forward, she pushed

Angie. "Don't be a fuckin' idiot. This fan will chew you up and spit you out!"

"I don't understand you. You're her favorite and yet you constantly try to hurt her!" Angie whimpered raggedly.

"I ain't some brainwashed whore gobbling up her shit. We're fuckin' *prisoners* here! Don't you get it?" Cece snarled at her. "She's collecting us like Barbie dolls and I ain't gonna sit back and wait until she decides we're all too much trouble." She took a step forward. "Sofía said if I didn't do her bidding, she'd kill my brother and nephew!"

Angie growled low in her throat. "She would never do that! You're warped!"

Cecelia snorted, "*I'm* warped? You're willing to kill me because she's brainwashed you! You're all sippin' the fuckin Kool-Aid." As she spoke, she inched further toward the other side of the duct. Angie was smaller and faster, but Cecelia was definitely stronger.

It just so happened that Angie was prepared for Cecelia to fight and brought her switchblade. The moment Cece leaned toward the door, she lunged with her knife outstretched. Cecelia elbowed her, taking a slit to the shoulder but managing to kick the girl away. The knife fell onto the ground and there was a mad scramble for the weapon. Angie went crawling for it but Cecelia grabbed her by her hair, wrenching her back as she grabbed the knife. "I don't wanna hurt you, Angie!"

Since Cece had been discovered, it seemed pointless now to try and go back for the others. She'd have to bust out and then bring Los Santos down to get her friends as quickly as possible. It wasn't ideal and she had no guarantee Sofía wouldn't kill all her friends, but if she went back now there would be far too many questions. Angie would narc her out and Sofía would make sure Cecelia never saw the light of day again—if she even let her live. There was no alternative.

No matter how hard Cecelia tried, Angie wasn't letting up; she tried to grab for the knife and pushed hard, trying to jump for her switchblade. Cecelia held her off with her other hand. It was then that Angie noticed the screwdriver at Cecelia's waist and all was lost. With one violent motion, she took the tool and slammed it toward the taller woman's eye. Cecelia felt the screwdriver enter her cheek and then twist as Angie tugged it downward. Blood spurted from her eye socket and around her face as she stopped trying to simply fend off the attack and countered with a violent shove of her own.

The sickening splatter of human bone and flesh against the fan rattled the entire infrastructure. The blowback splattered Cecelia's face, her clothes, and stained her clothes and hair. She covered her face with her hands, ignoring the pain and damage to her own body as she started crawling back toward the duct. Adrenaline kept her going for a little while, but she was wounded and blood flowed into her eyes, stinging bitterly. She was not even halfway before everything she'd been holding back seemed to leave her and she succumbed to her own injuries. The wounds at her back and arm were not clotting and it was no longer evident which of the blood was hers or not.

Cecelia's consciousness waxed and waned as she fought her way toward the end of that tunnel. Finally, she dropped the five feet onto the ground and lay there for a long time, crumbled and broken until finally someone came along. She didn't know who it was...or how many days it took for her to wake up. Cecelia was so delirious, she couldn't really make out much of anything. She started measuring time in surgeries.

Many weeks later, Cece finally cleared and realized what a horrible mess her face was. Bea's careful care managed to save Cece's eye but Sofía had been very clear about what she would allow. Cecelia had not been allowed any pain medicine or antibiotics. If she lived, she would be permitted to stay, if she died then it would be a blessed relief from the prison of her flesh. It was a true act of God she managed to make it through the fevers that ravaged her body, and the pain.

At first, Cece was too weak to walk more than a few steps to the commode...but with help from Bea, Candy, Julia, and Adela, she started to rebound. Every day she would sit in front of the mirror, staring at her reflection and the tangled, swollen, scarred remains of her cheek. Slowly but surely, Cece grew strong again on a tonic of rage and hate. Eventually, she was well enough to return to the general population with even more restrictions and more of Sofia's cronies keeping an eye on her. Even though the wounds started to mend on the outside, the festering infection inside was too much.

Cecelia wasn't just out to escape now. She wanted *blood*. Every shred of decency she'd been holding onto was burned away until she was a shell of herself, thinking only of survival. She had become an animal with an unspeakable hunger and, in time, forgot what it meant to be human. There was no love left, only loathing.

Chapter Twenty

Rogelio's joyous return to La Verdad was overshadowed heavily by Lazarus's decree. He had given Los Santos three weeks to pack their things and get the hell out of town and time was almost up. Cecelia was still adamant they play along and lull Los Lobos into a false sense of security. As it stood, she nearly had the entire house packed up and Ramón was returning from Florida today. The news of them moving out of town would spread like wildfire in the hands of the right gossips. Cece was counting on it.

What she was not counting on was her father-in-law trailing behind Ramón in the airport, lugging his oxygen tank behind him. Cecelia's heart leapt as she ran to Angelo, throwing her arms around him and hugging him tightly. They'd spoken on the phone since the man moved out of town but it had been far too long since she'd seen him.

Angelo kissed her cheeks, spinning her around happily. "*Ay, mija*, you are more beautiful that I have ever seen you," he cooed.

"You're a rotten liar," Cecelia replied, covering her scarred cheek with her hand. "What are you doing here?"

Angelo rested his hand on the small of her back as they headed out to the car and slipped into the front seat. "Ramón told me everything." He let out a heavy sigh and warm brown eyes were filled with annoyance. "Why didn't you tell me? I would have come sooner."

Cecelia eased her way into traffic and headed the familiar road to home. She cleared her throat nervously. "You seemed so happy, Tío. I didn't want you to get sucked into everything. That's why you left: to start a new life away from all this. I couldn't ask you to give that up for the club."

"My obligation is not to the club, it's to you!" Angelo scoffed. "I love you, Cecelia. You're *mi familia* and I will not let anything happen to you. Rogelio is like a son to me too. I was devastated to learn he had started a rehab program without the support of his whole family!" He shook his head.

A blush crept over her cheeks and stayed there. She hadn't told her Angelo anything about what was going on—mostly because she wasn't sure he was up to hearing the news. Health issues had been one of the major reasons Angelo moved out to Florida in the first place. They had a specialty clinic for individuals with severe COPD. He'd gone through a program that helped him map his lung function; he'd lost weight, got on a regimen of medications, and found the woman of his dreams. Estelle obviously cared about him, making a full regimen of low sodium meals and making sure he took all his breathing treatments. Cecelia had never seen him look better. "*Lo Siento*," she said finally.

When they got back to the house, Angelo headed into the bedroom to change while Ramón and Cecelia chatted. "*Hola, mi esposa*," he smiled. He inched toward her, kissing her gently on the forehead. Cecelia didn't push him away, but he got the impression she didn't want to be touched. He didn't have time to dwell on it, since the rest of the club started to trickle in. Rogelio arrived with Gina and Raphael in tow. Martín, Diego, and Luis chatted quietly in the corner. Last, but certainly not least, Danny showed up with a case of beer, pizzas, and salad for everyone.

Cecelia genuinely smiled as she helped him carry things into the house. Their shoulders bumped against each other casually as they worked. Danny glanced at her tenderly, his hand brushing over her arm as he reached over her to grab the salad tongs. Cece crouched to grab some paper plates and silverware, for those who needed it and doled out extra napkins to those who didn't. Danny grabbed a piece of pizza, nearly dripping grease on his cut and she scolded him with a sharp bark before hurling a wad of paper towels at him. To any outsider, the ease of their interaction wouldn't have been indicative of anything...but Ramón knew Cecelia. She and Danny were fucking each other.

Ramón felt his rage start to build. It simmered in his veins, bleeding into his stomach, and before it could reach a crescendo, he turned and stormed into the bedroom he once shared with his wife. Their personal items had been packed away and moved into a storage facility. Only the essential items were left in the drawers, closets, and suitcases were splayed out on furniture.

Something had to be done. Something *drastic*.

A soft cough from the doorway knocked Ramón out of his tailspin and he turned. "*Papa, está bien?*" Angelo looked fine, but he was wearing his oxygen again. The plane ride coupled with being back in the dusty La Verdad air was agitating his lungs.

"You've been quiet since we returned, *mi hijo*," Angelo replied softly.

"*No te preocupes*," Ramon interrupted. "It is between *Cecelia* and me."

Angelo settled on the chair in the bedroom, dragging more oxygen into his lungs and coughing to clear some of phlegm in his throat. "I have to say, I was quite surprised to hear you two had decided to give your marriage another try. After Cecelia gave you the divorce papers, I thought it would be a good chance for the both of you to move on."

Ramon clenched his fist tightly, his jaw following suit. "You don't know everything. You've been gone for a long time now."

"It does not matter how long I have been gone. I am your father and I know more than you think I do." Angelo narrowed his eyes. "Once upon a time maybe you and Cecelia were meant to be together but things change, Ramón. How long has it been since you two were happy with one another?"

Ever since his accident, Ramón didn't feel pleasure and joy the same way he once had. He couldn't give an answer and it infuriated him. "We made vows!"

Angelo shook his head sadly. "Vows cannot force the heart."

"She loved me once. She can love me again," Ramón growled, glancing toward the open door. Cecelia and Danny were standing out in the open and he swore they were purposely flaunting their love for all to see. "You're in on it, aren't you?"

Angelo's face creased as he took another long puff of oxygen, letting it seep down into his lungs before he coughed it back up. "In on what, *mijo*?"

"Cecelia cheating on me!"

Wizened grey brows flew up in surprise. "I don't know what you're talking about." Angelo frowned deeper. "*Ramón, mirame*," he urged, "Cecelia has grown and changed. She served you with divorce papers before the Black Jacks took her. Since returning, she has done what is necessary for this club—which means she may have made promises or alliances you cannot understand. Until you are el Presidente, you cannot begin to know the sacrifices that must be made for the good of the club." Angelo reached out, cupping his son's shoulder.

"None of that matters!" he hollered, wrenching away from his father's touch. "We pledged in sickness and health. Until death do us part!"

"The Cecelia you knew *has* died, just as the man you once were has died!" Angelo thundered, pushing himself to his feet once more. He let out a wheezing cough. "Heed my warning, Ramón: the wife you knew has been gone for a long time. Gather your strength, cut your losses, and move on or you will continue to destroy one another!"

Ramón stalked for the door, his heartbeat thundering in his chest and his rage blinding him. He hardly noticed that he knocked his father back into his chair, pushing his way through Luis and Horatio as he powered through the kitchen. He vaguely heard Cecelia call his name, but he did not stop. He grabbed the keys to his car and held onto the railing tightly as he descended the stairs.

"Ramón!" Cece yelled again, jogging out the front door, but he was already peeling off down the street. She hurried back down the hall to where Angelo was in the bedroom. He was half-hunched over the bed, trying to change over his oxygen tank. "Let me help you," she offered.

Angelo's face was ashen as he turned to peer at her while he continued to go through the motions of changing over his tank. "I am afraid of what he might do, Cecelia."

"I know," she replied softly. "But right now, I am concerned only for you." Resting her hands over his, Cecelia helped him open the new tank and change over the tubing. To her surprise, there was still a small amount of oxygen left in the other tank. She thought he'd run out and that's why he looked so frightened. When he cupped her cheek, she realized that wasn't the extent of it. "What happened?"

"Ramón knows..."

"Knows what?"

"*Cecelia*," Angelo warned, "He knows you've shared your heart—and your bed—with Daniel Harding."

Cecelia scrambled to her feet, heart pounding in her chest. "I—"

Angelo raised his palm to stop her from denying it. "There's no need to lie. I can see when a woman is in love. Daniel softens you, makes you feel safe, and you are frightened of those feelings...but you need to be willing to fight through your fear, you have to allow him to be in your life. I am an old man but I am not blind."

There was a long silence and, for a moment, Cecelia looked like she would argue. Suddenly, she sagged and leaned against the doorjamb. "I never wanted to hurt Ramón. He was my first love, a man I thought I would end my days with...but this is not the man I married. I can't be scared of my own husband." She licked her lips. "I'm sorry, Tío."

"Don't be sorry, Cecelia, be *careful*. Ramón believes you have betrayed him and your marriage. I am not sure what he will do in retaliation..." Angelo inhaled deeply, some of the color beginning to return to his face.

"I will," Cecelia promised. "But for now, we need to focus our efforts on Los Lobos. I'll deal with Ramón tonight." She still had the divorce ready and waiting to be signed. She'd given him every chance to show her he was the man she once loved, and it had still gone to hell. It was time to end the charade and let them both move on with their lives. "Come and get something to eat and then you should rest for a while. We will sort all this out."

Angelo followed her back into the living room where Los Santos were mingling. There was plenty of pizza and salad left, and Gina was making dessert. She tended to bake when she was stressed; it reminded Cecelia of Jenna, and her heart lurched again. Cece could only imagine what kind of horror the girl had been subjected to by Lazarus and Los Lobos. She made up a plate for Angelo and settled him in the living room before grabbing herself a bottle of water.

"*Oye!*" Cecelia whistled, settling down the rowdy crowd and motioning for them to take their seats. Luis, Horatio, Martín, and Diego were crowded on the couch. Rogelio was on the armchair with Gina at his side; his arm was wrapped tight around her waist, her head resting against his shoulder. Cece had a new appreciation for the woman Rogelio had knocked up by accident after a long, drunken night of partying.

Danny perched on a chair he'd grabbed from the kitchen, his arms crossed over his chest. He wondered where Ramón was, but decided not to bring it up. Cecelia had that look on her face and she wouldn't take kindly to being interrupted.

"We all know why we're here. Los Lobos have been encroaching on our territory, trying to stake their claim." Cecelia glanced around the room, her eyes landing on Rogelio and how guilty he looked. She didn't want him to

211

wallow in his failures and the bad decisions he made, but she needed him to remember so he never did anything like that again. "They don't have a moral code. They will abduct women as leverage. Although Jenna appears safe for now, we cannot be sure what they are doing to her out there." She swallowed hard. "We have played their game, we have made it seem as if we will pack up and leave…but now we have to follow through."

Chaos erupted in the room.

"*What*?" Luis snapped, sitting bolt upright.

"La Verdad is our home!"

"*No!*"

Cecelia slammed her fist down on the table, silencing them with a deathly glare. "If we do not make our surrender believable, they will smell it a mile off. We will pretend to exile ourselves, scatter to the wind. If Lazarus is a man of his word, he will return Jenna. Then we bide our time and when their defenses are weak, we strike."

"How long do we have to wait?" Luis pressed.

"As long as it takes," Cecelia replied coldly. "We cannot rush this or we will lose. They have power, money, and connections." She licked her lips. "We will use our own connections, ask them for help. They will be our eyes and our ears. The Devils of California and the Nightriders will assist us in this. But I need your cooperation, all of you." She glanced around the room again.

Diego cleared his throat. "It feels like we're giving up and that's not what this club is about."

"That's not it," Danny broke in. He could sense Cece's patience wearing thin and her anger beginning to grow. "We're pulling one over on them. It requires a shitload more effort than just fighting until we're all dead. We've got to fight *smarter*, not harder!"

Horatio peered over at Martín, and nodded. "We trust you."

"So do I," Luis replied. "Danny's right. We *do* have to fight smart...and Cecelia's always been smarter than all of us combined."

"That's for damn sure," Rogelio smirked. "We're all behind you, *hermana*. You just tell us what to do and we'll follow." He stood up, wrapping his arm around her shoulder. "We're family, blood, and we're going to come outta this on top."

Cecelia shot Danny a grateful smile and breathed a sigh of relief. "It's settled then. I'll contact Marco Caraway and we will ship out in time for the deadline." She hugged her brother closer. "We've got this." Cece put on a brave face but she wasn't so sure. The odds were stacked against them; the only thing she knew was that they had to try.

Los Santos settled back into socializing, eating, and catching up with Angelo. Danny gave Cecelia a little space, but he was never too far away. Ramón was still missing well into the evening and Cece was through

213

agonizing over it. Once she found her husband and ended things once and for all, perhaps she could begin to deal with the Devil in their midst.

Chapter Twenty-One

Sven was on to them.

Despite being identical, the Villeneuve twins were almost complete opposites in every other way. Petrik was cold and callous, violent to his core, and willing to do anything to get what he wanted. Sven was the sensitive brother, the one who went out of his way to walk little old ladies across the street; he was a very attentive lover and an excellent listener. Petrik and Sven had different styles of dress, different ideas on how to further Los Lobos' objectives, and even different sexual preferences. The one thing they did have in common was an inscrutable bond of brotherly loyalty.

Sven had known for several days that something was wrong with Petrik. His twin brother often went days without answering text messages or phone messages—that was nothing new. Petrik had once gone off the grid for a month after a trip to Shanghai and simply left his life behind. Sven had been angry, of course, but there was no aching void in his chest; this time he couldn't sleep, eat, or take pleasure in any of the things he usually enjoyed.

Pulling himself up over and over again on the pull-up bar made Sven's skin glisten with a sheen of sweat. He was aching and tired but he persevered, breathing even though his lungs were on fire. If not for a timid knock on the door, he might have continued that way until he collapsed.

It would've been the first rest he'd gotten in weeks...

A fluffy white towel sat neatly folded on the end table and Sven flung it over his shoulder before heading to the door. His eyebrow quirked up as he came face to face with a woman with flaming auburn hair and the clearest hazel eyes he'd ever seen. She was a hair over five feet tall and he dwarfed her by a solid foot, even in her sky-high heels. Unlike many of the women who had come to him in the past, seeking to entice, she revealed nothing of her body—which made him ache to divest her of everything she wore and explore the curves beneath. The silky black skirt she wore fell to her mid calf and she wore simple black stockings beneath. He found himself wondering if they were pantyhose or if she had secured the stockings with garters. Tucked into the simple skirt was a crisp white button down that was fastened all the way up her neck. He had to steel himself against the urge to undo the one at her throat to see if her pulse was beating as quickly as his. "May I help you?"

"No, but I can help you," she answered boldly.

Sven took a step back to admit her into the apartment. "Pardon the mess," he offered, but there was not a single stitch out of place. The room was immaculate, not a single object out of place. It was not inherently obvious he had been living here for nearly six months. All of his clothes were perfectly pressed and hung meticulously in his closet. The carpet was pristinely white, not a single object on the floor beyond what a very expensive interior decorator, or someone with exquisite taste, had purposely set there.

It was a studio apartment with Sven's bed on one side of the room and an apartment sized leather couch on the other resting against the long end of the kitchen island. The cooking area looked untouched, not a speck of food or dust or residue on any surface. Perhaps the most striking feature of the apartment though was the skylight that filtered light down, illuminating the man who stood in front of her. The way the shadows crossed his face made her stomach twist half in fear, half in anticipation.

"Who are you?" Sven asked suspiciously, his eyes narrowing dangerously as he grabbed a t-shirt out of the drawer and pulled it over his muscled chest. "Don't tell me Los Santos sent you to distract me." He laughed bitterly. "Do they truly think I would be so stupid as to fall prey to a pretty face?"

"My name is Julia Amos and I won't lie to you, I know Los Santos pretty well." She watched Sven's expression go from angry to surprised in a millisecond. "Do you remember reading about the Black Jacks and the hostages they kept in an abandoned prison in the Nevada desert?"

"Make your point," Sven replied testily.

"I was held there with Cecelia Santos and I got to know her quite well. I know how she thinks. I know how she operates. I know her weaknesses..." Julia explained. "There were women from across the country and the world. Sofía Salma wished to build an army and hand selected girls who she knew were angry or downtrodden or skilled in their fields of study."

Sven padded into the kitchen, grabbing two bottles of water from the fridge and extending one to her before taking a long swig of his. "Which one were you?"

"None, I'm afraid. I was just collateral damage." Julia flashed him a sad smile. Opening up the bottle of water, she took a long drink before flopping down on his sofa, kicking off her heels. If Sven minded, he didn't say anything. Instead, he sat on the edge of his bed, watching every move the girl made.

He watched her cross her legs daintily at the ankle, a soft flush of pink spreading over her cheeks. "Why would you come to me?" Sven stated. He laced his fingers as he leaned in to stare at her. "I do not trust you."

"I tried to get ahold of your brother first," Julia admitted and she watched his posture tighten. "A mutual friend gave me his name. I tried reaching him for days but he never called me back. So, I did a little digging and found out you were twins. I thought maybe if I met you, you could help me get to Petrik." She hesitated. "Maybe I'm wasting my time..."

"No." Sven exhaled sharply. "I am beginning to believe Los Santos have done something horrible to him and if this is the case, I wish to obtain any knowledge I can to destroy them all." He licked his lips. "I will need to investigate the claims you've made. I'm sure you understand."
"Of course," Julia replied, a slow smile tipping up the corners of her lips. "I'll cooperate in any way you wish. I'm looking forward to doing business with you."

Oddly enough, Sven found he felt the same way…and perhaps doing a bit more than business, if everything worked in his favor.

* * *

Every morning since McGruff's passing, Jenna awoke in Lazarus's arms. With a yawn, she stretched and rolled to face the man who had become her darkest secret and deepest desire. Wispy hair fell into his face, softening the razor sharpness of his cheekbones. He slept unperturbed, even as she slipped out of the bed they now shared.

Pulling one of his sweaters on over her head, Jenna eased down the stairs. They were running low on supplies, including her favorite kind of loose-leaf tea. She had taken to making a list so when Lazarus went into town, he could pick up groceries for them. He'd gone out a few days ago, to meet with Los Santos, but insisted on rushing back to her side. They made love long into the evening and when they were finally too exhausted to continue, she closed her eyes and let him overtake her.

The kettle whistled and Jenna began to pour the water into a teapot when a blur of movement in her peripheral vision startled her. Blazing liquid burned her skin and she cried out, pulling her hand close to her chest. She whirled to face Lazarus, her heart still pounding. "I thought you were still asleep!"

Lazarus reached out, grasping the injured hand to assess the damage. It was a minor burn, her skin pink but not blistered, thankfully. He dropped the appendage and moved to stare out the kitchen window. "Why are you still here, Jenna?" he asked, after a long time.

She froze. "What are you talking about?"

"I have given you time and space. I have left the door unlocked, and the keys to the Jeep in plain sight." He inched toward her, his hands sliding over her shoulders. "I have pretended to sleep so soundly you would not worry to wake me...but you are still here." Lazarus slid his arms around her waist, cradling her closer to him. "I see now why Los Santos are willing to give up their home, their legacy, to protect you. I would give up my life for the very same..."

Emotion choked Jenna like a rising tide, stealing her breath and leaving her eyes watering. "You want me to leave?" She could barely recognize her own voice. "After everything we've been through...after everything we've built?"

Lazarus's expression hardened. "What have we built, Jenna? I drugged you, stole you from your home, your business, and your friends. I have made you my prisoner here, I've frightened and intimidated you." Cupping her cheek, he leaned in and pressed a soft kiss to her lips. "If you love someone, you must set them free. If you choose to return to me...if I survive the wrath of Los Lobos when they have learned what I have done, then it is meant to be." He closed his eyes, unable to bear the pain in her eyes. "Jenna, I have never loved any person the way I love you. I could not live with myself if your feelings were tainted by fear or obligation." Lazarus pulled away from her.

Jenna staggered and watched him retreat to the other side of the kitchen. On another day, she might have followed and thrown herself back into his arms but he had the look of a caged animal, ready to strike at any moment. "Lazarus, you don't know what you're saying." Jenna choked again, her chest heaving with the pressure of her sadness. She leaned against the counter, desperate for the support a solid object would bring her. "The minute you opened your heart to me, you shared yourself, it ceased to be this torrid love affair that needed to be hidden in the shadows. I love you. I'll fight for what we have."

Lazarus smiled, but there was no mirth in his eyes. He only held her gaze for a second before he turned away, walking into the living room and opening up the front door to the house. He stared at her, his face a mask molded in pain. "If you wish to fight, return to your friends." He swallowed hard. "I am not a good man, Jenna."

"Bullshit!" she spat at him. "A bad man would've held him me in that dungeon in your basement. You would have tied me down, violated me, made me fear your very presence. You would've let Petrik have his way with me. You would *not* be keeping your word to Los Santos by allowing me to return. I would be the one hacked apart and burned alive...don't you see, Lazarus? You *are* good. You're just on the wrong side of this."

There was a moment when it looked like Lazarus would acquiesce and accept her assessment of him. "If you stay, that is the man you will force me to be. I will hurt you and I cannot abide that. I care about you too much to allow you to fall victim to what Los Lobos are about to do..." he swallowed hard. "The city will burn, the citizens loyal to Los Santos will be cast out or killed, there will be violence until nothing remains. Then we will rebuild La Verdad the way we wish for it to be. Out of the wreckage will be a citadel intended to distribute our products across the nation." He let out a shaky breath. "I will not see you go down in flames."

Jenna's crystal blue eyes were wide and horrified. "Is that what you want, Lazarus? You want to tear people from their homes and force businesses to shut their doors? You want to flood the streets with drugs and guns and watch everyone get hurt?"

"I am the leader of this empire. I have a responsibility—"

"*Fuck* responsibility!" Jenna hollered at him. "I refuse to believe you want this!"

Lazarus remained stoic in the face of her accusation. "I will never be a poor street rat again, unable to protect my family. I never want to know the fear of freezing in the winter and burning in the summer. I never want to know what it is to go hungry again."

Shaking her head at him, Jenna pressed herself tighter against the wall. "Isn't that exactly the fate you're sealing for the displaced residents of La Verdad? Refugees

222

without a home, lost jobs, families torn apart and scattered to the wind…" She wrapped her arms tightly around herself, hoping to keep herself from being ripped apart by the swirling vortex of her emotions.

Silence hung between them, the tension thick enough to be cut with a knife. Lazarus could not come up with an answer that would satisfy her—or *him*, for that matter. Putting the needs of others before his own was an entirely foreign concept. He'd lived hand to mouth as a child, and ignoring the rights of others had been the only way he'd been able to survive. Then again, it had been quite some time since his basic needs hadn't been met; he always had enough food, clothing to spare, and a roof over his head. He was never cold in the winter or hot in the summer. As a matter of fact, he had such an excess that he spent it on ridiculous things he didn't need. Having money and status had been the most important things in his life. Now, this one little woman was changing everything for him. "I do not know what you wish me to say, Jenna…" he trailed off.

"I want you to say you'll stop this!" she cried. "Walk away and we can go somewhere, *anywhere!*"

A heavy sigh rumbled from Lazarus's throat. "If I were to do what you are asking, there is nowhere I could run or hide. I would be hunted to the ends of the earth. Even if I were to stay ahead each and every time. It's no life for you." He strode forward, finally closing the distance between them. He reached out, cupping her cheek. "You are a talented chef. You deserve to be settled somewhere and to have a real life."

Jenna's skin sizzled the moment he touched her and she leaned into the pain searing inside of her. "So rat them out! Turn state and bring these guys in. Then you could enter witness protection and we could start over somewhere. There are always other options! You don't have to give up so easily, Lazarus. You built this empire, you can take it apart brick by brick!"

If only it were that easy...

Lazarus held her tighter and pressed a kiss to the top of her head. "I can make you no promises, Jenna. I can only ask you to run far away from here. Take the Jeep, follow the road to the fork and stay to the right. It will bring you to the main road, and then you can follow the highway to La Verdad. *Please*, Jenna..."

For the longest time, neither of them moved. The sun rose higher in the sky, warming their faces. Jenna was determined not to be the first to pull away and eventually, Lazarus found the strength to do it. Pressing one last chaste kiss to her lips, he pressed the car keys into her hand, and turned his back.

Jenna stared at the open door for the longest time before she finally gathered up her strength to leave. She took only her memories with her as she slid into the driver's seat of her Jeep, slid Lazarus's aviator sunglasses over her nose, and started the journey back to the place she used to call home.

Chapter Twenty-Two

Even though Los Santos had been up late last night, Danny got up far earlier than he wanted to. Rubbing his eyes, he sat up and padded into the bathroom only to find Cecelia brushing her teeth. She turned to glance at him before rinsing and spitting. He leaned against the doorjamb, his lips curved up as he watched her finish her morning routine.

Cecelia furrowed her eyebrows. "Can I help you, *vaquero*?" He was just standing there, leering at her. Well, that wasn't exactly fair. She wasn't uncomfortable with him staring at her; unfortunately her lack of discomfort made her feel awkward anyway. She was still in her pajamas: a soft blue tank top and a pair of black yoga pants. She didn't have on a bra or underwear beneath her sleepwear. Her blue hair was mussed and she didn't have on a stitch of makeup. It didn't stop Danny from wrapping his arms around her and pressing her against the sink. A sly smile slid over her features and she nudged him. "We shouldn't..."

"Nobody's up yet," Danny admonished. He licked his lips, bending to kiss her sweetly; she tasted like mint and smelled like the fabric softener she used on the sheets. Sighing softly against her lips, he brushed a wayward strand of blue hair from her cheek. Her locks were pink when he first arrived in La Verdad but the blue reminded him of Cecelia when he first met her. It was cathartic for both of them.

Snuggling against him for a brief, weak moment, Cecelia finally gathered her strength and untangled herself from his grasp. "There are eyes everywhere." Heading into the kitchen, she cleaned out the coffee maker and waited for the heady brew to finish percolating. Cece found herself sighing. "Ramón didn't come home last night. He knows."

Danny's head cocked in confusion. "Knows what?"

"About *us*," Cecelia admonished.

"Fuck!" The curse tumbled from his lips and he dragged a hand through his hair. "'I'm guessing that's why he stormed off?"

Cece rubbed her temples, aching for an extra strong cup of coffee. "Yeah, he's pretty pissed." She exhaled sharply. "It's kinda a relief, though. I'm sick of hiding things. I'm sick of lying. I'm sick of being trapped in this loveless marriage just for the sake of the club!" As soon as the coffee was done, Cecelia filled herself up a hearty mug and handed one to Danny. "At some point, I gotta start living my life for myself." She licked her lips. "The shit could hit the fan any time with Los Lobos. I don't want to end my days lying to myself and everybody else about how I feel."

Danny's mouth was bone dry even after taking several slugs of the vilest coffee in existence. He gathered his courage. "How do you feel, Cecelia?"

"You *know*, Daniel."

"I want to hear you say it." He inched toward her, setting his mug of coffee down on the counter. Slipping his arm around her waist, he grinned predatorily at her. "*Say it*, Cecelia."

"You're a fuckin' dick, you know that right?" Cece growled. She slid her hands up his chest, tracing the muscles that hid beneath his t-shirt. "Oh well, I love you anyway."

Danny widened his stance, tugging her so she was flush against his chest. "That's how you're going to tell me you love me for the first time? I'm a fucking dick but you love me so it's alright?" He dropped a kiss to her nose, smiling as she wrinkled it at him. "That's not very romantic."

Cecelia nudged him playfully. "I never promised you romance," she sniggered. "Don't tell me you need flowers and chocolates and all that pussy shit?"

"Of course I do!"

"I never pegged you as the type, Danielito. Luis *is* still single, you know." For the first time in a very long time, Cecelia genuinely smiled. Unable to resist, she devoured his lips again. There was no hesitation this time, no pulling back. Danny pressed her against the cabinets, his fingers already tugging at the waistband of her pajama pants.

A loud cough from the other side of the kitchen dragged them out of the moment. Cecelia glanced around Danny to see Angelo smirking at them. Her cheeks darkened with embarrassment and she tugged away from him. "You want a cup of coffee?" She asked, her voice slightly strained.

"Nah, I quit the stuff years ago," Angelo replied. "Not good for *mi corazón*. Estelle lets me have a cup of herbal tea before bed. For now I'll have a cup of water, if you're offering. I've got to take my pills." Sitting down at the table, he sifted through a bag of meds and inhalers, taking each of them methodically while smirking to himself.

Danny cleared his throat. "I'm going to take a shower," he lowered his voice, "A *cold* one." He half-limped for the stairs, glancing back at Cecelia. Now wasn't the time to consummate their love; there was a battle to be waged and a war to be won. Plus Cecelia was still technically married to Ramón and there was no way that man was going to take such an insult lying down. Danny and Cece needed bide their time.

He didn't want to, of course. Danny ached to drag Cecelia upstairs and claim her in any number of locations and positions until everyone in the house knew he belonged to her. Instead, he gathered his things and hurried for the bathroom without anyone being any wiser to his current predicament. Turning the shower on as cold as it would go, he dragged off his clothes and stood beneath the icy blast. The shower didn't last long and he slung a towel around his hips before walking, still dripping, back into the bedroom. Shaking off like a dog, he sat on the edge of the bed and reached for his phone. Marco had sent a text letting him know their crew would be awaiting their arrival whenever. There was also a popup reminding him of something important...

Lucy's birthday.

Danny's heart twisted and he stared down at the text reminder. He hadn't talked to his baby sister since their awful fight and his defection from the Devil's Own. She thought he was a traitor and a fool. Perhaps he was. It didn't change the fact this was going to be the first year he was not going to be spending her special day with her. He should at least call her though, right? Danny struggled. He almost pressed the call button a dozen times. He popped up from bed, hurriedly and jerkily getting dressed, trying to keep his mind occupied. Did she even want to hear from him?

"You're a chickenshit," Danny muttered to himself. He grabbed the phone again and this time he pressed send before he could talk himself out of it. It rang once, twice, but on the third ring, he heard her voice and his heart ached. "Happy Birthday, sis..." There was a long silence on the other end before he heard her sigh. "I hope your husband is treating you like a princess."

Lucy's voice sounded strained, despite her best efforts. "I got breakfast in bed, but I can't seem to get the breakfast tray close enough to myself to eat, thanks to my belly." She laughed nervously. "Now that I'm not nauseous all the time, I've really popped."

"That's what pregnant chicks are supposed to do, Luce. Eat up while you've got an excuse." He found himself smiling. God, he missed her. Archie might've been his official best friend, for propriety's sake, but Lucy was the one who actually held that title. "I'm a jackass, I didn't get you anything—"

"I don't need anything," Lucy interrupted. "The only thing I want for you to come home. I don't like the way we left things. You're my *only* brother. I love you, even if you make stupid choices sometimes."

Danny snorted. "Just some of the time?"

Lucy chuckled despite herself. "I miss you, Danny."

"I miss you too, Luce." He could hear the tears in her voice and it tore a hole in his chest. Danny drew in a deep breath. "I promise as soon as I get a chance, I'll come up to see you. I'm a patched member of Los Santos now and they need me here. "

Lucy's shock came through the phone in waves. "Cecelia actually let you wear Los Santos colors?"

"You don't have to sound so surprised," Danny scoffed. "I had to earn it but yeah, I'm a full member now. Things are good with Cece and me. She...told me she loves me this morning. I'm not going to mess this up, Luce. I'm sorry I fucked up your life and betrayed Archie but...this is what I needed to do."

Nearly a minute passed before Lucy spoke again. "As long as you're happy, that's all that matters to me, Danny." There was a screech from the other room and she sighed.

"Amelia's up and I've got to get going. Call me soon, okay? And tell Cecelia I'm sorry."

Danny nodded to himself. "I will. I love you, sis. Happy birthday." He could hear his niece wailing for mommy before Lucy's side cut out and he was left with beeping in his ear. It felt as if a weight had been lifted from his chest, easing the suffering he'd been feeling since he severed ties with his club and, in the process, his family. He could make amends, which was something he scarcely felt he deserved but had hoped for beyond all hope.

The rest of the house was just beginning to stir. Luis and Diego were sipping coffee and chatting with Angelo in Spanish when Danny appeared downstairs. Cecelia had changed out of her pajamas into a pair of worn jeans and her cut was tossed over a chair while she prepped the morning meal. He refilled his coffee cup and winked at her before jumping in where he could, his Spanish broken and sad, but infinitely improved from a few weeks ago. Horatio jogged down the stairs, pitching in eagerly to help make breakfast; 'helping' really meant sampling the food as it came out until Cecelia slapped him and told him to sit down.

Just as she was getting everything on the table, the sound of a car pulling into the driveway caught Cece's attention. Something about the heavy, low engine noise piqued her senses. That wasn't what Ramón's car sounded like. His BMW purred like a kitten. This was a deep rumble, seeming to flow through her bones. "*Oye!*" She snapped. "Somebody's here."

Danny's hand was at his gun in an instant. The Jeep's windows were deeply tinted, obscuring the person inside. Luis and Diego were at his side in an instant, weapons drawn and teeth gritted. "Get the fuck out of the car!" Danny snarled, kicking the tire of the car. He had no way of knowing if the person inside was armed, but he was prepared nonetheless...but this was not his first standoff.

The door opened timidly and Danny ducked low, crouching to give him the best vantage point to wound— but not kill—his foe if they came out with guns blazing. He expected to see leather pants, combat boots, or even stilettos. Instead he found himself staring at fleecy pink pants, black flip flops nestled between toes, the nails coated in chipping pink polish. His shoulders straightened and he stood all the way up. "Stand down," Danny ordered.

"Fuck no!" Diego snarled. "It could be a trick! Ain't the first time a club sent a hooker here to get us to let our guard down..."

"It's not a hooker, *cabrón*," Danny snapped back. "It's Jenna!" The woman's face was red and puffy from crying, tears gathering in her crystal blue eyes. She was shaky on her feet as she stepped forward. He reached out to comfort her but she shrugged him off, wrapping her arms tightly around her body. Danny wasn't offended. He had no idea what kind of trauma she'd been through. He turned, hollering for the house. "Cece!" he cried. "*Cecelia!*"

While the boys checked out front, she made sure Angelo was away from the action. She couldn't bear it if anything happened to him. All the activity had caused his breathing to become heavy and she sent Horatio into the bedroom to get the man's nebulizer. He could supervise Angelo's breathing treatment while Cecelia dealt with whatever was going on. Danny was yelling for her and fear crawled in her veins. Of course she didn't want anything to happen to her cousins, but the thought of something happening to the man she loved was almost too much for her to bear.

Without her cut, without her gun, Cecelia flew down the stairs and her heart slammed into her ribs. Standing in the middle of the three men was Jenna. "Fuck…" she muttered under her breath, jogging out to wrap her arm around the girl. "It's alright, you're safe now," she murmured, leading the distraught woman upstairs into the spare bedroom, barking orders the whole way. She sent Diego to find the first aid kit, Luis to get Jenna some clean clothes, and told Danny to keep out of the way.

Jenna sat down on the bed, her chest and head aching with sorrow. Cecelia was digging through the medical supplies, looking for something—anything—to help ease her pain. It was almost enough to make her smile through the haze of her tears. "Cecelia, I'm not hurt," Jenna assured her.

"I don't know how you escaped but whatever he did to you, he's going to pay for it a hundredfold," Cece vowed. To her surprise, Jenna didn't seem any worse for the wear. She didn't have cuts or burns or bruises; her body

233

didn't bear the marks of a woman who'd suffered at the hands of her captor. If anything, she seemed well hydrated and the few pounds she'd put on made her look hale and healthy. It only stood to reason that Jenna's affliction was emotional rather than physical. And that was something Cecelia could relate to. "Do you want to talk about it?"

"Not yet," Jenna begged. "I-I've made such a fool of myself." Standing quickly, she moved toward the door. "I shouldn't be here. I don't belong."

Cecelia furrowed her eyebrows. "You're one of us, *chica*, whether you like it or not." She rested a hand on Jenna's shoulder, shepherding her back to the bed. "That means I'm gonna look out for you. You're clearly exhausted. Take some time and rest...when you wake up, we'll make sure you get something to eat." Hopefully Jenna would be able to tell her a bit more after that. She'd stayed with Lazarus for quite some time and had likely overheard something that could be of use.

Jenna allowed herself to be led back to the bed, swinging her legs onto the fluffy mattress. She rolled onto her side, avoiding Cecelia's gaze. "You'll never forgive me..."

Pausing for a moment, Cece glanced down at the woman before her with empathy spilling from her every pore. "I don't know what you're talking about. You don't have any Los Santos secrets to spill. There ain't nothing you coulda told him that he ain't already figured out for himself. Whatever he made you believe, we're gonna protect you." She moved toward the door.

"I love him."

Cecelia froze. "Who?"

"You *know* who." Jenna's voice cracked painfully. "Lazarus Caine…" She wrapped her arms tightly around her waist, praying to God she wouldn't shatter under the weight of her pain. "He let me go, gave me the keys to the car and told me to start over but I can't, Cecelia. I love him so much." Bitter tears splashed down her cheeks. "He's not a bad man. He doesn't want to hurt people deep down. He just wants—"

"Money. Power. Destruction," Cecelia interrupted. "I know the type." Her eyes lifted, staring at the picture of Ramón and Cece on their wedding day hanging on the wall. "You think you can change him. You think you can save him but you *can't*," she replied harshly. "You can fool yourself for a little while. Hell, even a *long* while…but one day you'll wake up and it'll be a stranger looking back at you in the mirror. He'll be the one to change *you*, Jenna, and you'll hate the person you've become." Cece closed the distance between them, settling at the edge of the bed. "You'll find yourself thanking God that you never had children with this man, that you've never exposed any innocent person to his slow poison." Cecelia's hand splayed over her belly instinctively. "It hurts now but one day you'll realize just how lucky you are." With that, she strode for the door. "Get some sleep."

Jenna rolled onto her stomach, face into the pillow and let Cecelia's words wash over her. She didn't want to hear any of it. She didn't want to hear the dark fairytale

235

she'd been living was nothing but that, a story she'd be forced to keep stuffed down inside of her, hiding it from the light of day. A fresh set of tears burned in her eyes, soaking the pillowcase as she pulled the covers up over her head and wished the world away.

Cecelia stalked back down the stairs, finding herself face to face with the several worried men. Brushing past them, she settled down at the table and started filling her plate. The eggs were cold and she had to wipe congealed grease off her bacon, the toast was dry but easily fixable with butter.

"Are you going to tell us what she said?" Luis piped up, leaning against the counter as he watched Cecelia eat.

Raising her butter knife menacingly, Cece pointed it at each of them. "You leave her the fuck alone, you got me? We all want to get the upper hand on Los Lobos but pushing that girl too hard ain't gonna help anyone. *Entiendes?*"

Diego sat down beside her, tucking into his breakfast without a word. Luis was rolling his eyes but he didn't argue. The rest of the group chatted idly, avoiding the elephant in the room. The only person left standing was Danny, his guilt clawing at him as he stared out into the sunlight. Bringing Jenna into this was his fault. All of what she'd endured was his fault and he could never undo that.

Chapter Twenty-Three

Los Lobos went by many names and were called something different depending on where they settled. In some parts of the world they were known as the Vilks, in others Leloo, Nekran, Ye Lang, Ze'ev, or Nodi. The thing each faction had in common was the fear they struck in the hearts of citizens near and far whenever one of the pack got close to their homes. Their name had become synonymous with violence, destruction, fear, and death.

The men—and women—who took up the moniker and joined the regime were highly trained, intelligent, well educated people. That was perhaps why they were so dangerous. These people were not thugs motivated by feeding their families and protecting their loved ones. Los Lobos were a brigade of wealthy crooks looking to get richer off the suffering of others.

Julia Amos dragged a crisp white sheet against her body as she moved to stare out the window. It was strange that she'd gone from a wild child, raging against authority and the law which had done her father no favors, to being a certified, ranked member of the FBI.

Jules had spent months helping Steve clean up the mess Sofía Salma and the Black Jacks left behind. Rounding up the last of the perpetrators and overseeing the destruction of the compound took months but for Julia, it felt like a blink. She completed her task and was suddenly adrift in the breeze. Steve Ellis—her full-time overseer and sometime bedfellow—suggested she apply for the program and wrote her a glowing recommendation to go with it.

Julia never thought she'd pass the background check, let alone get through to the interviews but she managed it, somehow. It didn't seem to matter that her father had been executed on death row when she was two years old or that her half-sister had deep ties to Marco Caraway, the President of the Devils of California. Julia herself was clean...except for shoplifting a candy bar from a drugstore when she was five. The FBI was nothing if not thorough.

Six months at Quantico prepared Julia as much as it could for this moment. She was not their first choice; she wasn't their second, either, as a matter of fact. With both the other agents out of commission, the opportunity arose and Julia grabbed it with both hands. Having contacts with the local MCs had proved to be an asset to this case. Falling into bed with Sven Villeneuve had its perks as well...

Glancing over her shoulder, she stared at the chiseled man asleep beneath the covers. He'd run a full check on her, as promised, and turned up exactly what she'd expected him to. When he learned about her father and her family, he dropped his guard completely. There was simply no way the daughter of a convicted serial killer would be in law enforcement...

Sven was prettier than any sculpture she'd ever seen. She could trace the lines of his muscles with her fingers. He had close-cropped hair that was so blonde it almost looked white and the rest of him was completely and utterly smooth. Whatever he saw in Julia, she'd never know. He seemed to revel in her imperfections the way she marveled at his lack of them. He spent hours tracing every curve, as if mapping her topography in his memory. She'd been prepared to kneel before him and please him, anything to get him to trust her. Instead, Sven seemed perfectly content to lavish his attention over her body until she was languid.

In fact, that's all he ever seemed to want. He hadn't penetrated her once, and seemed unnerved at the idea. The only thing Julia knew without a doubt was that Sven was damaged in ways she couldn't begin to comprehend. There was a reason they said he would be the easiest target, and in some ways that was true…in others, she was left with so many more unanswered questions.

A piercing alarm suddenly rang out through the room and Julia startled, narrowly avoiding reaching for the gun she had stashed in her purse. In an instant, Sven was up and out of bed. He grabbed a fresh set of clothes before he turned to face her. "I've been summoned by the Chancellor."

"Should I come with you?" Julia pressed, following him into the bathroom. He turned on the water but not to warm. Instead, he cranked on the icy spray before he stepped under it, his body tensing like a wire getting ready to snap. "I can tell them all the information—"

"No," Sven cut her off swiftly. There was no malice in his eyes or his posture as he finished his shower and stepped out, accepting the towel Julia held out to him. "You are not part of the pack. You will not be welcomed. I fear you would be in danger if I brought you along. Another time, perhaps."

Julia had hoped he'd simply take her to where Los Lobos conducted business, but that would've been far too easy, she supposed. She climbed back onto the bed like a good little one night stand and watched him towel off. He brushed his teeth viciously, stealing glances at her out of the corner of his eye now and again. "Should I leave?" She asked softly.

"No!" Sven replied with more force this time. "I will be gone only a short while. You are welcome to anything in the fridge. I will expect you primed and waiting for me when I return..." This time there was something predatory in the way he advanced on her, his lips meeting hers in a brutal kiss. "You are quite unlike any woman I have met. I can trust you, a rare quality in anyone. I won't lose you, Julia."

Well, that was a little ironic...but Julia just smiled and giggled and hugged him tightly like she was expected to. "Hurry back, okay? I'm not sure I can wait for you to finish me off," she teased and watched him tense.

"You best be a good girl, or I will be forced to punish you when I return," Sven's voice came out as a growl. He wrapped his arm around her waist, kissing her hard before he turned and stormed away.

It was a goodbye kiss unlike any Julia had ever experienced. It truly felt as if he was going to walk out of her life for good and never return and, oddly, there was a niggling spot of hurt somewhere in the back of her mind. The man was strange, but he had skills…

It was just the sex, Julia told herself. She'd been celibate for quite a while before the Black Jacks took her, part of a pact she'd made after a string of one night stands and a pregnancy scare in her twenties. When she got out of Reno, she had been in need of a friend and Steve Ellis was there for her emotionally, at first, and then physically.

Julia knew the score…but with Steve it felt different. There were little signs: a note left on her pillow telling her he'd gone to grab coffee or serving her breakfast in bed. It wasn't always sex with them, either. Sometimes they'd sit in his den with a frightening amount of Chinese food and enjoy a movie. It started to feel more like a relationship than just a fling, which was probably why Julia was looking for any little spark of something in this stupid assignment with Sven. Steve was still hung up on his ex-wife and he always would be. Maybe it was better to get over him with a handsome stranger who didn't love her and never would.

Waiting until Sven was out of the apartment, Julia grabbed her phone and turned it on. The tracking device she'd planted on Sven was working like a charm. She got dressed and set a leisurely pace as she followed him along the main drag of the street and then down the back roads. When he pulled off down a dirt lane, she kept going and parked her car out of view before she followed on foot.

Even though she'd been working out, Julia found herself exhausted and out of breath when she finally tracked the car to a cabin in the middle of nowhere. There were six cars and a motorcycle taking up the entire length of the driveway. Inside the house she could see people milling around, sipping tea or coffee, and chatting. With the amount of people and vehicles around, she easily sidled up to the house without being noticed. The leader of the group, Lazarus, was the tallest among them and looked haggard—as if he hadn't slept in days. There was something about the way he walked that made her stomach churn. Other voices were low murmurs but his voice boomed above the rest.

"Los Santos have agreed to leave the territory and so, I have released the hostage." More murmurs erupted, clearly questioning the decision. "There is honor among thieves, there should be some amongst warlords as well." There was a sharp, protective edge to his voice when he started talking about the woman. "Jenna Dayton is not our enemy. She was a pawn in a larger plan. She served her purpose and was released per the terms of the bargain I made with Cecelia Santos. They have been nothing but cooperative."

"But Lazarus, she's a liability. She has seen this place! She could bring them here and ambush us!" A razor-sharp female voice spoke up.

Sven readily agreed. "I, too, am concerned. I have not heard from Petrik in days and I believe some horrible fate has befallen him!" he cried. "What of that? Los Santos must have taken as retaliation!"

"Petrik is the least of our worries. I don't need to remind you the last time your brother went missing. Sven..." There was something in Lazarus's voice that was panicky, although he cleared it and was solid as a rock in his next breath. "In two days time, Los Santos will have met their deadline and we can secure the borders. I am hoping by this time next week we can show our suppliers this is *our* town and begin the process of establishing contacts. Once that is done, I anticipate our reach will extend quite far." He paused. "Are there any questions about your assignments?"

Julia could tell the meeting was starting to come to a close and she crawled back toward the trees, her heart pounding from adrenaline. She intended to be back in the apartment, just the way Sven wanted her, before he got suspicious. There was a bit of traffic into the city, but she made it in time to make the bed with pristine hospital corners—just the way the Black Jacks had taught her. Stripping down to her birthday suit, she arranged herself on the comforter, hands between her legs as he stepped through the front door.

Sven looked as if he'd been beaten up, his eyes weary and his posture slumped. He seemed to perk up a little bit at the sight of her and plunked down on the bed, pulling off his shoes. Leaning over, he stared down at the white carpet. "I need your help..."

"With what?" Julia froze, her eyebrows rose in shock.

"I believe Lazarus is hiding something and I wish for you to help me find it out." Sven turned and crawled toward her slowly, lowering himself to kiss her fleshy thigh. "Can you do that for me, dearest?" His lips grazed higher until he was poised at her center, his grey eyes flashing with desire. "I will more than make it worth your while…"

As Sven's tongue plunged into the center of her, Julia fell back, spasming as she cried her 'yes' to the heavens. She would help him and, in turn, she would stop Los Lobos from spreading their terror across the nation. After everything her father had done, it was time to bring some good back to the Amos name…but maybe not tonight.

Chapter Twenty-Four

Lazarus had lived in dozens of places all around the world, the majority of them much nicer than the little shack removed from civilization. Yet somehow the cabin was the first place that had ever felt like home. Or at least, it had until Jenna left...

Once, a few years ago, Laz had seen a doormat that said: '*Home is Where the Heart is*'. He hadn't thought much about it, since he was at that residence to murder the occupant and claim his share of drug money the thief had retained. It stuck out in his mind now that he had a chance to think about it. Lazarus found himself expecting the shuffling of slippered feet on hardwood floors, the whistle of the teakettle, and the soft noise Jenna made in the back of her throat when she slept soundly. Now that she was gone, he missed her as acutely as if one of his limbs had been severed off.

Lucian had made several comments about Lazarus being distracted but he brushed them off. Moving out of that cozy love nest and trading it for a room filled with sleek black wood and chrome finishes gave him some reprieve. Dinner was delivered from a local restaurant but Lazarus couldn't stop thinking about how much better Jenna's food had been. After several hundred pushups and a scalding hot shower, he was only slightly more focused on the situation at hand. The deadline they'd given Los Santos to get out of town expired tomorrow...and although they'd made a good show of packing their things and finding new places to exist, Lazarus knew better than to trust anyone but himself.

The clock had just struck three when he gave up pretending to sleep and slipped out of bed. As usual, Lazarus slept in the nude but there was a pair of blue silk pajama pants at the bedside. He pulled on a t-shirt that hugged his lean body, palming his keys to his brand new sports car. Unlike the rugged Jeep with a rumbling engine that made him feel powerful, the sleek black Jaguar was deadly silent.

Easing his way through the light traffic, Lazarus wound through back alleys and neighborhoods until he got to the house. Los Santos were keeping close company and he hardly blamed them for that. He could see two keeping watch. Lazarus killed the lights, idling just a few houses down and focused. Despite the late hour, Cecelia's place was lit up and people were milling around. He was a long ways off but he was certain he could see Jenna sitting among them, keeping very close to a shape that could only be a man.

Jaw ticking furiously, Lazarus gripped the steering well. He was livid...not at Jenna—although he wished she'd have waited a little bit longer before she threw herself into the arms of another man. The real fury was at himself for letting her go, for pushing her away, and not listening to what she had to say. Turning state's evidence and living happily ever after in the land of witness protection certainly had its appeal, but Lazarus was a realist at his core. If he talked, there was no way he'd survive the week. Los Lobos were everywhere. There was nowhere he could run or hide. He'd never be safe...and neither would she.

Perhaps one day Jenna would return to him of her own accord, after they'd finished taking over La Verdad. She could reopen her restaurant and they could go on a real date. Or maybe he should cut his losses and leave this place in Sven's hands. It was what was expected of him to be the leader, after all. Then again, didn't he deserve happiness? This life didn't lend itself to settling down and starting a family, putting down roots, but it wasn't impossible to find love in a cruel world…

Right?

Lazarus sighed heavily and shook his head. He'd stayed here too long. Los Santos were not stupid; if he lingered any longer they'd get suspicious and come after him. So, he backed up and went around the cul-de-sac. He caught sight of his Jeep parked in the driveway and his heart leapt. Jenna *was* there, so close and yet so far away. As he watched the home recede in his rear view mirror, he felt as if he'd left his heart right there on the curb with her.

Although it was warm and balmy, a chill crept over Lazarus and he shivered against it. He'd never let anyone close enough to him before to get his heart broken, but he had to assume this was what it felt like. He hated every agonizing second. Somehow, someway, he'd have to find a way to be strong for what was to come. Until Jenna was safe and settled, Laz could never let himself succumb to his own weakness. He could keep his eye on the prize and stay the course.

Even if it killed him.

* * *

Jenna had slept for most of the afternoon, so when everyone else was ready for bed, she was wide awake. She'd spent the evening sitting with Cecelia in the living room, sipping tea, and going through every second of her time with Lazarus. Once she had divulged every dirty detail of their torrid love affair, Jenna felt as if a huge weight had been lifted off her chest. Cecelia hadn't judged or condemned her for any of the choices she'd made while under the spell of a man she shouldn't love.

Unfortunately, Jenna didn't feel as if any of her information was worth anything to Los Santos. She knew the location of his hideout but when Luis had ridden out there, it was empty and abandoned. Jenna didn't believe Lazarus could leave the place for good; not after losing McGruff there and burying him up on that beautiful hill. He may have left the home for now, but he would return...she'd bet her life on it.

Perhaps the only thing Jenna could offer was the confirmation that Petrik Villeneuve was dead. Cecelia took the news surprisingly well, only a slight lift in her eyebrow as she noted it in the documents she was compiling on Los Lobos. So far, she had a few pages of scribbled notes and strategies laid out. The engineer in her was already going through a plan and numerous backup plans. It wasn't going to be easy to defeat Los Lobos but Cecelia Santos was not a quitter...and she was willing to sacrifice everything to protect the people she loved.

At first, Cece kept the boys away from Jenna, but it was inevitable their paths would cross eventually...especially since Danny wouldn't leave her alone. He kept trying to find excuses to be near her and eventually she broke down and went to him. He wrapped his arms around her, his voice tight with emotion as he apologized over and over again. Jenna said nothing, letting the hot tears run down her cheeks as he held her against his chest.

Jenna didn't blame Danny. Los Lobos had been the ones to make contact with her first and they'd been demanding collateral for months now, forcing businesses to give up their hard earned money or see their livelihoods destroyed. It just so happened her restaurant was one of Los Lobos' favorites; she and Lazarus would've come face to face eventually and who knew how everything would've panned out. The 'what ifs' would only lead to more heartbreak.

What surprised Jenna the most, however, was how little had changed. After spending all that time with Lazarus, she expected the world would be turned inside out and upside down when she returned to it. It wasn't. The ground was still solid beneath her feet, birds still flew and chirped overhead, and there was still always an accident on the 405—no matter what time of day it was. As Jenna paced around the house, listening to the conversation and the laughter and the murmuring voices on the television, she felt removed from it all.

Ramón had been missing for more than twenty-four hours and Cecelia was worried. She sent Horatio out to look for him with little success. There was no evidence that anyone had been at Black Ink, he hadn't gone to her condo, and his car hadn't been spotted at any of the local bars or strip clubs. He wasn't answering his phone for Cece or his father, and eventually it just started going to voicemail. Cece started calling emergency rooms to find out if Ramón had perhaps had some kind of accident but nobody seemed to know where he was. It was as if he'd dropped off the face of the earth.

Jenna had been shocked to learn Cecelia and Danny were *involved* with one another. It wasn't exactly a secret now since Ramón found out. Suddenly it made sense as to why Danny had come to La Verdad and screwed her with such ferocity. He was trying to forget the woman he really loved...Jenna was starting to understand the appeal in that. She didn't want to feel sad and lonely anymore, she wanted to wake up in a stranger's arms, exhausted and sore.

Of course Jenna knew she wasn't supposed to drink on her medication, but right now she just needed a little something to take the edge off. She had a glass of wine, picked at one of the burgers Diego had grilled for dinner, and avoided eye contact. Cecelia coaxed her to eat a few bites but mostly spent her time bossing around the rest of the boys and prepping to move out of La Verdad tomorrow. It was going to be emotional for all of them, and it showed on their faces. After most of the crew turned in for the night, Jenna was still in the kitchen staring into an ice cold cup. She heard a whisper of footsteps behind her and turned, finding Danny standing behind her. "I told you, I'm fine," she murmured.

"Yeah, I heard you. I just don't believe you," Danny replied and plopped down next to her. He wrapped his arm around her shoulders and pulled her against him. "Look, I know you're pissed at me but I need you to know how sorry I am."

"Danny!" Jenna snarled. "I heard you the first hundred times you said it!"

"But you haven't told me you forgive me!" Danny argued.

Silently, Jenna stared down at the table, her fingers laced around the cup. "What's there to forgive? You weren't the one who kidnapped me. You weren't the one who made me open my heart to a monster and you weren't the one to crush me either. I used to think I was one of the smart ones, but you know what? I'm not. "

Danny shook his head. "Don't say that! I'm the stupid one." He exhaled sharply. "The heart wants what the heart wants, Jenna. And if yours is anything like mine, it ain't very reasonable." Resting his chin on the top of her head, he exhaled sharply. "I've been in love with Cecelia since the moment I laid eyes on her. Blue hair, bad attitude, and balls the size of California...she's all kinds of scarred, inside and out, and I fell head over heels for her. I don't care about any of her shit. I want her and my damn heart won't take no for an answer."

A fresh set of tears burned in Jenna's eyes. "Lazarus is the enemy and I just keep wishing he'd pull up in front of the house, throw the door open, and drag me out of here so we can start a life together." She buried her face in her hands. "I told him I'd go with him. I told him to abandon Los Lobos and we'd start over somewhere and he wouldn't...he chose them over me."

"Well, then *he's* the fucking idiot." Danny squeezed her tighter as she cried. "It's going to be okay, Jenna. We're all here for you. Nobody's going to hurt you ever again." There was such an overwhelming lump of guilt in Danny's throat as he continued to rub her back. Jenna's cries only grew more plaintive and her body was wracked with sobs until she slumped against him, exhausted.

Brushing a strand of platinum blonde hair away from her cheek, Danny lifted her as if she weighed nothing and carried her into the guest room. Cecelia was standing there, watching him and he shifted guiltily. She must've seen him comforting her and he was worried she might be jealous... instead she threaded her arms around his waist and kissed him deeply. "Let's go to bed," she whispered, and Danny didn't need to be asked twice. It wasn't about sex tonight but about being physically close with her. As they lay there, wrapped around each other, there was a sense of hope lingering between them.

Tomorrow they would leave La Verdad, let Los Lobos get comfortable, and shore up their defenses to strike. It was the calm before the storm. Cecelia and Danny intended to soak up every minute of it.

Chapter Twenty-Five

The sunrise over La Verdad was blood red, crimson rays cutting harshly through a fine mist of fog that had wrapped itself around cars and fixtures. Cecelia was not a particularly good Catholic—at least not anymore—but she found herself crossing herself, whispering softly to *La Virgen*, and praying for strength.

Moving trucks rolled in at eight and the boys filled them with the last of the boxes, exactly as Cecelia instructed. While they did the heavy lifting, she was consumed with finding Ramón. By now, all her calls were going straight to voicemail—either because he had blocked her number or because he'd run out of battery. She wasn't sure which reason was worse. Cecelia was worried that he'd driven himself off the road and was laying in a ditch somewhere. La Verdad wasn't exactly a rural area but the closer to Mexico he drove, the less populated the roads became.

By noon, the rest of Los Santos's belongings had been packed. Cece sent Luis and Diego ahead with the personal effects she didn't feel comfortable hauling in the truck. Horatio was driving the big rig with his bike safely secured in the back. Cecelia put her most prized possessions in a rucksack she'd carry with her during the trip. There had been a vote on whether to just stash everything in storage somewhere local but she needed everything to look authentic and this was the best way to do it.

"Still nothing?" Danny sidled up beside Cece, mopping his brow with a handkerchief. When she shook her head, he

253

scoffed. "Asshole! What the hell is he thinking, disappearing when he knows we've got to get out of La Verdad today?"

Cecelia leaned against Danny, her eyes fluttering closed as she took a deep breath. "Ever since the accident, he's had trouble with this stuff. He goes off half-cocked and I'm afraid he really stepped in it this time. I mean, we got a treaty with the Redhawks and the Nightriders—if he ends up in their territory, he won't be killed on sight but they aren't going to put up with his crap." She chewed her bottom lip. "He's probably off on a bender, balls deep in some slut who's name he don't know, and enjoying himself. He'll get in touch when he's ready...at least I hope so."

Danny smiled grimly. "I hope so too."

Jenna eased down the stairs, careful not to trip on the hem. She was wearing a pair of Cecelia's jeans which were two sizes too big secured with a belt from Danny—since he never wore one anyway—and one of Luis's tank tops. They'd offered to take her home to get clothes but she'd declined. The thought of going back made her feel physically ill. That was the home Lazarus had taken her from and she wasn't ready to go back there yet. It was better this way...

The only thing she'd asked Cecelia to do was to pick up her prescriptions at the pharmacy. Jenna had already called her oncologist to let her know she would be out of town for a while. She didn't have repeat scans for another six months. Hopefully by that time, Los Santos would reclaim La Verdad and everything would go back to normal…

Well, as normal as her life could be now.

Inching toward the edge of the driveway, Jenna's stomach sank when she saw the brigade of shiny sports cars coming down the road. "They're here," she breathed.

Cecelia didn't stop to ask questions. She unholstered the gun at her belt and put herself bodily in front of Jenna, pushing the blonde back behind the Jeep. Hand steady and posture tight, Cece kept her gun level as she watched the smug bastards step out of their vehicles. There were more of them than Cecelia had seen before. Lazarus, of course, led the pack. Sven was to his left, sans his twin brother, of course. Lucian and Harriet brought up the rear, along with a woman who Cecelia almost didn't recognize at first… "*Jules*?"

Danny had met all the girls who had been locked up with Lucy. He didn't know all their names and he couldn't be trusted to accurately pick them out of a lineup but he remembered one had red hair; he was guessing this was probably that one. "What the fuck is this?"

"Yeah, Cece, why don't you tell him what the fuck this is!" Julia snarled, her face and posture tight. "Did you think I was just going to forget all the nights we stayed up and talked? All the promises you made?"

"I'm not sure what kinda dope this guy has been stirring in your coffee but I didn't promise you a damn thing!" Cecelia fired back.

The redhead shrieked like an irritated banshee, stamping her feet. Sven's arm snaked out and wrapped around her waist, which did little to calm her. "You told me you were going to let me patch. You promised me I was part of your family and that you were going to give me a new start in La Verdad."

Cecelia groaned. "I told you a million times, *chica*, you're better than this. You coulda gone and talked to Lucy, gotten yourself in with the Devils and the work they're doing in Errol. Down here, we ain't got nothin' for you. We can't even keep the fuckin' wolves at bay."

"Yeah I can see that," Julia laughed, but it was not a happy sound. "Well, I'm getting my piece of the pie—with or without you." She leaned into Sven, finally looking comfortable. "Maybe *you* can go join up the Devils because you aren't going to be welcome here ever again."

While Cecelia and Julia argued, Jenna stared at the monster wearing the face of a man she loved. Lazarus had clearly not slept last night and she could certainly relate. His soft blonde hair fell over his forehead and she wondered if it had gotten longer since she'd seen him last. It was a ridiculous notion, of course. He'd let her go twenty-four hours ago...but it felt like years. Lazarus had changed. He was not warm and soft and expressive; his demeanor was cold and rigid and his face was like slate.

Danny clenched his jaw, agitated at the sight of Lazarus staring at Jenna and Cecelia's argument with Julia getting more intense. "That's enough!" he snapped. "I'm not sure why the fuck any of you are here, since we're doing exactly as you asked. If you're going to kill us, it's going to be a little disappointing since most of our club has already left."

Lazarus turned suddenly. "If it was my intent to kill you, it would have happened a long time ago." He took a step forward. "I came to offer some words of advice. You have been spared certain death and destruction. If you look back or think you will outwit us, you are not only guaranteed the aforementioned fate, but it will be slower and more painful than you could ever imagine."

Jenna couldn't believe the staccato threats coming from a man who had kissed her so tenderly before. He had the look of a madman, ready to strike at any second. The sharp bark of laughter that erupted was startling and she realized, after a moment, the noise had come from her. "Go away." Jenna glared at him. "You made your point," she dug her hands into the pockets of her jeans, "and I mean this in the nicest possible way, Lazarus: go *fuck* yourself."

If the sun fell out of the sky at that very moment, it would not have been as shocking as Jenna cursing at Lazarus.

Cecelia stared at the scene unfolding, her arm physically restraining Danny from stepping forward. If the leader of these animals even thought about hurting Jenna, she'd kill them all herself without remorse. It wouldn't be the first blood on her hands. But Lazarus's position suddenly shifted and his expression changed. Inclining his head, he ordered his crew to retreat silently. They started moving back to their cars, except for Lazarus. He stared Jenna down, his lips softly parted and his fingers half extended as if he was going to reach out and touch her.

Much to Jenna's relief, he didn't. Lazarus breathed out, his warm breath fanning her face. They seemed to stand there for hours, suspended. It was Laz who moved first but Jenna had the last word. "And I'm keeping the Jeep."

A smile tugged at his lips. Seeing her now, strong before him made Lazarus feel weaker than he'd ever been in his entire life; weaker than when he'd been a child starving on the streets, when he'd given his life over to a drug lord and took up his mantle when he passed, even weaker than he had been when McGruff died and his entire world crumbled around him. Without Jenna, nothing mattered… he move forward now with no remorse.

Cecelia watched Los Lobos pull away but her shoulders were still tensed. She turned toward the warrior woman who had emerged before them. From personal experience, she could tell Jenna didn't want to talk about anything right now. Instead, Cece pulled her sunglasses out of her saddlebag and threw her leg over her bike. "We ready to go?" Jenna was already in the driver's seat of the Jeep. Danny hurried to kick his bike into gear. He had to just go with the flow. That didn't mean he wasn't muttering about crazy shit going on in his life all the way until they hit the 405.

From there, they had to navigate carefully through traffic. What should've been a three and a half hour trip ended up being closer to seven hours. Jenna had to stop to get gas after an hour on the road and they grabbed a bite to eat. By the time they got to Marco's estate, the rest of the team was already assembled. Rogelio and Gina had rented an apartment in the area. Luis, Martín, and Diego would be staying with a few of the Devils, Horatio had chosen to bunk down at a local motor lodge with a few choice prostitutes, and Danny, Cecelia, and Jenna were guests in the Caraway home.

The minute Cecelia got through the front door, without bothering to remove her helmet, she hollered for Candy. Marco didn't say a word when Cece met her in the hallway, grabbing the woman by the shoulders. "You didn't fuckin' tell me Julia's in bed with Los Lobos!"

Candy stood there, horrorstruck. "What? Last I heard she was still in Reno tracking down the last of the Black Jacks. Then she decided to join the Peace Corps for a while. I thought it would be good for her to go away..." She covered her face with her hands. "She doesn't know what she's doing, Cece. She doesn't understand!"

"She seemed to fuckin' understand when she said this was payback for me not letting her patch with us!" Cecelia hollered. "I'd have let her, you know. You were the one who told me not to let her and I get it! She's weak." She paced the length of the floor, the dust from the road floating to the floor as she did. "At least if she'd been one of mine, I'd have some control over her now."

Marco stepped in, pulling Candy against his chest. "This isn't her fault. It's not any of our faults!" he growled. "Julia is a grown ass woman—a point I have been trying to get across to you since the first day I met you! She's had it tough, I get that. Your mom had issues and it isn't fair she took them out on Julia." He cupped Candy's face, forcing her to look at him. "You couldn't have protected her. And trying to make up for that now does no one any favors, least of all Jules." He exhaled sharply. "We'll proceed with our plan and ensure she doesn't get caught in the crossfire. End of story."

Cecelia wasn't happy with being told what to do but Candy was openly weeping now. Continuing to press this subject would do no one any good. Instead, she nodded and faced Danny again. "I need a shower, some pain killers, and to sleep. I feel like my head is going to explode."

Three rooms had been made up for their use, but Danny didn't intend on sleeping anywhere without Cece. He followed her into the room they'd been locked in the last time and made sure she was safely in the shower before he popped in on Jenna. She had changed into a pair of pajamas and was slumped over on the bed. Danny knew he wasn't the brightest bulb in the tanning bed, but he could tell she was pretending to be asleep. He decided not to press the issue and slipped out of the room, closing the door behind him.

Standing beneath the warm spray, Cecelia let the water untangle the knots in her back and shoulders. The ibuprofen she'd taken was starting to sink in and it was lovely to relax. When Danny slipped in behind her, she found herself smiling and snuggled against him. "This is going to work, right?"

Danny nuzzled her neck, pressing soft kisses to her slick flesh. "Yeah. It is," he said with a confidence he wasn't sure he believed. He must've been convincing enough for Cece, because she let his statement hang and, instead of giving him that look, her lips met his instead. Pulling her against his body, he felt her shudder and realized after a moment she was crying. "Shit, Cece." Danny clung tighter. He'd seen her angry, violent, guarded but never as vulnerable as this. She had been kept at the hands of a madwoman, scarred, hurt in every possible way, and she'd never shed a tear...

Cecelia had worked so hard to stop those things from hurting her. She grew stronger in the wake of each insult. But the loss of her home felt like the loss of her identity. Burying her face in Danny's shoulder, her nails slid down his back. "I don't want to feel this pain anymore. Make me feel something else, *anything* else. Danny, *please*."

Tilting her chin up, Danny kissed her hard and deep, pressing her against the wall. Her sharp intake of breath was more a response to the icy tile against her warm flesh, but it inflamed him nonetheless. He pressed her arms back, lacing his fingers with hers as he pistoned his hips forward, entering her in one swift motion. Cecelia gasped again and this time he knew it was in pleasure. The water rained down upon them, lubricating their bodies as he pounded into her.

The comfort of Danny flooding her insides took away the hurt that clawed in her veins. Pleasure superseded the pain of losing her identity for the moment. Even though he had finished, Cece was hardly done. The next time they made love it was when they were toweling off and he bent her over the sink, sinking into her from behind. By the time they made it into the bedroom, she was sore and exhausted. They fell into bed without another thought, wrapped in each other's arms.

"Thank you," Cece croaked, her eyes red and her heart wide open.

"I love you, Cecelia Santos. I will always be here for you, whether you like it or not. And I should be the one thanking you." Kissing the tip of her nose, Danny closed his eyes. "Get some sleep." On any other day she would've chastised him for telling her what to do, but tonight she simply settled in. For the first time in days, Cecelia slept unperturbed.

Chapter Twenty-Six

Three weeks passed in rapid succession. The Devils of California really rolled out the red carpet for the displaced members of Los Santos. Cecelia was more than grateful for all of Marco's hospitality and considering she'd never liked the bastard all that much, it was a bit of a shift in their dynamic. Seeing how the older man interacted with Danny, Candy, and his son gave her new insight into how he was as a person instead of an MC President.

There were many club-wide dinners followed by brainstorming and plotting their revenge against Los Lobos that felt more like social events. Narayan Bosko and the Nightriders were following peripherally, offering their support wherever possible. Sometimes Adela would come to visit, smiling and laughing as she greeted her sisters in arms with adoration. Cecelia was so glad to see the young woman was coming into her own. When Adela was at the Black Jacks compound she never talked, let alone smiled or made eye contact; now she was a high school graduate and had finished her first semester at a women's college. She was going to be a teacher and Cece could think of nothing more perfect for such a sweet girl.

Cecelia had been at one of these events when she got the call. She always knew deep down something wasn't right but she continued searching far and wide for Ramón. He wasn't using his credit cards, checks, or even his cell phone. When an unknown number popped up on her phone, she eyeballed it skeptically. "*Qué pasa*?" she answered brutally.

"Cecelia..."

"Ramón!" she breathed. "Where the fuck are you?"

"Don't pretend like you care," he wheezed. "I ain't going to sign the divorce papers. It'd just make everything harder for you anyway..."

Cecelia tightened her fist. "We made a mistake getting married when we were young and stupid but that doesn't mean I don't love you. You're my family, no matter what." She heard his breathing grow heavier on the other line. "What are you doing? You sound like shit."

Ramón coughed into the receiver. "I made a big fuckin' mistake." It was an effort to even speak. "That real pale one, Sven or something. He met me at the border, said you and the rest of the crew cleared out but told me I could come in under a few conditions. It started out as just a taste and I...I can't stop..."

"Can't stop *what*, Ramón?"

"I'm sorry, Cecelia..."

The line cut dead and chaos erupted. She didn't even care she was inciting a riot in the middle of three MCs. She tried again and again to call the number, she called the police to trace it, but it was no use. It was almost eight hours later that she got a call from the Albuquerque police chief that her husband had been found dead of an alleged overdose. He'd written a fairly rambling suicide note that indicated he wanted to be cremated and his ashes were to be sent to his father for disposal wherever Angelo deemed fit. He wanted no funeral or service of any kind to mark his passing. The only thing he seemed to want was for his wife to know how sorry he was.

Anger burned in Cecelia's chest brighter than any she'd ever known. Lazarus Caine and Los Lobos were responsible for this. Giving a man like Ramón heroin was worse than handing him a loaded gun. They'd tried the same thing with Rogelio and had very nearly succeeded. Her brother was clean and sober now but that story could've ended just as tragically.

Danny knew he wasn't the right person to comfort Cece during this time. He was the man who had filled her heart with love it hadn't felt in a long time but their relationship that had driven Ramón to do something stupid and reckless. Now he was dead.

Cecelia slipped away, finding herself in Marco's backyard with two of his little dogs running around her feet. They stilled and turned when the man himself swept out of the house, hands in his pockets.

"You look like you could use a drink." Marco extended a glass of amber colored liquor. Cecelia shrugged him off, turning away to stare across the lawn. Marco just smiled at her, picking up the squirmy Chihuahua who immediately snuggled against his chest. "Chip likes you," he offered.

Cecelia eyeballed him, her lips curled into a frown. "Look I ain't trying to be rude but I'm not in the mood for small talk." She turned her attention back to the lawn, saying nothing as he plopped down into the seat beside her.

"Me either." Marco leaned back, stroking the small dog's fur. "I like you, Cecelia. You cut through the shit and say what you think. It's a quality I admire in anyone. It's one of the very reasons I encouraged Danny to return to La Verdad and assist in taking down Los Lobos. I knew it wasn't going to be easy but it's a worthy endeavor." He cleared his throat. "In the pursuit of greater good, sacrifices need to be made."

"Ramón isn't a sacrifice! He was my fuckin' husband!" Cecelia snarled at him. "I didn't want this to happen to him."

Marco didn't flinch despite the violence lurking in her hazel eyes. "That's not what I was implying...but you already knew that." He narrowed his gaze. "I won't bore you all the details of how drugs have ruined my family, but I am willing to do anything to make sure it happens to no one else. I know you will work that much harder to make sure Los Lobos do not succeed in their mission. We are going to be the victors and when they tell our story— years after we've died—they will immortalize those who sacrificed their lives for the cause. Ramón Diaz will be remembered as one of those heroes."

Cecelia wasn't sure if she wanted to murder Marco or hug him. What he said was infinitely agitating, and yet somehow comforting at the same time. Standing abruptly, she glanced down at him. "That'll be great, years from now. Today, I'm going to fucking mourn the loss of a person I loved."

"And we're here to support you," Marco replied warmly. "Take as much time as you need."

Cecelia straightened her posture. "I appreciate it. You mind telling me where you've been hiding the good stuff?" she asked, sniffing at the glass he'd offered. On any other day, she might've wanted to get blasted but her stomach was off and she already had a headache brewing. She needed to keep her wits about her, now more than ever.

Marco smiled, setting Chip back down. The little dog stayed right by him, prancing around Cecelia's feet as they headed back into the house. "Linen closet, behind the stack of towels...but if you tell anyone it's there, you'll be sorry."

Smirking, she inclined her head. "Your secret's safe with me." There were still people milling all over the house and it felt nice to blend into the crowd. She chatted quietly with Candy and Adela while she ate far too much. Marco enjoyed cooking but Jenna was a professional chef, and she was enjoying having full use of the kitchen. Cecelia swore she'd put on ten pounds since they had all started living together. She almost couldn't zip up her jeans this morning.

Danny was sitting on the other side of Diego. After his last little run in with Luis, he made sure he didn't send the man any mixed signals. He was doing a good job of staying under the radar and giving Cecelia space, even though he wanted nothing more than to wrap her in his arms and kiss away her pain.

Rogelio was sitting across the living room, his arm wrapped around Gina tightly. Ever since getting out of detox, he'd stopped being such a dick to the woman who had given him a child and started to be the man his family deserved. He shot Danny a comforting smile and inclined his head. "Let's take a walk, *ese*." Leaning in, he pressed a chaste kiss to Gina's lips before he stood up.

It wasn't his idea of a good time, but Danny followed anyway. They headed toward the other side of the house. "Look, man—"

"*Callate*," Rogelio interrupted. "Cecelia is my sister and I ain't exactly been the best brother around." He dragged a hand over his face. "I never had a say in her relationship with Ramón. If I did, she would never have married that jackoff..." he sighed. "Don't get me wrong, I loved Ramón like my own brother but he was never good enough for Cece. She never had a chance to see it before he wrecked himself. You can be a different kind of husband for her, Danielito."

"Look, I'm not rushing Cecelia into anything." Danny raised his hands in mock surrender. "Of course I want to marry her. She's the only woman I've ever loved. But it ain't about a ring and a piece of paper. It's about being there when she needs me, about giving her space when she doesn't, and being her partner."

Rogelio took a sip of his lemonade, turning to glance back toward where Cecelia was sitting. "She plays tough but she ain't. She doesn't give her heart up easy and she will *never* say die...underneath all that, she's just as sweet and warm as any other girl you know." He raised a finger menacingly. "If she thinks you're worthy that's all that matters. You guard her heart, always protect her and if you *ever* hurt her, I will hunt you down and I will murder you in the most horrible way possible. *Entiendes*?"

"If I hurt Cecelia, you'd have to get in line because she'll kill me first," Danny replied with a sly smile. "I'm not afraid of you, Rogelio, but I'm fuckin' *terrified* of her. I love her so much, I'm not even sure what I'd do if I ever screwed up." He licked his lips. "I'm in this for the long haul."

Clasping Danny on the shoulder, Rogelio dragged him into an overly tight hug. "You're a good man, *hermano*. I'm glad Cecelia found you." Everything the former Devil had said gave Rogelio hope that Danny would be the one to make his sister happy. She'd been putting everyone else first for so long and deserved a man who would do the same for her. Plus, he could stop worrying she'd succumb to unhappiness just to make everyone else happy. "It's only right you're wearing Los Santos colors now. You're one of us. Brothers. And don't let anyone tell you otherwise."

The tender moment was over almost as quickly as it came, and both men were grateful for the distraction as Raphael ran over to show off an odd Lego building he'd made. Rogelio oohed and ahhed over the crude structure, listening intently as the boy explained his design. Danny gave them both a warm smile before heading back into the living room. The sun was starting to dip in the sky and Narayan had taken his wife and daughter home; that left the Devils and Los Santos alone again.

Candy and Jenna orbited around each other, picking up discarded plates and cups. They had become fast friends, bonding over their mutual love of good food and crappy *telenovelas*. Cecelia wished she made friends so easily and found herself watching Danny. Maybe it was just the grief talking but she loved him more in this moment than any other before. His willingness to give her space was amazing. She wasn't sure she'd have had the same control if he'd lost someone close to him. But Cece had needed time to process…and now she needed the man she loved.

Pushing herself up off the couch, Cecelia sidled over and plopped down in his lap. Danny grinned and wrapped his arms around her waist. "I missed you," he murmured as he pressed sweet kisses to her neck. "How are you doing?"

"I don't know," Cece replied honestly, "But I'm getting there. Thanks."

Marco tugged Candy against him, urging her to stop cleaning for a moment. "It's been two weeks since we implemented our plan against Los Lobos and things are coming together. With the Nightriders being our eyes and ears, we have insight into their movements. Los Lobos are already starting to get their drugs on the streets but, thankfully, it takes a little bit longer than anticipated to open up that pipeline. According to Sanjay and his crew on the shore, Los Lobos are starting to make upgrades to the marina." He exhaled sharply. "That construction will take at least a month, maybe a month and half depending on the weather. They need to be able to get their ships through and that includes upgrading the security out there too."

Cecelia remained silent as Marco recapped the day's discussion for those who had not been involved. Unlike most club business, which was kept under wraps—especially from people like Jenna and Candy—it felt wrong not to include everyone. Jenna was just as involved as any of their club members, if not more so. Anyone could see she was struggling with this more than anyone else. "All eyes are going to be on the projects and on getting their product on the streets."

"So, when are we doing this?" Diego piped up.

"We gotta be ready to move at any time. Los Lobos are still patrolling but they ain't got the numbers to protect the harbor *and* the border. Once they get far enough along, they are going to need to pull a lot of those gunners to keep their merchandise safe. That transition is going to be our key. Sanjay is giving us updates. He's set up at Jenna's restaurant, which gives him the perfect vantage point."

Jenna tensed and her stomach clenched painfully. La Trattoria had always been her place and with someone else at the helm it felt as if the very soul of the place had been defiled. It was all necessary, of course, but she couldn't bring herself to be happy about it. "So, we wait."

"Yes," Marco replied without emotion. "It shouldn't be long now." He swallowed hard. "There's something else I want to bring to a vote." He glanced over at Danny. "Lucy has been in contact with me recently. She knows you're here and...she's growing suspicious. The Devil's Own are our comrades in arms but more importantly, they're our friends and family."

Danny shifted. "We're not telling them. Lucy is six months pregnant and Archie has his hands full keeping the club in line now that they've shifted their mission. There's dissent in some of the ranks. If they spread themselves too thin, everything will implode. I won't let my sister get hurt!"

Marco narrowed his eyes. "Having something to do other than running the shelter might be a good thing, Danny. Lucy doesn't have to come down and neither does Archie."

"But they *will*! It's everything we've been trying to avoid!"

"I'm not making the decision. I'm putting it to a vote," Marco explained. "We can use all the help we can get. This extends beyond La Verdad, Danny. Los Lobos are all over the country. Hell, they're all over the world!" He frowned deeply. "Even if we take out the head of this organization, a new despot will rise from the ashes."

The bottom fell out of Jenna's world. "You're going to kill Lazarus?"

"What else can we do?" Cecelia glanced over at her.

"You could turn him over to the police, let them handle it!" Jenna cried.

A snort from the other side of the room dragged everyone's attention away from Jenna's outburst. "You really think Los Lobos haven't already bought the police? Why do you think nobody can bring these guys down? They're out in the open doing this and everyone turns a blind eye. We have no other choice. We've got to kill them all..." Rogelio huffed.

Silence hung in the room for a moment before Jenna stood up. "I don't have voting privileges but I'm not going to sit by and watch you vote on killing people."

"This is a special circumstance," Cecelia interrupted, "you get a say."

"Since when?" Horatio sat up straighter.

"Since I fuckin' said so!"

Marco cleared his throat. "Everybody can vote, alright?"

"Even me?" Matthew piped up, his eyes lighting up. He was still the youngest member of the group and, although he wanted to be a Devil more than anything, his father wasn't letting him participate as much as he'd like.

"No," Candy answered coolly. "*We're* not voting." She could tell Matty was annoyed, but it was better to be the bad guy than force Marco to do it. They'd already lost so much time together thanks to her insecurity, she wasn't going to let any more distance come between them.

Cecelia slid off Danny's lap, moving to stand in the middle of the room. "All those in favor of killing Lazarus, raise your hand."

Unsurprisingly, Rogelio, Martín, Horatio, and Luis's hands went up right away. Danny perseverated for a moment before he raised his, and Marco followed suit. Diego shook his head, "I abstain. I can't choose whether somebody lives or dies." Cecelia respected him for that; he'd always been the peacekeeper in the group. Marco's team was clearly in favor of making this a bloody battle...but Cecelia couldn't tear her eyes away from Jenna. The woman was curled almost in a ball, her arms wrapped around herself and her eyes wet with tears. Several moments passed and Cece shook her head.

"It doesn't pass. It wasn't unanimous." Cecelia decreed. "Los Lobos live...but we still gotta decide what to do with them. And we're leaving the Devil's Own out of this. Danny's right. The risk outweighs the benefit." Danny breathed a sigh of relief. Tears of relief splashed down Jenna's cheeks and she stood abruptly, hurrying to her room to hide her emotion from everyone. Cece didn't blame her, and continued on as if nothing happened. "We'll come to the table tomorrow night with more ideas."

With the meeting adjourned, the group scattered to the far corners. Candy resumed cleaning up; Marco and Matthew pitched in to help. Rogelio and Gina packed up Raphael and headed back to their apartment for the evening. Luis, Diego, and Horatio left together, heading out to grab some drinks. Cecelia was more exhausted than she could ever remember being and fell quickly asleep while Danny washed the day off him. He stopped in on Jenna, offering her a hug before he headed back to the room and curled up with Cece.

For the moment, all was calm...but there was no telling what tomorrow would bring. All they could do was take things one day at a time.

Chapter Twenty-Seven

Julia was exhausted.

Sven had some deep-seated intimacy issues and while he rarely allowed her to please him, he was forever grabbing at her. Jules never thought she'd get sick of a man going down on her but she was chafed in places she never even knew it was possible and walked with half a limp. It was a relief when he got called away for a meeting. She planted a bug on his phone and she listened in on Los Lobos while sipping a glass of chardonnay and taking a nice, long Epsom salt bath.

Just like a pack of wolves, Los Lobos had one alpha and the rest of the members fell into line—at least, that's how it should've been. Jules was quickly learning not everyone was happy with Lazarus's decisions. Lucian wanted to focus on getting the pipeline opened at the expense of guarding the border. In his eyes, if Los Santos returned, they would be quickly identified, rounded up, and destroyed. Lazarus was not so easily persuaded. He continued to split his assets wisely but as the construction lagged on the harbor, he was having a hard time convincing even himself that staffing the borders so heavily was in their best interest.

It had only been a few days since Ramón Diaz's death and Lazarus knew retaliation was coming. He was not so naive as to believe Cecelia Santos would take the death of her husband lightly, even though they had been estranged. Then again, Lazarus's control was slipping little by little. The man was still a formidable foe, but it seemed his heart wasn't in it. Rumors swirled that he had lost his edge and become weak, but there were still very few in the world who were willing to check and see for sure. So, Los Lobos soldiered on, working on their mutual goal of flooding the streets of La Verdad—and eventually, the rest of the country—with the most potent drugs an addict could buy.

Sven returned to the apartment shortly before nine with takeout from La Trattoria. The restaurant had recently reopened under new management and Lazarus refused to step foot inside. Sven found that to be infuriating since he enjoyed Italian food and the restaurant had several nooks and crannies that were perfect for conducting private business. Instead, Los Lobos were meeting in an abandoned warehouse near the docks. It was dank, smelled like fish, and most certainly did not serve cannoli cake. So, Sven ordered takeout and picked it up as an act of protest.

Setting the food on the table, he dragged off his suit jacket and hung it on the back of his chair. Julia was still lounging in the bath. Sven turned on the shower to warm up while he peeled off the rest of his clothes. "I grow tired of meeting in the dark. We own this town, we could go to the courthouse and hold senate there if we wanted. Who would stop us?"

Julia finished her wine, standing so the water sluiced down her naked body. She moved toward him, her pruned fingers sliding over his biceps. "I'm sure the Chancellor has his reasons."

"Lazarus has changed," Sven snarked, his pouty lips curving down in a sneer. "At first I forgave his foolishness. He is only a man, not above the temptations of flesh." Bending his head, Sven pressed kisses to the curve of her neck, his thick fingers palming the globe of her breast and then sliding lower to drape across the curve of her hip. "Yet he has allowed it to make him weak. Even when he speaks of greatness and expanding our reach, there is something holding him back." Sven's expression turned cruel. "Not something...*someone.*"

"Cecelia?"

"That brash whore holds no power over the Chancellor," Sven laughed, but the bitter edge froze the blood in Julia's veins. "Jenna Dayton. The hostage he took from Los Santos, whom he lived with and, I believe, fell in love with in the process. There's certainly enough evidence to corroborate the theory." He pressed one last kiss to Julia's lips before he slipped into the shower. "I need to wash the smell of the sea off me. Would you care to assist?"

Julia smirked. "I'm tempted, but I'm turning into a prune." If she joined him, she was certain he'd end up with his face between her legs and that would defeat the purpose of the Epsom bath. "I'll get dinner on the table and pour you a drink. Take your time." Heading into the main living area, she slid a robe around her shoulders and belted it at the waist. She grabbed two ivory white plates and settled them on the black table that was nestled up against the window. She put out napkins and silverware, and was poised to pour them both some wine when her phone buzzed. It wouldn't have been unusual except the Morse code spelled out SOS.

Peering around the corner, the shower was still going and Julia answered the blocked number. "Hello?"

"Jules, what the *hell* are you doing?" Steve's livid voice seared through the phone. "I've been calling and texting you for weeks. I thought you were dead!" he snarled at her. "Then I got a strange call from Cecelia Santos. Do you know how many favors I had to call in to find out what's going on? Why didn't you tell me?" There was a long pause and Steve let out an angry growl. "You have nothing to say for yourself?"

"Not really." Julia wanted to pat herself on the back for how level she kept her voice. "You told me I should go after what I wanted, as long as it wasn't you. So I did." She sat down on the bed, her arm sliding around her waist. "I don't even know why you care."

"*You don't know why I care?*" Steve yelled back at her. "Jules—"

"*Don't!*" She cut him off. "I'm a big girl. I can take care of myself and, in case you were worried, I've got a man now who isn't afraid to show me how he feels. And he sure as hell isn't hung up on his ex-wife!" She realized she was practically yelling...and even from the bathroom, Sven could probably hear her. She lowered her voice again. "I'm fine without you. I don't need you to protect me anymore..."

Steve groaned. "I'm just worried about you, J. You just disappeared off the face of the earth and—"

Julia tightened her first, nails digging into her palm. "And how long did it take you to notice, Steven?" She was deadly quiet now, her entire body tense and shaking. "Days? Weeks?"

"That's not fair, I am in the midst of preparing everything for the trial! Sofía Salma should never going to be a threat to anyone ever again. I need to make sure I have everything in order; it's got to be a slam dunk." He sighed heavily.

"*How long*, Steve?"

"A month."

Stabbing the red 'end call' button on her phone, Julia felt as if her heart was falling in on itself, like a star collapsing and being absorbed into the universe. She barely noticed when the bed dipped beside her and Sven crawled over, wrapping his arms around her. "Are you all right?"

Resting her head against Sven's shoulder, Julia closed her eyes and absorbed strength from him. She didn't love Sven. Hell, she didn't even like him very much...but right now he was good enough. "I'm sorry..." she choked out. "My ex found out my new number and I—"

"Say no more," Sven soothed, kissing her sweetly. "Do you wish for me to kill him?"

Julia smirked. "Tempting...but I think I'd rather be the one." Cuddling Sven closer, she exhaled. "Let's just have a nice dinner and some wine, and forget this ever happened." To his credit, the man didn't say another word on the subject for rest of the night. Julia had feared Sven might be turned off but uncovering this little sliver of truth in her beneath the façade made him feel more comfortable in their own relationship.

They ate pasta, sipped wine, and then settled into bed to watch a movie. Julia was half-asleep before the opening credits finished and when she snuggled closer to Sven, she found him staring down at her so lovingly. It...did something to her. She didn't expect to feel anything for this man who was so broken. This time when they kissed, he poured all of his soul into it. That night, for the first time, he buried himself inside her. Julia couldn't help but think they'd forged a bond she'd be hard pressed to break...

After they'd made love, Sven cradled her in his arms, his breathing soft but even. His fingers tangled in her auburn locks, twisted in the silky strands. "I wish you could have met my brother," he whispered into the darkness of the room. "Petrik would've hated you.

Julia tensed. "What? Why?"

"Because you are everything he would have wanted and I *have* you." Sven laughed. "My brother was always a jealous man, coveting anything he could not have. He was full of rage, and hate, and violence. The only thing in this world he ever loved was me..." His eyes filled with tears that spilled down his cheeks. "Petrik was not afraid to take what he wanted and he let his baser urges rule him. I believe Lazarus killed him in a fit of rage." Sven shifted, his voice growing more urgent. "Petrik was on his way to meet with Lazarus and suddenly, I felt empty inside. I know my brother is not out there somewhere, shirking his duties. I know he's gone...I could be tried for treason and ripped apart for such a statement but I will not go another day without saying the truth out loud."

This was more than Julia could ever have hoped for. Any group was only ever as strong as its weakest link, and Los Lobos were tearing apart at the seams. Between Lazarus's brooding, Sven's doubts, and Lucian's anger, there were three threads she could tug to unravel all of this.

Julia needed to gather enough proof to build a case and take the entire organization down. She knew illegally tapped phone conversations, second hand knowledge of clandestine meetings in warehouses, and hunches galore were not nearly enough. Sofía Salma's case was airtight with dozens of eyewitness testimonies and an entire fortress of legally seized evidence, but there was still a chance the legal system could fail them. It was why Steve was so invested, not wanting to miss a single detail...

Jules needed to do better if she wanted this to work.

"Petrik was your brother," she whispered dangerously, "You can't just let it rest. We need to prove what Lazarus did!" She caught the flare of something in his eye and her heartbeat kicked up. "I'll be the bait. He will be

282

suspicious of me and expend his resources trying to figure out what *I'm* up to while you actually do the detective work." She sat up on her knees. "We can do this, Sven."

Crushing her in his embrace again, he turned and pinned Julia to the bed once more. "Where did you come from?" Sven whispered. "My wildest dreams?"

This time when they joined, it was to seal the deal they'd made. For Sven it meant avenging his brother and learning the truth. For Julia, it was about her mission and the vow she'd made to protect the people she loved. She was going to show everyone—especially Steve—she was good enough. Julia wasn't going to waste the opportunity.

Chapter Twenty-Eight

Narayan Bosko had been a godsend. The moment Lazarus started to pull resources away from the border, the Nightriders let Cecelia know and Narayan increased the manpower he'd promised them by nearly double. Cece was certain she had Adela to thank for that, and would absolutely make sure she understood the depth of her gratitude at a later date. For now, la Presidente de Los Santos had much more pressing matters at hand.

For one thing, Cecelia was having a hard time keeping her cousins from imploding. They were not used to living in such close quarters and fights were breaking out over the stupidest things. Pistols had been drawn this morning over who got the last Pop Tart...Cece knew it was time. They'd end up killing each other if they waited any longer.

Despite everything else around them going to hell in a hand basket, Cecelia found comfort in Danny. She was seeing a whole different side of him. This version of Daniel Harding was calm, collected, and worked to foster peace among their ranks. He gave her space exactly when she needed it and knew instinctively when he should be close by. He helped Marco out around the house, was extra nice to Jenna—who was still struggling with everything that had happened these last few months—and still managed to find time to mentor Matthew. The shirtless menace she'd met in Reno was growing and changing right before her eyes...and she liked the man he had become.

Danny had no idea he'd made any changes at all. He lived every day to its fullest potential. His goal was to keep some of the heat off Cece as she worked with the Nightriders to secure their future. Between Martín, Horatio, Luis, and Diego, he had his hands more than full—throw in Rogelio and it was a whole new brand of chaos. Gina had been a huge help in keeping things calm, but she only held power over Rog...that proved to be a huge asset unto itself. The only thing Danny cared about was keeping Cecelia happy and so far, so good.

Then there was Jenna, who was overwhelmed by the people all around her. Since her mother passed away, she had been mostly alone in the world. Of course there were her employees or passing acquaintances, she had a few close pals from college...but nothing like *this*. Every day Jenna was thrown into the middle of five dueling cousins, a cheeky kindergartener, two baby mamas, all of Marco's dogs, and Cecelia Santos. It was a lot to take.

Danny had been Jenna's rock. He was the only one she really knew and he'd been incredibly supportive. It wasn't romantic between them; if she was being honest, it never had never been. Even when they were screwing each other, it was simply to fulfill a physical need. She didn't love him the way a woman should love a man...she loved him like an annoying older brother.

A part of Jenna always knew this was going to be temporary but when Cecelia announced they were going to siege the gates of La Verdad, it ached in the pit of her stomach. She wasn't going to be taking up a weapon, of course. In fact, it had been suggested not so subtly that she should remain behind until the danger was gone but Jenna wasn't going to let Los Santos return to La Verdad without her. The time away had given her a chance to rethink her priorities. She'd let seven of the Nightriders reopen La Trattoria and, although she watched from afar, she itched to get back into the kitchen. Home was where the heart was and, after some soul searching, Jenna realized home had always been her restaurant.

"Saddle up and be ready to ride out at dawn tomorrow," Cecelia announced, storming into the living room where the group was amassed. "We're finally takin' back our home."

"Why we gotta wait? We can get there tonight and it'll be safer..." Diego furrowed his brow.

"They're gonna expect us under the cover of darkness," Rogelio interrupted. "Cecelia's right. We walk up in the middle of the day, nobody is going to be any wiser. The Nightriders are already in place and that's when we hit the marina. Best chance we got to cripple these bastards is by taking out the pipeline they're building. It's almost complete, so taking it down at this stage will be devastating. But they've got money to rebuild, which is why we gotta take it a step further."

Cece glanced over at Jenna, briefly making eye contact. "We ain't killin' nobody. Not this time. Protect yourself if you gotta but we gotta keep this legit. I called an old friend of ours who's got some FBI contacts. They ain't sanctioning this but he's got our backs. We're gonna need a pretty fuckin' good lawyer when all is said and done."

And if what Steve said was true, Julia was going to supply the rest of the information to take Los Lobos out of California for good. They'd still have other outposts, but that was the government's problem...not Los Santos. "We all in agreement here?"

A chorus of affirmations in English and Spanish echoed around the room.

It was a three and half hour ride and if they were on the road by five, it would be smack dab in the middle of the morning rush. Nobody was going to stop them riding right up to the harbor, setting the implements Cecelia had acquired, and blowing that shit sky high. The months she'd spent in Georgia learning about remote detonation and fissionable materials had really paid off and, despite her dislike for the assignment, Cece was grateful for everything she learned. Once this was over, she was going to find some steady engineering work in the area, and really make a name for herself. They'd reopen Black Ink, and remind La Verdad that Los Santos were their family and their friends. It wasn't going to be drugs and violence and stupidity anymore. They were going straight, just like the Devil's Own had.

Cecelia wrapped her arms around her waist, feeling slightly off kilter for a moment. She inhaled deeply, giving her final decrees: "Pack up your shit, get some sleep, and say your prayers. We're gonna need them." With that, the group was dismissed.

Rogelio went off to spend the evening with Gina, tasking Horatio with watching Raphael. Martín, Diego, and Luis

287

decided to scatter to the far corners of the house to avoid each other; there had been some grumbled apologies over the breakfast pastry incident but it was better if they stayed out of each other's hair for now. Marco and Candy had dinner plans and were clearly looking forward to a little bit of alone time. Danny took the opportunity to grasp Cece by the elbow and lead her upstairs.

"Hey," he murmured, pressing a soft kiss to the contour of her neck. "How're you holding up?"

Cecelia rested against him, her hands curled around his biceps. "You want honesty?" She looked into his warm blue eyes and sighed. "I'm worried about how calm I feel. I should be nervous to go up against these fuckers but I'm just tired. We've been up and down these plans and if we fail now, there's nothing more we could've done." She licked her lips. "With Narayan and Marco working with us, we've got good backup. Without everything you've done, I don't think we'd have that so...thank you." She chewed her bottom lip. "After all this is done, I'm handing my Presidente patch back to Rogelio and I was going to recommend you for *Segundo*."

Danny furrowed his eyebrows, cupping her cheek to hold her gaze. "What are you talking about?"

"I been thinking lately about everything and I just...want more." Cecelia cleared her throat. "I'm an engineer, Danielito. I never wanted to be just a fuckin' biker bitch my whole life. That's why I went to college and studied hard and worked to make something of myself." A sad smile tipped up the corners of her lips. "I got a little lost along the way but it ain't too late for me."

"Whatever makes you happy, you need to do it," Danny offered. "But there's something you should know: No matter where you go, no matter how far you travel, I'm coming with you." He bent, capturing her lips sweetly. "I love you, Cecelia Santos. I will follow you to the ends of the Earth and back. You're not going to get rid of me again. You hear me?"

Chortling softly, Cecelia deepened the kiss before she pushed him onto the bed. "That's another thing. I ain't going to push you away anymore." Throwing her leg over him, she slid her hand down his chest. "I love you Danny. I've loved you since the fuckin' day I met you, I was just too afraid to admit it. I didn't think I deserved what you were giving me." Sighing heavily, she snuggled into his arms, "I still ain't sure I do. But I'm going to spend the rest of my life trying to be good enough for you."

Danny crushed her in his embrace. "I don't think I'm as great as you think I am." He rubbed her back in slow circles. "You make me want to be, though. Before I met you I was listless, restless, bored with everything and I didn't give a shit about anything or anyone. You made me want to do more." Letting out a low whistle, he smirked, "Man, we're fucking sappy as shit."

"No!" Cecelia mocked. "Anything but that!" Tugging at the button at his jeans, she smirked. "Quick! Fuck me before somebody thinks we're one of those old boring couples." Danny had her divested of her clothes and pressed into the soft mattress before she even knew what hit her. She laughed, dragging her nails down his back as he slammed into her molten center. As they made love, it felt more like a goodbye to the past they were closing the door on and, during the second round, it was the opening act to a brighter future...

If they both survived the siege.

* * *

"We're weeks behind schedule on this project!" Lucian scoffed, pacing the length of the room. "We need all the manpower we can get work on getting a client base established. These townies are not so easily fooled. They've been led by Los Santos for a long time and they aren't going to lay down easily." The warehouse they were holed up in was oddly cold and it was startlingly obvious none of them wanted to be here.

Lazarus was perched on the edge of a crate, scraping his hand over the three-day stubble on his chin. He wanted to say his heart was in this; it was everything he'd ever wanted since taking over this empire but, truly, he just kept thinking this wasn't the right place. La Verdad was the home to quiet, God-fearing folks who held down jobs and lived quiet, fulfilling lives. They were fisherman, restaurateurs, lawyers, policemen, and artists. Los Santos had fostered a sense of peace in this place and it had flourished under their rule. Sure, they had access to a slice of the seaport that wouldn't tip off the DEA...but Los Lobos weren't going to make friends here. They were going to wreck a lovely place. Soon the junkies would crawl out of the cities and poison this once-thriving place.

It was sickening, really.

Sven's arm wrapped around Julia's waist and she dug her hand into his pocket. Her presence at the last few meetings had been unwelcome...but nobody but Lazarus had the right to throw her out. He seemed ambivalent to Sven fostering a relationship but, as expected, he began to probe into her background. Harriet had been tasked with sussing out Julia's intentions; while she was distracted, it gave Sven the opportunity to sneak off and search for any trace of his brother, Petrik. So far he had confirmation that his brother had met Lazarus at the cabin in the woods...but there was no evidence to suggest he had ever left once he arrived. The car had been dumped in the long term lot at the airport. They didn't have answers just yet but they were close. Everything was coming together, as far as Julia's agenda went. It wouldn't be long now before she had all the evidence she needed to put an end to Lazarus and Los Lobos for good.

Turning away, Lazarus clasped his hands behind his back. The sun skimmed low on the horizon, casting purple shadows on the rippling blue water below. There wasn't a cloud in the sky but he couldn't help but feel like there was something shifting in the atmosphere. "You will have your manpower, Lucian...but I do so only reluctantly. Los Santos—"

"Los Santos are finished!" Lucian snarled. "They are sniveling cowards who left town with their tails tucked between their legs."

Lazarus remained still as the grave, his face molded into a mask of anger. "If you truly believe we've heard the last of them, you are more foolish than I thought. We've discussed all that needs tending to tonight." The muscle in his jaw ticked dangerously and his shoulders squared. "You each have your assignments. Get out of my sight before I lose my temper!" The very slight roughness to his tone sent the group scurrying for cover like rats.

Sven tugged Julia's wrist, his eyes flashing dangerously as they stepped out of the meeting. Gravel crunched beneath their feet as he looked around. "Shh," he murmured, tugging her toward the nondescript vehicle parked around the back of the warehouse. Julia followed behind him, glancing around to see if anyone else was following them. If Sven tried to pull something, she was well aware of his weaknesses by now but this didn't feel like an attack. He was taking her on a clandestine mission somewhere.

"Lazarus is going to be tied up all night reallocating resources. He hasn't been to the cabin for a while now. We'll be able to do some digging without him being any wiser." Sven smiled boyishly and herded her into the car.

The opportunity to look around Lazarus's residence while he wasn't home was just too good an offer to pass up. Julia had been hoping for a chance to get down there and case the place; this was her shot. Julia couldn't dare turn him down. Los Santos were going to retaliate against Los Lobos soon. Since her goal was to keep the body count low on this whole roundup, she was hoping she'd be able to obtain enough incriminating evidence on Lazarus Caine to put him away for a hundred lifetimes; once they took down the head of the beast, they would press him to give up the rest of his cronies for a slightly reduced sentence that might let him out in time to die at home.

It was a solid hour's drive along the back roads and deep into the forest before they reached the cabin. The first thing that struck Julia was how eerie it was. The cabin looked as if Lazarus simply walked off, leaving the house exactly as it rested. The satin sheets on the bed were crumpled, as if someone had just slipped out of bed. There was a white towel resting on the top of the sink and a toothbrush beside it. In the living area, there was a teacup with dried leaves in the bottom and a stagnant pot sitting on the coffee table. The newspaper was neatly folded and rested on the couch cushion. If not for the soft blanket of dust over the house, she might've thought they stumbled upon a home. Instead, it was a shrine to the life Lazarus had been living before everything went to hell...

Sven was clearly not as attuned to their surroundings. He was opening up closets and drawers, looking for a paper trail or clues to indicate his brother had been there. They scoured the basement first, finding nothing but a nest of mice and an old set of free weights. The upstairs similarly held nothing but some discarded clothes, toiletries, and towels. Even the main living area seemed to be completely devoid of any indication Petrik had been there.

Plopping down on the couch, Sven buried his face in his hands with a groan. "There is nothing here!" he lamented. "I was so sure." Bending down, his spine bowed and he seemed to sag under the weight of his body. As he shifted, his foot nudged something jammed beneath the couch and he furrowed his eyebrows. Bending down, he hissed, his fingers coming back bloody. He knelt, lifting up the couch and his eyes widened. "This is Petrik's knife..."

Julia hurried over, her eyes widening. "Are you sure?"

"Positive. He would *never* have left this behind. It was his favorite. They must have fought and Petrik lost his blade..." Sven glanced outside. It was already past dusk, but the moon was casting shadows. He scanned the yard, coming across an area that was scorched and his heart slammed into his ribs. "He's here. He has to be here..." There was nothing on the surface, but neither of them expected that. The minute he started digging, the soil moved away and suddenly there were remnants...

"Sven," Julia's voice was shaking as she inched toward him. He didn't respond at first, his fingers digging into the soil as he pulled out bone, holding the warped fragments in his hand. "Sven, stop!" She grabbed him by the shoulder. He lashed out, pushing her back and she tumbled, hitting the ground so hard her teeth rattled. The breath was knocked out of her lungs and she tightened her fists in anger. Sven watched her, suddenly frozen in place. Julia took a moment to catch her breath before she crawled to her knees. "This isn't helping anything."

Sven's eyes filled with tears as he clutched charred remains in his hand. "This is my brother, I know it..." He took a shaky breath. "Lazarus killed him and *lied* about it."

Julia couldn't tell if Sven was angrier his brother had been murdered or that Lazarus had not outright told him so. These people had sick, twisted morals. She wondered: if Sven had known the truth all along, would he even have cared that Petrik was gone?

"What are you going to do?" Jules asked, inching closer. She needed to get a sample of the bone for later. Despite her focus on the mission, she still felt a pang of compassion for Sven. He was hardly the worst criminal in her acquaintance...if anything, he was simply too weak to go off on his own and followed his brother into this depraved lifestyle instead.

A low fog rolled over the valley, moisture settling over the grass and chilling their skin. Julia and Sven stayed there, kneeling on the ground for what felt like hours. He hadn't actually cried over the loss of his brother but kept a tight leash on his emotions. When Sven finally stood up, it looked as if he'd fought a war...his face was pale, his shoulders were tense, and he was walking erratically. Julia took the opportunity to grab a shard of bone before she stood, wrapping her arm around him and guiding him back to the car.

The trip home was deadly silent. It wasn't until the little sign proclaiming they had entered La Verdad that she even heard Sven breathe. She looked over him, his face ashy and his palms were sweaty. She could see there was something dark in him. "Sven, what're you going to do?" Julia asked again.

"I'm going to kill him," Sven answered without fanfare. "Tomorrow, once everyone goes home for the night. I'll go to his new apartment. I'm going to slash him to bits and then I'm going to burn him exactly like he did my brother!" He gritted his teeth. "Are you going to help me?"

Julia pulled up to the apartment, easing into a spot where the car wouldn't be towed. She rested her hands on the wheel, her heart and stomach aching as she looked out into the street. If she said no, she risked her position...but she couldn't let Sven kill Lazarus. He was the only one who could tie every single person to Los Lobos and help the FBI dismantle the organization. He was like a son to the founder and had been molded in his image. They needed him and the only way Julia could ensure Lazarus was safe was to play along. "We're in this together," she soothed. As soon as they were in the apartment, Sven went to take a hot shower and Julia sat in the kitchen watching the moon set over the city.

Tomorrow was the day she would apprehend Lazarus Caine and secure her place as an FBI agent for good. For some reason, she didn't feel excited or happy about the prospect of closing this case, though. She was worried and uneasy; something told her this wasn't going to be cut and dry. Closing her eyes, Jules focused on her training and on the promise that when all of this was over she could take some time off, maybe spend some time with Candy and Matty, and head a normal life. That was, if she could ever figure out what normal was...

Chapter Twenty-Nine

It was still dark outside when Jenna was startled awake by the rustling of men getting ready to do battle. She was honestly shocked that she'd managed to fall asleep at all given what lay ahead of them...and it didn't help that her room was right next to Cece and Danny's. They'd gone after each other like animals last night. Not that Jenna blamed them. Nobody knew what was going to happen when they rode back into La Verdad and making love seemed the right thing to do, in her opinion. If something happened to either of them, at least they'd have said their goodbyes.

Slipping out of bed, Jenna showered and then put the last of her personal items into the suitcase she'd been living out of for far too long. Although she was troubled, there was a deeper part of her that was looking forward to being home again. The separation had given her time to think about what she wanted out of life. Jenna had been so focused on her restaurant and making her business a success, she'd completely forgotten about a personal life. The time she spent with Lazarus made her consider what she wanted and deserved. Despite all the uncertainty surrounding her, she decided not to live in the shadows anymore.

By the time she got downstairs, Cece and Danny were packed and ready to go. Rogelio, Horatio, Luis and Diego had gotten a head start. It would be far less suspicious to ride in a few at a time than to storm the bastille and draw attention. Martín was still sleeping, which surprised no one. He'd lead the Devils of California to La Verdad later on in the morning, when they were all amassed.

That left Jenna to travel with the lovebirds...

It was bad enough she had been dragged into this, but she always seemed to be the third wheel when it came to Cece and Danny. Of course, they tried not to let her feel that way. Jenna still knew it was true. She slipped into the driver's seat of the Jeep, pinning her blonde hair up in a bun to keep it out of her face during the drive.

"Hey," Cece said gruffly, cuffing Jenna's arm before she got into the car. "I know I said it already but I want you to hear it again: I'm sorry about all this shit." In the hazy light of dawn, the scar on her face looked more pronounced as her dark blue bangs swept into her eyes. "The fact that you got dragged into it is something I can't ever make up for. But what I can do is make sure you're safe. Why don't you stay and we'll call you when it's all over—"

"I already said no," Jenna interrupted. "Sitting in the back seat is exactly what got me here in the first place." She tossed her bag into the back, tightening her grip on the keys. "If I was strong, if they knew I could defend myself, I would never have been taken in the first place." The word 'taken' was more than just in the literal sense, and her cheeks flushed in response. "I'm going to be there when we take back La Verdad. I'll do whatever I can to help but mostly, I'm showing them I'm not afraid."

Cecelia wanted to argue. This was Los Santos business, it was dangerous and would likely turn bloody. Then again, she couldn't tell Jenna to stay away without being the worst kind of hypocrite. She had earned her place and her voting rights, and was as much family as any of her cousins. Reaching out, Cece squeezed Jenna's shoulder tightly. "Don't get yourself killed."

Laughter bubbled up from somewhere deep inside and Jenna turned the gentle touch into a tight hug. "You either." To Cecelia's credit, she simply allowed the hug to happen, giving a couple of pats on the back. After a moment, she pulled back and Jenna smiled. "Let's go give them hell."

Cece inclined her head before she moved to Danny's side. She stole a quick kiss, turned the engine over and revved it before taking off down the road. Danny was in perfect sync, riding just to her right and a foot or two behind. Jenna brought up the rear in the Jeep, blocking anyone from getting too close.

They stopped once to refuel but nobody wanted to dawdle. Danny shoved a couple candy bars down his throat, Cecelia chewed a piece of gum, Jenna bought herself a cup of the vilest gas station coffee available in America, and they were off again. As expected, they arrived at the border of La Verdad just after ten in the morning. They remained vigilant coming through, but there wasn't anyone manning the border...it seemed that things were going according to plan, at least for the moment.

Narayan Bosko's crew had set up a safe haven at La Trattoria and they headed that way. Jenna's heart twisted as she pulled her car into the parking lot. It was strange how nervous she was walking into her own restaurant. To her relief, nothing had fundamentally changed; the tables were in the same spot, the tablecloths pristinely pressed and white, and the smell of lemon and herbs permeated the atmosphere. Tears welled in her eyes as she went to the kitchen, her apron hanging exactly where she'd left it. The Nightriders had kept everything perfectly clean and well oiled. She slipped into her office, allowing herself a moment of weakness before everyone else arrived.

Sanjay was prepping meals for the crowd but Jenna took the reins easily, stepping back into her role as head chef like a second skin. Pasta was a bit heavy for a crew that was about to go out and fight for their freedom, so she made a bunch of chicken and roasted vegetables and enough cannoli cake to feed an army. Narayan and Cecelia were sitting at a booth, maps spread out before them. Danny was napping on top of a table, but that was to be expected. Rogelio, Horatio and Diego were watching the game on the TV in the bar, and Martín joined them halfway through after he arrived with Marco and the Devils.

Several of Narayan's crew patrolled the outside, keeping an eye out. It was a shameless show of force and Jenna was sure Lazarus knew they were here by now. If all went according to plan, they'd start to pull men away from the construction site in anticipation of a fight. Cecelia slung her backpack over her shoulder, smirking over at Danny as he snored. It was time to set the explosives and there was only one engineer who could possibly do the job. With everyone fed and relaxed, Jenna suddenly stepped forward. "You're going to need someone to drive, right? You shouldn't be on your bike with bombs strapped to your back."

Narayan looked up, his expression pensive. "She's right, you know," he said, in heavily accented English. "It would be less conspicuous to go by car."

"We can take the Jeep—"

"I don't want you in the middle of this," Cece argued.

"I'm already in the middle of this," Jenna snapped and grabbed her keys. "I told you, this is as much my fight as yours. So shut up, get in the car, and let's go!"

Cecelia's expression darkened, but she made no further comment. They headed down to the Jeep, slipping inside. Jenna's fingers were poised to start the car when Cece grabbed her wrist. "I don't know if you got some kinda fuckin' death wish but if this goes South, you get out and you don't look back. You hear me?" She frowned.

"Yes," Jenna said blankly and pulled onto the main stretch of road leaning to the marina. She pulled into the public side, where fisherman and beachgoers parked. Cecelia was out of the car before Jenna could stop her and she watched the blue-haired Presidente walk toward the construction site as if she owned the place.

There were men with guns swarming everywhere and Jenna's stomach tightened. She lost sight of Cecelia after she went around a corner and uneasiness curled in the pit of her stomach. Slipping out of the car, Jenna headed toward the edge of the sidewalk, her shoulders tensed as she stared out into the ocean and prayed to whatever God would listen that this was going to work. There were more lives at stake than just theirs...

Lazarus gazed out from his post, his heart seizing in his chest at the sight of a woman he could have sworn was Jenna. Even with time and distance separating them, he had missed her as fiercely as the day she left. He thought about her parting words to him a million times or more and it had clouded his judgment. Everyone thought so...

When the woman turned, the world fell out from beneath him. She didn't just look like Jenna. She *was* Jenna. Rocketing out of his chair, Laz nearly tipped off the guard dogs that had been hired to watch the area. He cleared his throat, "I'm going to take a walk." No one knew what to expect from the great and powerful Lazarus Caine, so it didn't bother anyone when he hurried down the steps from the watchtower and jogged across the parking lot.

Inhaling the salty scent of the ocean, Jenna turned just in time to see Lazarus barreling toward her. If she had been smart, she'd have run; instead, she turned and faced him. There was something altogether different about him, though she couldn't exactly put her finger on what it was. They stood there, staring at one another. Jenna's mouth was glued shut, since they'd said everything that needed to be said to one another the last time they parted ways.

He knew what her presence here meant. Los Santos had returned, just as he thought they would. One part of him knew he should put everyone on high alert that they were under siege…but a larger part of him needed to spend just a few minutes more with Jenna. "I'm glad to see you're looking well."

Jenna sighed. "You said something to me a while ago, Lazarus, something I didn't really understand until this very moment. You told me I was part of this and I needed to pick a side." She chewed her bottom lip. "I spent so much time thinking I'd wake up and realize this was all a terrible dream. But it's not. It's a real, live nightmare…" The sun was starting to dip in the sky as time ticked by. "So, I finally picked a side. I picked the *right* side."

"I know," Lazarus replied. His shoulders hunched as he exhaled, as if he were too tired to stand straight any longer. "Which is why I'm not going to stop you." He took a step away. "Do what you must, Jenna."

Jenna furrowed her eyebrows and closed the distance between them again. "Doing nothing is the same as helping us, Lazarus." It was in that very moment she realized the error she'd made. Cecelia had finished setting the charges and was heading back to the Jeep. Her hand was already on her weapon, safety off and ready to fire. "Wait," Jenna begged. "Cecelia, don't do anything rash!"

Sweat beaded on Cecelia's brow. She'd set the charges along the gas line that ran parallel to the water main. Four perfectly placed, mathematically precise bombs would do the maximum amount of damage with the least amount of material and lowest risk of tipping off the bad guys. It just so happened that all of her work was for nothing because Jenna was standing there with the leader of them all. "Rash?" she repeated incredulously. "This *asquero* is the reason we're all here, Jenna."

"You said you weren't going to kill him!"

"I said we'd try an' avoid it. He's fuckin' standing right there." Cecelia exhaled. "If we let him go, it's all over." She chewed her lip for a moment before striding forward. "This is gonna hurt, *cabrón*." Before Lazarus could react, she reared back and pistol-whipped him. The first blow didn't take him down...but her backhand afterward certainly did. Jenna looked horrified as Cece wrapped her arms beneath Laz's. "Get his feet. I'm putting him in the back."

Horrified and terrified were two emotions Jenna had become quite well acquainted with as of late.

"Hurry the fuck up!" Cecelia snarled at her. "We got three minutes before those charges blow and I, for one, ain't looking' to get blown sky high." Dumping the Chancellor's body in the back, she took the keys from Jenna and put the pedal to the metal. They were nearly a mile away but when the blast hit...

Everything stopped.

Sirens and alarms started blaring, and a thick plume of black smoke erupted and continued rising toward the sky. The smell of burning rubber hung thick in the air. All around the city, people stopped to stare and marvel as the harbor burned. Lazarus began to come-to just in time to glance out the back window as fire engines screamed down the road, hurrying toward the wreckage of the pipeline they were building. Jenna was sitting in the front seat, alerting Cecelia the moment he awoke. A trickle of blood had woven down his temple and he was left feeling nauseous.

That feeling didn't abate any as Lazarus was dragged out of the car and prodded up the stone steps into La Trattoria. There were two dozen men standing around, eyes wide as saucers as he was thrown in front of them. Cecelia strode in behind him. "Don't just stand there!"

The whisper of switchblades erupting got Lazarus's attention and he sat up on his knees. Jenna stood a few feet in front of him, her arms slightly extended as if she meant to protect him. She couldn't, of course, if they rushed her. But these men moved on Cecelia's command alone and it was clear she had laser-focus and precision. "We took out the headquarters but now we need to round up the stragglers. Go!"

Lazarus's hands and feet were secured with plastic ties and he was put in a corner. Jenna paced in front of the table, chewing her fingernails as Sanjay and the Nightrider team went to the North, Marco and the Devils of California headed to the South, Los Santos split and went to the East and West with Danny and Rogelio leading their teams. The fire had smoked out Los Lobos

306

and if they didn't catch them quickly, they'd scatter to the wind and regroup.

Darkness covered La Verdad like a blanket, spidery fingers sliding through the smoky streets. Firefighters were still knocking down the blaze that completely wiped out the harbor and had evacuated several miles of the beach. The found Lucian first and hauled him in, Harriet wasn't far behind—they had been preparing to run away together. Next, they found a horde of gangsters who had recently come from Europe to lay down their roots. It didn't take a genius to find and raid their hotel rooms. Danny was glad they came easily. Sven, though, was the wildcard...they scoured every inch of La Verdad and short of going door-to-door, it was impossible to find him.

Night started to eek into the wee early hours of the morning and everyone was at their wits end. Lucian was making such a fuss they stuck him in the freezer to cool off a while, which had only made Harriet act out. Lazarus, though, was eerily silent. He sat in the restaurant, alternating his attention between the table and Jenna. She was keeping constant vigil, not letting anyone get too close to him in case they tried anything.

Cecelia was so exhausted, she started to get dizzy sometime around three in the morning. Danny made her sit down, got her some leftovers and a big cup of coffee. He'd never seen her look quite so fragile than in the soft lighting in the booth. He rubbed her back gently and sighed. "We've been at this all damn night. We should regroup and look for Sven Villeneuve in the morning. We only have one of these bastards left…"

"No," Cecelia's eyebrows flew up, "We've got two!" She slammed her hand on the table. She went to stand up but Danny was giving her 'the look'. "Get *mi teléfono.*"

Rogelio groaned. "*Que coño*! Who are you texting?" He snapped. "Now ain't the time!"

"*Callate*!" Cecelia snarled at him. She wasn't texting anyway, she just had to find the number she was looking for. Within moments, despite it being the middle of the night, a voice on the other end picked up. "Candy? I need you to do something for me." After explaining the situation, she hung up and less than five minutes later had a ping on Julia's cell phone. "What the hell are they doing all the way out there?"

"The cabin," Jenna said softly. "I bet they found Petrik." She licked her lips, turning her gaze to the man sitting at the booth so silent and stoic. His eyes were horribly bruised from getting hit and it was clear he was still dazed from the blow.

"Do it…"

"Wait," Lazarus snapped. "Sven knows what's going on. He's going to expect an ambush. You don't know what he's capable of. But I do…I *trained* him."

Cecelia shook her head, "What're you suggesting, *cabrón*? We let you go?" She snorted. "Not a fuckin' chance in hell."

Jenna shifted in her seat. "Hear him out. He knows Sven better than anyone. And he won't be going alone. Cecelia, I know how to get there. I'll take Danny and whoever else wants to go. I don't want anyone else getting hurt. *Please.*"

Before Cecelia had a chance to dismiss the idea outright, Danny flopped down beside her. "Hey," he murmured. She was already giving him that look that said to guard his junk, and that was exactly the right move. "Cecelia, listen," he rested his forehead against hers. "This is his house. He knows the booby traps or whatever shit they got. He knows Sven and how he operates. I've got Jenna and we'll take a couple of the Nightriders and it'll be fine." He sighed, "You need to get some rest. You look like you're about to pass out."

As much as she wanted to argue, Cece knew it was a solid plan…and she did want to rest a little bit. She felt like crap and she needed a chance to eat a whole lot of cannoli cake without anyone judging her. "I want hourly updates. Alright? And I'm sending a backup team behind you." She glanced around Danny. "You pull anything and he's gonna fuckin' maim you and then I'm going to finish you off."

Lazarus shook his head as much in agreement as in agitation. It was not as if he was in any position to argue. He didn't even bother tugging when they dragged him down to the Jeep that had once belonged to him. He was almost surprised to see Jenna hadn't sold it or traded it in for something better. She handed over the keys and they were off.

Danny drove the Jeep, Marco Caraway was in the front seat. Jenna had opted to sit in the back with Lazarus and nobody was going to argue with her. The SUV behind them held three of the Nightriders and Luis, who was more than a little interested in striking something up with Sanjay after this was all done. It was nice to know that something good could come from all of this.

As they pulled down the dirt road, Lazarus sat up. "Slow down," he commanded. "He secured the base."

"What's that mean?" Danny frowned.

"In the event we were ever found out, there are tire spikes. You go any further by car and you'll wreck and end up hitting a tree," he explained.

"So we have to go on foot, how convenient," Danny snapped. "Fine." He grabbed his gun and was already out of the car. Marco was not far behind and they strode ahead, ready to leave Lazarus behind when they heard Jenna calling after them.

She slipped out of the car and opened the door on Laz's side. "You need him with you. Didn't you hear what he said? He knows the terrain and he knows Sven. You can't go in there half-cocked, Daniel."

Danny pinched the bridge of his nose. "Damn, you sound just like Cece..." He sighed and glanced over at Marco. They seemed to share a silent thought before the older man walked around the car and cut the ankle restraints impeding Lazarus's movement. "You try anything and it'll go down just like Cecelia said." Marco pushed Lazarus forward, and all three men halted when Jenna started following behind. "Oh no, *you* are not coming."

Jenna folded her arms over her chest, her eyes narrowing dangerously. "Oh, yes I am. I'm a grown ass woman."

"Okay, seriously, now I'm *sure* you've been bodysnatched."

"I'm just a quick learner. I'm not getting left behind and I'm not letting anything happen to you." Jenna brushed past the two of them, walking ahead and forcing them to follow after her. "Let's go, we're wasting time." It was almost two in the morning and even the moon looked tired. She was about sixty feet from the cabin when suddenly Lazarus halted her in place.

"Stop," he commanded. "It's too quiet. There's something—" Shots rang out in the darkness, filling the eerie silence with the shattering scream of a semi-automatic weapon. The chemical twang of fired rounds lingered in the air and he inhaled it deep into his lungs. Sven was not a very accurate shot and given how dark it was, he was grateful nobody seemed to have gotten hit. It had, however, given away the man's position. "Cut these off me," Lazarus demanded, holding out his hands. "I can help you."

Danny rolled his eyes. "Do I look stupid to you?"

"Yes, as a matter of fact, but that is neither here nor there," Lazarus replied coldly. "You need all the help you can get here." It was obvious no one was listening to him. He was still the leader of Los Lobos, even if most of them were under lockdown at a restaurant in La Verdad. He pulled forward, not realizing Jenna was directly behind him. "Sven!" he barked.

A wheezing laugh echoed in the brush. "I was hoping you would come...you see, I'm going to kill all of these bastards but I have something special in store for you. I'm going to tear you to pieces and burn you alive. Just like you did to my brother..."

The soft thud of the magazine falling to the ground and the subsequent click told Lazarus to get down. When he turned and saw Jenna at his side, he panicked. "What are you doing? You're going to get killed! Go back!"

"No," Jenna hissed, "You have no hands and there's a crazy man trying to kill you for protecting me."

"Just as I suspected. My brother came to get his pound of flesh and you wouldn't let him play with your toy." Sven sounded much like a madman as he laughed. "I don't mind killing both of you. After all, you're both responsible." There was no end to his chuckling, as if he was a scratched record, doomed to make the same horrible noises over and over. "Why don't you do us all a favor and come quietly. I'll make her death painless, if you cooperate."

Danny crouched beside a tree, his entire body tensing when someone moved behind him. He turned with his gun drawn to find Julia with her hands up. She motioned for him to be silent and he gritted his teeth. Who the hell was he supposed to trust now? The woman who had been tooling around with this crazy fucker? She wasn't armed, as far as he could tell, and he moved toward her. "You got a plan?"

"I need the Chancellor alive," she whispered, almost inaudibly. Julia reached into her pocket, and flashed her FBI badge, ignoring Danny as he rolled his eyes. "Look, this is bigger than you and me. I'm *this close* to cracking the case and I need you to buy me some time."

"So what do I have to do?" Danny scoffed.

There was a pause and Julia glanced over her shoulder. "Just make sure he doesn't die."

"I hate this plan..." Muttering a string of curses under his breath, Danny moved around the tree to try and figure out where Sven was hiding. There were trees galore and tall grasses, plus it was still dark and a low fog had settled over the area. Danny understood the logic behind keeping Lazarus alive, but he also wasn't interested in losing his life for one asshole. He had Cecelia now; he wasn't going to do something stupid like getting killed. Then again, if they didn't destroy the entire Los Lobos gang, they'd eventually creep back into La Verdad and terrorize their peaceful town all over again. Danny would never be safe and Cecelia would never be free.

Sighing heavily, Danny raised his gun and fired it up into the air. Julia gave him a bright smile and he flipped her the bird.

Jenna found herself at Lazarus's side as they moved closer to the house. If they could get in, they might be able to get a better perspective. Without his hands free, Lazarus wouldn't be able to fight. She had taken a handgun from the glove compartment and it was in her shaky hand. The moment Danny's gun went off, her hand was on the trigger but, thankfully, the safety was on or she would've shot Lazarus by accident. Her breath hitched in her throat as she looked over at him. They were coming to the clearing where the house was settled now and her heart was pounding. "What's the play here?"

"He's close," Lazarus explained. "I can feel it...stop moving for a second." He closed his eyes, relying on his other senses. Suddenly mercury eyes snapped open. Sven took a running leap and tackled Lazarus to the ground. Sven's body was so tense he couldn't even get his hand to tighten around the weapon he'd stolen just for this occasion.

"NO!" Jenna screamed, drawing the attention of everyone else.

Lazarus's hands were tethered and he could do nothing as Sven's fists crashed into his face, his abdomen, and his groin. Bile caught in his throat as he tried to roll away and the man tore at the blonde strands of his hair as he pulled him back. A roaring cry echoed from his throat as he tried in vain to defend himself. With another couple of rolls, Lazarus managed to get back on his feet and kicked Sven away from him, trying to get away without leading him right toward Jenna.

Danny cursed, rushing out to join the fray, but Sven was thickly muscled and wily as they came. Danny took a punch that left him seeing stars and he spat blood.

But Sven didn't care about Danny and went right back to Lazarus, grabbing a knife from his pocket this time. "This was my brother's blade. It's only right I end your life with it." Reaching down with one hand, he grabbed Lazarus's bloody shirt and pulled him up, positioning him on his knees. "This is for Petrik." His arm rose, poised to strike when a gun fired once, twice, and then more…fifteen times the gun went off until nothing but the click, click, click of an empty weapon.

Lazarus looked up, incredulous at Jenna. Her feet were planted, her face ashy, and she couldn't stop pulling the trigger. Sven started back at her with derision, stepping toward her before he staggered. Not all of the bullets hit him, but four had gone into his chest, two into his leg, and one tore a chunk out of his shoulder. The shock of adrenaline lasted only a second and then he fell, his face contorted into a silent scream of death.

Jenna dropped the gun, taking a step back in horror. She was terrified for Lazarus and that Sven intended on killing all of them. Ending his life seemed her only option, but once she started firing, she couldn't stop. Sven didn't go down as easily as she thought he would. A gentle hand against her shoulder dragged her away and she let out a horrified noise. Jenna had seen the redheaded woman at Sven's side and she panicked and flailed.

"Stop!" Julia cried. "It's over. You're safe now!" She was glad there were no more bullets in the gun Jenna had dropped, since she was fairly certain there would've been one with her name on it had there been anything left to give. Lazarus was covered in spatters of Sven, he didn't look at all perturbed by the violence. He was more concerned with Jenna's reaction, something that surprised Julia. She hadn't been sure the rumors about the leader of Los Lobos being in love was true but now she could see for herself it was.

Grabbing her cell phone, Jules in her location and the FBI deployed teams to La Trattoria and the cabin. A helicopter landed in a field half a mile away, and within two hours, they had raided everything Los Lobos had ever touched. Jenna and Lazarus were airlifted back to a local hospital to be looked at, Danny and Marco headed back to town immediately, while Sanjay and Luis snuck off for some alone time.

Cecelia had practically worn a hole in the floor with her pacing by the time Danny got back. Narayan had called in the big guns...Adela and her mother had made sure Cece was full of tea, cake, and dogged her every step. The moment he walked through the door, he ran to her side and wrapped her up. "I said fucking HOURLY updates and I don't get a single text? You're so fucking dead," her chest heaved and her body convulsed as the tears she'd been holding back for months, maybe even years, came spilling out.

"Hey," Danny hugged her tightly, rubbing her back as best he could. "Cecelia, I didn't even use my gun! Well, I mean I did fire it up in the air once...but I'm fine." Seeing her so distraught tore a hole in his chest. "It's over, honey. Los Lobos have been rounded up, Julia's leading the FBI investigation, and we don't have to worry anymore. It's just you and me against the world," he whispered, his fingertips sliding over the scarred curve of her cheek. "We're safe now. And I'm never leaving your side again..." He exhaled sharply. "I never plan any shit ahead but I'm telling you now, I want you to marry me, Cecelia. I'll wait for fuckin' ever if that's how long it takes because I love you. I want to be with you forever."

"Do you ever stop talking, *pendejo*?" Cecelia sniffled, smiling through her tears. She didn't care that everyone was staring at them or that she had shown weakness. She was ready to let go of her pain and Danny was willing to shoulder the burden. "I guess I gotta make an honest man of you." She licked her lips. "While you were out dickin' around in the woods, I've been doing some math."

"Math?" Danny wrinkled his nose. "That sucks. I *hate* math."

"Yeah well, thankfully you knocked up an engineer..." Cece dragged a hand through her multicolored hair. "I been thinking about how I been angrier than usual, worried more, and nauseous as fuck every once in a while. We are definitely in trouble, Danielito."

All the motion in the room ceased as Danny let out a whoop of joy. "I'm going to be a father?" He hugged her tighter. "I have to call Lucy! She's not going to believe this." He suddenly clasped his hands together. "We gotta get married fast, no kid of mine is going to be born out of wedlock." Danny's face was sore from grinning. "Didn't you say the doctor told you it would be hard to get pregnant after everything?"

Cecelia couldn't help but laugh out of sheer joy. She wasn't expecting him to be so excited about everything. "I guess you're just that good, *cabrón*." She snorted. "It was never impossible, just...improbable. Then again, so is my falling in love with a Devil." She smiled. "Although you do make a pretty good Saint."

Wrapping his arms around her waist, Danny kissed Cecelia long and deep. "We need to get the fuck out of here. You and my kid need sleep and I need a shower. I'm pretty sure I stepped in bear shit out there in the woods..." Danny shook Marco's hand on the way out, waved at Rogelio and Los Santos, the Nightriders and Narayan Bosko. As Cece and Danny stepped out into the murky twilight, he took a long, deep breath. "What do you say we start off our new lives with a long ass vacation?"

"I'd say you read my mind," Cecelia grinned broadly, suddenly lighter. Order had been restored in La Verdad and in their lives. No matter what happened now, she had Danny by her side and a new chance at a family. For the first time in a long time, Cecelia was truly at peace.

Epilogue

It took a month to start piecing La Verdad back together.

The harbor was completely destroyed and would take a long time to rebuild, but the citizens of the town didn't seem too concerned. Los Santos had saved them from a horrific fate and they would be eternally grateful. With Cecelia and the MC restored in the community, the entire town breathed a sigh of relief.

Black Ink had been cleaned up and reopened their doors to an extremely enthusiastic client base. How their citizens had gone so long without getting their nipples pierced or a brand new work of art on their buttock, Cecelia had no idea. The minute Black Ink started taking appointments again, they were booked solid for the foreseeable future. Rogelio was not only getting his business back in order, but his personal life too. Although his and Gina's relationship had been tempestuous at best, they shared a son. This whole experience had tested the mettle of their staying power and Rog knew, without a doubt, he couldn't live without her.

So, he decided the best thing to do was to cement that for the rest of their lives. Rog had proposed to Gina and they were married in a civil ceremony later that week. Cecelia presented him with a massive wedding gift when she signed over the deed to her house on the cul-de-sac. Everyone Cece spoke to said it was so generous of her but honestly, she was relieved to have gotten rid of it. Rogelio, Gina, and Raphael would fill up the place with love and give it a new purpose. It wouldn't be a shrine to Cece's unhappiness anymore.

Cecelia was so happy to be back at condo by the beach. She rolled over, taking a moment to stare at Danny as he snored beneath her down comforter. The rush of waves was soothing, drawing Cece outside to dip her feet in the surf. For the first time in her life, she was truly and uncompromisingly happy. Her brother was married and settled, Martín had moved down to Florida with Angelo to enjoy his retirement, Diego and Horatio were planning a nice long vacation, and Luis had found new love with Sanjay Bosko. They decided to invest in Jenna's restaurant and had franchised a second store, with plans to open in the LA area the following year.

As good as life was for Los Santos, it was the exact opposite for Los Lobos. Steve Ellis showed up in force hours after Julia had called in her position. A knock down, drag out fight ensued between them for the first three days. Eventually the stubborn fools realized they needed each other and reluctantly agreed to play nice— at least for the sake of the case. After that, Julia and Steve seemed to fall into a routine.

Lazarus gave up his entire organization in exchange for minimal jail time—whether out of pure selfishness or a misguided notion he was righting wrongs, no one could be sure. He'd go to a minimum security facility for fifteen years, with possibility of special probation after five for good behavior. If Laz played his cards right, he could walk away from prison without a single grey hair and begin his life anew. The rest of his crew would never see the outside world again and—after a particularly spectacular psychotic breakdown—Sven would live out his days in a detention center for the criminally insane.

Now that order and balance had been restored to La Verdad, Cecelia breathed easier. Her hand caressed the new swell of her belly, cradling the child within her. According to the doctor she was fifteen weeks pregnant and the picture of health. The baby was firmly planted in her uterus with no chance of this being another ectopic pregnancy. Thankfully, losing one ovary and fallopian tube posed no threat either. As far as symptoms went, Cece breezed through the first trimester with minimal discomfort. These days, she simply wanted to eat everything in sight—which was perfect, because Jenna was keeping them well fed.

A whisper of movement behind Cece dragged her attention away. Danny's arms threaded around her waist and he rested his chin on her shoulder. "Mornin'," he murmured, pressing a soft kiss to her cheek. "More like afternoon, I guess." He glanced out over the water, his fingertips tracing lazy circles over her tummy. "You shouldn't have let me sleep so late."

"Thought about waking you up but you were a busy boy last night," Cece chuckled knowingly. "The least I could do is let you sleep." She pressed a soft kiss to his cheek. "Besides, we'll miss the traffic if we leave now." Slipping her hand into his, she tugged him back toward home. Their suitcases were ready by the door, except for the last few personal items. Cece and Danny showered together—which didn't save them any time at all. At least they were both ready to go around the same time…

They had a pretty lengthy trip ahead of them, so they had packed a large bag of snacks. Cecelia didn't even argue about his unhealthy choices, since she'd recently found a new affection for sour straws that wouldn't be deterred. Settling into the seat of their new SUV, she buckled in and they were off. Cecelia would've loved to say she was a good copilot but once they were on the highway, her eyelids started to droop and she was fast asleep against the window. When she finally awoke again, it was dark outside and her bladder was aching.

Danny pulled off at a rest stop, grinning as he watched Cecelia darting through the parking lot. He took his time, grabbing a cola and a couple of burgers for them as they got back to the car. "We've made pretty good time. We're about an hour outside of Errol."

"*Qué*?!" Cecelia practically shouted. "I've been asleep for eight hours?"

"Yeah," Danny snorted, "Some travel companion *you* are." He slung his arm around her, pressing a kiss to the top of her head. "Don't worry about it." For the first time since he'd met her, Cece's hair was actually a normal color. She had vowed not to use harsh dye during her pregnancy and he was surprised to find her natural hair was caramel brown with chestnut highlights. He asked her once why she hated it, to which she'd replied that she simply enjoyed a brighter, more colorful existence. It was one of the ways she showed her defiance, and now that she wasn't constrained by a loveless marriage or a madwoman, the gesture hardly seemed necessary. Her elbow pressed sharply against Danny's ribs made him smile and Cecelia found herself following suit.

The ancient wooden sign welcoming them to Errol filled them both with a sense of excitement and dread, in equal measure. Danny hadn't been back to his childhood home since he'd ridden down to La Verdad and he'd changed a lot since then. He wasn't sure how this reunion was going to go. Although he had spoken to his sister a few times, he hadn't heard from Archie at all. They'd been like brothers since they were children and not having him around to talk to had been horrible. He hoped this could be the beginning of mending fences.

As Cece and Danny pulled down the street where he'd grown up, his heart leapt into his throat. The home he had lived in his entire life was familiar and yet so very different. Lucy and Archie kept the integrity of the house with its wraparound porch and the steps that led to a stone walkway but they'd completely redone the place. Those wooden stairs had been creaky and rotting for years, but Archie had replaced the wood and repainted the house in a soft cream that accented the newly whitewashed porch beautifully. The original stones of the walkway had been preserved but instead of having to carefully walk around the loose ones, they had repaired and sealed the concrete so it wouldn't be a hazard for the kids.

The grass was perfectly manicured. Lucy had planted flowers in the front and tended a small vegetable garden in their back, just as their mother used to do when they were alive. As he pulled up in front of the house, Danny's eyes misted at the nostalgia. Lucy's bike was parked and covered with a tarp in the garage, next to Archie's, and they had a sleek grey minivan that Danny would have to rib him about later. Once they made up, of course.

Several members of the Devil's Own were milling around on the porch, including Beaver and PJ. Someone was grilling in the backyard and Danny would put money that it was Mort. The pink balloons on the mailbox blew gently in the wind as Danny stepped out, walking around the car to open the door for Cece. She slid her hand up his chest. "You alright, *mi amor*?" Tugging her leather jacket, she zipped it up to hide her bump. Today was about Lucy and Archie, and she didn't want to draw unnecessary attention to herself.

"Yeah." Danny cleared his throat in attempt to dislodge the lump there. It didn't work. "Let's just go in." As they headed toward the house, he felt the stares. He was the defector, the one who had abandoned them at a critical time for the Devils...but he was also the man who had helped take down Los Lobos before they spread their poison throughout North America.

Marco and Candy were chatting in the kitchen and greeted them warmly. It was slightly less friendly when Julia appeared behind them. Of course they understood what she had been doing, but it was hard not to think about it when they saw her. Thankfully, she seemed to take the hint and disappeared from sight.

Pushing past Kyle and Hunter with warm greetings, Danny smiled at the sight of his sister resting on the couch with the newborn. Archie was chasing Amelia around the room, swinging her and cuddling her close. He was a bear of a man at six foot four, thickly muscled and his close-shaved blonde hair made him look just as formidable as he actually was. He stopped, staring hard at Cecelia and Danny as they moved closer.

Lucy shifted, the blanket falling away from the chubby-cheeked newborn in her arms. "Danny!" she called, eagerly sitting forward. "I'm so glad you're here."

"Take it easy, sis." He closed the distance between them, resting a hand on her shoulder and easing her back into her spot on the new couch. It seemed the outside of the house wasn't the only thing that had been redone. The old couches that were falling apart had been hauled out and replaced with easy to clean leather and the worn blue carpet had been torn up and replaced with a softer blue one. It looked lived in and, despite the longing for the old and familiar, he liked what Lucy had done with the place. "You look great."

"You're so full of it," Lucy snorted. Her ebony hair was piled up on the top of her head and secured with a Hello Kitty hair bow she'd found in the bathroom. It was definitely one of Amelia's, but nobody seemed to mind. She was wearing a simple tank top and a soft black sweater with the Devil's Own insignia on the back, only because she didn't want to leak on her leather vest. There were dark circles under her eyes and she didn't have on a stitch of makeup, but she looked so deliriously happy.

Danny grinned at her. "Yeah well, you just had a kid." He knelt in front of her, staring down at the tiny little bundle in her arms. "She's perfect, Luce." The tiny baby was so much smaller than he remembered Amelia being, which could've been because she was born at thirty-seven weeks, instead of two weeks overdue—like Amelia had been. She was clearly healthy though, as evidenced by the hollering scream that emanated from her when the newborn realized she needed a diaper change.

Archie set Amelia down with a smile. "It's my turn," he murmured.

"Let me," Danny found himself offering.

All the chattering in the room stopped as Lucy and Archie stared at the redheaded menace they'd once had to remind to put on pants before leaving the house. Lucy raised an eyebrow. "You're volunteering to change a dirty diaper that's *probably* poop?"

Danny stood to his full height. "Yeah..." He looked around. "What's wrong with you people? Is it so strange I'd actually want to do stuff for my niece?"

"Yes!" was the resounding chorus from at least ten different directions. Danny scowled at all of them, easing the baby from Lucy's arms and cuddling the newborn close. He found his way to the nursery easily, considering it used to be his old room.

"I'll supervise," Cecelia hurried after him, leaving Lucy and Archie shocked in her wake. Cece pulled a diaper out of a bag on the side of the changing table. She'd changed Raphael before but that seemed like a million years ago now. As Danny eased the blanket away from the baby and carefully undid the onesie, Cecelia's heart twisted at the sight of the perfect little feet and toes that were uncovered. The infant was still screaming but calmed almost instantly when Danny peeled back the diaper.

To his credit, Danny only gagged a little bit when wiped the baby down. It took both him and Cece to figure out which way the new diaper went on...but without any untoward events, they got the baby changed, her onesie snapped closed, and wrapped up in her soft pink blanket. Once she was clean, the tiny girl was calm and he got a chance to really look at her. "God, she's perfect." He let Cecelia snuggle her close. "Just think, in a few months, we're going to have one of these."

"You're *pregnant?*" Lucy gasped from the doorway. Cecelia turned, her face threatening to crack with how wide she was smiling. "I didn't mean to eavesdrop, I just didn't hear any crying and I was worried something happened to the three of you." She inched forward. "I've been wanting to call you for so long but with everything going on with my pregnancy and Amelia and the Devils, it's been crazy. And then...I guess, I was worried you were still angry at me."

"That's all in the past, *chica*," Cecelia soothed. "I didn't know the score then and I was going through some sh—"

she paused, glancing at the baby before she cleared her throat, "—*stuff.*"

Archie padded in the room. "Marco filled us in on everything you were doing in La Verdad and, although I'm *pissed* you didn't tell us what was going on, I understand your reasoning." He exhaled sharply. "I want you both to know you're part of our family and that's always going to trump club business." He reached out, clasping Danny on the shoulder. "And you're always going to be a Devil. I talked to the guys and they agreed, we've still got your cut and, if you want it, that Vice President spot is still yours. You'll always be one of us, Danny."

The men embraced briefly, patting each other on the back a little too hard before stepping back—both with tears in their eyes. Cecelia and Lucy shared a look, laughing softly as they shook their heads. "If you need some tampons, I got one in my purse, *cabrón.* I won't be needin' them for a while," Cece teased. Danny just laughed and kissed her sweetly.

Archie smirked, cuddling Lucy closer. "What do you say, Danny? You ready to be a Devil again?"

Danny looked over at Cecelia holding the baby and shook his head. "We're always going to brothers in arms but Los Santos is where I belong." He was wearing their colors and their patch, he was going to marry their ex-Presidente, and they'd make their home wherever Cece wanted. Archie seemed to understand and they shook hands cordially.

Cecelia's heart swelled with love and she snuggled against Danny. "Hey, you never told us what the baby's name was."

"I wanted it to be a surprise," Lucy explained. "Meet Danielle Cecelia Archer...she's named after the two very best people I know." This time, it was her turn to well up with tears, but nobody said a word as she embraced her brother and her best friend. "Although, I almost feel bad now that I know you're pregnant. You might've wanted those names."

"Nah," Cecelia smirked. "I got something picked out."

"You do?" Danny raised an eyebrow at her.

"Yeah and I ain't telling you what it is neither," Cece teased.

"Hey, that's not fair!" Danny argued. "I'm the father!"

Just like that, they were back to bickering like an old married couple. Lucy smiled and kissed Archie sweetly on the lips. They were happy and whole, and their families were growing by leaps and bounds. All the sins of the past had been washed away and the slate wiped clean. Finally, Cecelia and Danny could make a fresh start and judging by the way they kissed and made up, they meant to take full advantage.

The End